MW00613006

DEAR SULLY

a novel

BY JILL COX

TOWER
19
PRESS

ISBN 978-0-9982200-4-8 (print)
ISBN 978-0-9982200-5-5 (digital)

Cover artwork and design by Sarah Huggins Oister

Author portrait by Mike and ReJana Krause | BluDoor Studios

Tower 19 Press logo by Tarran Turner

Vintage keys set vector | Vectorstock (Artist: Seamartini)

Vintage padlock vector | Vectorstock (Artist: Vectortatu)

Florentine journal pattern | Avalon Rose Design

Printed in the United States of America

to Sharon Duncan
for three books' worth of editorial magic
and for a lifetime of friendship

JUNE

TUESDAY, OCTOBER 16TH

DEAR SULLY,

NIGHT AND DAY TOLD ME YOUR SIDE
OF OUR STORY, SO MAYBE THE
LETTERS IN THIS JOURNAL WILL TELL
YOU MINE. WELL, THE JUNE VERSION
AT LEAST. THE OCTOBER JOURNAL IS
IN THE MAIL. (I HAD A LOT TO SAY.)

LOVE,
PETE

PS - NICE BOOK COVER, BY THE
WAY. WHO DO I THANK FOR MAKING
LUKE RESEMBLE CHRIS PRATT? ☺

#DUCKYSLINCRACKERS4EVER

DEAR SULLY

DR. KEATING

Once upon a time, a long time ago, I read that the average American male feels twenty-five years old (no matter his chronological age). Let's hope that's a lie, because today's my twenty-fifth birthday, and guess what? I spent the whole day blubbering like a baby.

I'm a wreck, Sully. I have been for six years, but when you left Paris forty-eight hours ago without saying goodbye, I think you took my swagger with you. If you don't believe me, ask Kelly, Anne, and Harper – they spent the rest of Saturday night and most of Sunday bullying me out of my funk. They even enlisted Kathy Beauchamp.

Which is why this morning – Monday, June 25th – my quarter-life crisis brought me to a small office near the *Gare Montparnasse*. It belongs to Dr. Campbell Keating, a rosy-cheeked Irishman with bright blue eyes and the same soft brogue your parents have. "Tell me, Peter," he said, eyes softening as he leaned back in his chair. "What brings you to see me today?"

Dude, I wanted to say. *Get ready to earn your paycheck.*

I started with my parents' accident and two hours later, I ended with you. My own words sounded robotic inside my head, like they belonged to some narrator on the audiobook of my life. But when I finished, Dr. Keating said something I'll never forget.

"You're a warrior, Peter," he smiled. "I can see that your soul is brave. Your heart is true. But you protect yourself behind an armor, because you're terrified to lose anyone else. But what if that armor has finally betrayed you? What if the armor has become your own personal prison?"

Fifty words, Sully. Fifty words is all it took for Dr. Keating to summarize your boy, Peter Beckett Russell. Can you believe that? I might have felt terrible that I was so transparent if I wasn't so relieved.

"I'd like to see you every day this week," Dr. Keating stated, clasping his hands together in his lap. "I can work you in on my lunch hour for now, and we'll adjust the schedule going forward, depending on your progress."

"But… I've just told you my whole life. What else is there to say?"

"Maybe nothing, in terms of facts. But I'm afraid the facts aren't what's troubling you. We'll need to go deeper to sort out the rest."

"Okay." I dragged those two syllables out like a melody. "How deep, exactly?"

"That depends. You see, the brain is a fascinating organ. For example, did you know that if you type words into a computer document, you only build six hundred neural pathways, but if you write it by hand, you build ten thousand?"

"Really? Then why do schools keep eliminating handwritten assignments?"

"Excellent question." He grabbed my patient folder from his desk. "I noticed on the intake paperwork that you have rather nice penmanship, Peter. Are you by any chance left-handed?"

"Uhhh, yeah," I gaped. "How'd you guess that?"

"Because your handwriting is so precise yet unique. It's the style a person develops when he's spent a lot of extra time in his life learning to write correctly with his left hand under the tutelage of right-handed instructors. Your style is quite upright and straight, like an architect's, but with its own little quirks. For example, do you realize you print in all caps except when you write a preposition? You write prepositions in lowercase, every single time."

Dude. I'm not going to lie. Dr. Keating was freaking me out. Who notices details like that? "I guess that's true," I stammered. "I don't really think about it, though. I just write."

"Precisely my point," he answered, tapping his fingers on the mahogany desk. "When we write things out by hand, we tend not to overthink them in the way we do when we can hit that little backspace bar. So when you leave here today, I'd like you to buy yourself a notebook. Nothing fancy, mind you; any old notebook will do. Once you've settled down somewhere comfortable, pick a person – any person, living or dead – and write them a letter. Tell the mystery person a story about yourself that he or she doesn't know. It doesn't have to be serious or significant. Just start somewhere. Bring your notebook with you tomorrow and we'll move forward from there."

"Listen, sir, if you think I'm going to start journaling – "

"I'm not asking you to journal. You'll simply write a letter to someone you trust."

I chewed on my lip. "Will you read it?"

"Of course not. You never have to show *anyone* what you've written. It's simply a cognitive exercise to get your subconscious working. If my theory is correct, the warrior I see on the outside has reached a crossroads with the young man you were before your parents died. From what you've told me today, you've *survived* the last few years. But you haven't really lived."

"No?" I huffed. "Sure *feels* like it. I feel ninety years old."

He smiled knowingly. "Just write five pages. Think of the one person you trust most in the world, even if he or she doesn't populate your current day-to-day life. I'll see you tomorrow at noon, okay?"

When I left Dr. Keating's office, I walked north up the rue de Rennes all the way to the Seine. At the first *bouquiniste* stand, I saw this fancy blue journal. How cool are those skeleton keys on the cover? I don't know why, but they reminded me of you, Sully. So I bought two, then climbed the stairs to the Pont des Arts, where I sat down on our usual bench. Because even before Dr. Keating finished doling out my assignment, I knew who my audience should be.

It's you, Sully. You're the person I trust most in this world.

Besides, this is *homework*. If anyone can appreciate the importance of an assignment, it's you, right? In fact, I'd bet five hundred euros that you already know about the handwritten word and its cognitive importance. It's just the sort of random factoid that's your stock in trade.

So here we go – you, me, this fancy new notebook, and my trusty Bic pen.

This was my first letter. Let's see where these ten thousand new neural pathways take us next.

LINCOLN CITY

I've never really told you much about my parents. I've wanted to tell you. So many times. Believe me, I could probably talk for a week straight about all the million little things that made my mom and dad *mine*.

Like how Jim Russell rented a stick-shift car the weekend after my thirteenth birthday because "everyone needs to learn to drive a standard transmission before they learn to drive an automatic." For the rest of the weekend, we drove around an empty school parking lot with the windows rolled down, sucking in the smell of burnt clutch and gasoline until I finally busted through all five gears like a boss.

Or how whenever I went sullen about missing a goal at a soccer game (or worse yet, about a girl), my mom would make oatmeal chocolate chip cookies. If it was really bad, she added butterscotch chips to the mix, because complex carbohydrates are my love language.

My dad loved U2 so much that Liz Russell called Bono his side piece.

My mom reread Jane Austen's *Persuasion* every single year over Christmas break.

Jim Russell may have been a photojournalist of modest renown, but his guilty pleasure was watching NASCAR with Gigi. (You read that right, sister. My fancy-pants grandmother was the reigning queen of the Talladega Nights.)

Liz Russell spoke French with no discernible American accent, yet she had subscriptions to both *People Magazine* and *US Weekly* because she liked her celebrity gossip fair and balanced.

My dad's eyes were hazel. My mom's were dark brown like mine (and Gigi's).

I miss them both so much that I still wake up in the middle of the night a couple of times a week with an aching heart.

And listen, I know I opened up to you while we flew home on spring break junior year, but the truth is I only skimmed the surface details of the night my parents died. Please don't take it personally. I've never told *anyone* the details of those final hours before my parents died.

Not Gigi and Pops. Not Dan or Brooks.

No one, Sully. Not until today.

The Russell clan rolled into Lincoln City on July 8th around four in the afternoon after a full day of driving up the coastal highway. I have no idea why my parents settled on Lincoln City, or why we didn't stop one town south in Depoe Bay. But stop in LC we did, at a hotel on the south side of town.

Our room opened onto Taft Beach, so my parents ducked out for a quick stroll in the sand while I took a shower and shaved. I didn't hurry. I figured it was a relief for all three of us to get out of each other's space for a bit.

I'd be lying to you if I said I've never second-guessed that decision. Most days, I'm glad they had one last walk together. But then I wonder: what if I'd hurried to get ready? What if we'd gone south to Depoe Bay for dinner? Would Alicia Baldwin have arrived home safely, or would she have drunkenly plowed into someone else instead?

Who knows why I still bother asking myself these questions? I'm sure you understand.

Around six o'clock, my parents and I drove north to Sullivan's Restaurant. For the record, I was pissed about it. I was hangry, hungover, and I wanted tacos – the greasiest tacos we could find. The kind you eat in the car and then head back to the hotel to sleep off.

But Liz Russell didn't believe in eating in cars (or in hotel rooms for that matter, even if it was a five-star establishment with top-notch room service). So we drove north, north, north until she spotted Sullivan's. My parents had a weakness for fish and chips, and bonus: your place was right on the ocean. Plus, as my dad so kindly pointed out, Sullivan's was casual enough that my still-damp hair wouldn't be a distraction.

Why yes, I did stick my head out the window that night in an attempt to dry my wild curls. How else does one achieve what you once called my Portuguese water dog look?

(Spoiler alert: this is where you come in, Sully. Cue the swooping, anthemic soundtrack.)

When my parents and I walked into your restaurant that night, you were standing behind the hostess's desk with a stack of menus in your arms, flirting with some guy.

Hold up… now that I'm replaying this story inside my brain, I'm seventy-three percent certain the flirty dude was Sutton. Why have I never connected those dots before now?

(Whoa. Well done with the "cognitive exercise" trickery, Keating.)

Now listen, I could lie and tell you that the first time I laid eyes on you, the world shifted to super slow-mo while the goofy hero (me) drooled all over himself just as a volleyball pinged him in the forehead. You know, like those 90s rom-coms you secretly love.

I *could* lie to you, but that's not the purpose of this assignment. And since I actually *want* to do the brain dive Dr. Keating prescribed, I'll just be blunt: the first time I saw you, all I could think was *holy long legs, Batman.*

That's right, Ginger Spice. My gaze got stuck on your lower body for so long that my mother elbowed me in the ribs. But in my defense, you're a championship-level dancer.

That night, you wore shorts and a green Sullivan's t-shirt. I noticed the freckles along the bridge of your nose and cheekbones – Irish glitter, you call them, which fades every winter and pops out every summer. Your hair was pulled back in a ponytail, and maybe it was just the lighting, but your hair looked copper in the setting sun, with streaks of gold near your face.

Except that's not your actual hair color. In fact, until I went with you to Ireland after we studied in Paris, I'd never seen any human being with your particular shade of red. How can I describe it – auburn, I guess? Cinnamon flames? Titian? The most beautiful thing I've ever seen in my life?

If you ever read this, you will definitely laugh at that last paragraph. If anyone knows how obsessed I am with your hair, it's you. After all, you've endured a lot of time with my fingers exploring every single strand just to figure out its magical hold on my heart.

The mystery-kid-who-was-probably-Drew-Sutton scurried away to bus a nearby table, and when he did, you finally made eye contact with all three of us – first with my mom, whom you smiled at, followed by my dad, and then me.

I'm not sure what I did to earn the blink-and-you'll-miss-it scowl I caught on your face that evening, but it might have had something to do with the St. Francis Friars Varsity Soccer t-shirt I wore. I'm guessing you disapproved of the rotund monk chasing a soccer ball across my chest.

In any case, you led us to our table without a second glance my way. You handed us menus, but you somehow failed to notice the killer smile I gave you.

Rude, Sully. So very rude.

After you sashayed your way back to the hostess's stand, you put yourself to work doing something important, like filling salt shakers or restocking sugar packets. And I never once let you out of my sight. Which explains why I didn't notice that my dad was laughing at me.

No wait, not laughing. CHORTLING.

"What's so hilarious?" I could already feel the blood rushing into my cheeks.

My dad glanced at my mom. "How long do you reckon he's been staring at the redhead? Thirty seconds?"

"More like forty-five," she grinned. "Looks like Brooks Darby finally has some competition."

"What the – Mom! I told you that in confidence."

"Relax, kiddo. Your mom would never sell you out." My dad knocked his foot against mine under the table. "But FYI, your Brooksie crush is the worst kept secret in Portland and its suburbs."

Just then you reappeared, Sully, balancing three glasses of water on a tray. You still refused to look at me as you doled out those drinks. So my mother took charge.

"Are you open tomorrow for breakfast?" She said in her sweet-yet-authoritative educator's voice, and you fell for it, Sully. Hook, line, and sinker. (You are such a teacher's pet, dude.)

"Yes, ma'am," you replied with a smile. "But only in the summer. This town doesn't get much traffic from September to May."

"You work here year-round?" My dad asked.

"Yes, sir. This is my parents' restaurant."

"Oh!" My mother clapped her hands together. "Are you actually Irish?"

"Mom," I growled, sliding lower into my seat.

"Yes! Well, sort of," you shrugged. "I have dual citizenship. My family and I moved here when I was little."

"To Oregon?" My dad's face lit up. "From which part of Ireland?"

"County Clare," you smiled. "Doolin, to be specific."

"Hey, I've been there!" My dad's grin was so wide, it must have hurt his cheeks. "There's no better place to hear traditional Irish music than the Doolin pubs, right?"

You beamed at him, Sully. "I can't believe you've been there!"

"You'll have to excuse my husband," my mom said in her warmest tone. "He doesn't get out much. Don't let us keep you, Miss Sullivan."

"Call me Meredith," you said, finally casting a tiny glance my way. "Oh, and my brother Ian will be your server. He doesn't get out much either."

And just like that you bounced off, and my parents and I sat blinking at one another, each of us laughing a little under our breath, because you'd just knocked all three of us out in one blow.

My mom went all starry-eyed. "Oh, I *like* her, Pete. You should ask for her number."

"What? Why would I do that?"

"Um, because you're into her?" My dad frowned. "Seriously, kid, what's with the sudden case of the nerves?"

"There's a big difference between nerves and rational thought," I frowned back. "Dude, this girl lives, like, a hundred miles away! Plus, I'm going to college next month. *In California.*"

Liz Russell had three personae, Sully. The first one was "Liz," a.k.a. perpetual girlfriend of Jim Russell. The second was "Mom." And the third was "Madame Russell," empress of the classroom, destroyer of all chill. You weren't too far off with your Romanov theory back in the day. Maybe she did have *tsarina* blood coursing through her veins. Someone with my mom's *chutzpah* would laugh in the face of a Siberian winter.

"How do you know," she asked frostily, "that our hostess isn't headed to college herself?"

"Mom, cut it out. Someone will hear you."

"No, I'd like an explanation, Pete. Are you under the impression that the only people who end up at college are those who attend twenty-thousand-dollar-a-year private schools?"

"Of course not. I just meant –"

"Surrender, Dorothy," my dad whisper-shouted at me. "Mama Lizzie always wins."

I shifted in my seat, then looked my mom in the eye. "You're right. Maybe that redhead's Yale-bound, or maybe she's America's next top model. Either way, we've both got our whole lives ahead of us, probably on opposite sides of the country, so why should I talk to her?"

My mom's eyes narrowed. "Listen, honey, I know you think we're old and out of touch. But in my experience, when a person makes your face light up like yours did just now, the very least you should do is find out that person's *phone number*."

"Okay, you guys have officially lost your minds. What you call a lit-up face was actually a sign of hypoglycemia. I'm in need of greasy carbs, that's all."

My parents turned to face each other, and for a split second, they looked sixteen instead of forty-six. Jim Russell slid his arm around the-artist-formerly-known-as Liz Beckett and pulled her closer to him. "You know I watched your mom from the sidelines for a year before I asked her out, right?"

I dropped my head in my hands. "Not this story again."

"Hey, you kept us awake all night last night," my dad said, tugging gently at my curls across the table. "If the worst punishment you receive for underage drinking is the story of how your parents fell in love, you should count your lucky stars."

"Fine." I rubbed my eyes and propped my elbows on the table. "But can we fast forward through the part where you tell me someone as cool as Elizabeth Beckett would never go for you? Because she's sitting right here, Dad, which makes your story revisionist history."

"Hey, if it weren't for Scott and Becky and their matchmaking skills, you might not exist."

Scott and Becky are the Logans. Scott was my dad's roommate, and Becky and my mom grew up down the street from each other. In fact, their son – the famous Shanghai James – is named after my dad. They're family, you know? The people I turn to nowadays whenever I need a safe place to land.

My mom laid a hand on my dad's chest and smiled. "What your father is saying is if he'd simply asked for my number the first time we met instead of watching me from the sidelines all those months, he could have saved us all some time."

"But if he'd asked for your number, we wouldn't have this charming anecdote to rehash over and over again, now would we?"

My dad chuckled under his breath, shaking his head. "Sorry, Lizzie. Looks like our son inherited my chickenhearted genes."

After some serious maternal side-eye, we eventually moved on to the topic of what I'd actually learned during Stanford orientation. Phew. I thought I was in the clear... until we passed you again at the hostess' desk on our way out of the restaurant.

And I tripped over my own feet.

Between the front door and the car, Liz and Jim Russell spiraled out of control, cackling at their only child and his total nincompoopery. So I buckled myself into the back seat of the SUV – something I rarely bothered to do – and buried my face in my pillow, hugging it tightly against me, like a fortress against the madmen at the helm.

Which is why I didn't see Alicia Baldwin's car careening toward us as we turned south onto Highway 101. A few days later at the hospital, after I'd had time to settle into the news, a detective explained that I was the only one in the car whose body was relaxed on impact. He said if I hadn't been hiding behind that pillow – if my eyes and brain had forced my body to react to the oncoming danger – well, I wouldn't be alive today.

So maybe this explains in part why I freaked out after your brother's accident. I'm not a superstitious person, but when Ian died, the whole thing suddenly felt all *Final Destination*-ish, like Death skipped me that night of the accident, and four years later, he took your brother instead.

I know that sounds ridiculous now, but it didn't to me at the time. Because I shouldn't have survived that car accident, Sully. I shouldn't have, but I did. All because of you.

SIGMA PHI SUTTON

Within ninety minutes of the accident, a helicopter had medevac'd me to Portland.

On impact, my dad's seat hurtled backward, pinning my left leg and shattering it in three separate places. Somehow in the melee, I broke my right wrist and damaged my spleen. To complicate matters, I had a dozen cuts on my face and a goose-egg contusion on the left side of my skull from where my head hit the window as our car spun into oncoming traffic.

I was a hot mess, Sully.

For eight weeks, the only non-medical people I spoke to were my grandparents. By the time I was fully discharged, Labor Day had come and gone, and all my friends had started college without me. I moved in with my grandparents, did rehab for my arm and leg, and felt sorry for myself every second of every day.

Which is why I ran away to Shanghai the first time. But you already know most of that story.

So how about I fast-forward to the first few days at Highgate? I think you'll like this letter, Sully. I'm about to blow your mind, because guess what?

Your boy Andrew Sutton and I were *almost* best friends.

Whaaaaat? I know, man. Mic. Drop.

In the days leading up to freshman year, Pops convinced me to give fraternity life a shot. "You need structure, Peter," he said. "The Greek system at Highgate seems healthy enough. And besides, everyone needs friends."

Which is how it came to pass that once upon a time, during the halcyon days of fraternity recruitment, I shared your favorable opinion of Andrew Sutton from Lincoln City, Oregon. I know this will shock you, and it would probably shock him as well, but here's the truth: those first days of freshman year, I freaking *loved* that kid.

I'm sure this goes without saying, but for dudes, Greek life is fairly low key. You hang out, play video games, shoot pool at the frat house… you know the drill. And yeah, okay. There are weekly meetings and charity commitments. But my point is that despite what you see on TV and in movies, fraternity life has very little to do with beer pong or keg stands.

At least, not at the Sigma Phi Beta house. They're the only dry house on campus.

Highgate allowed freshmen recruits to move into the dorms early, and thanks to a potluck miracle, Dan Thomas became my roommate. All four days of recruitment, Dan and I attended every event together alongside your favorite housemates, Braden and Ben.

Dear Sully

You know who else tagged along? The one and only Drew Sutton.

To keep the playing field level, recruits aren't allowed to talk about their past during the festivities – not with the upperclassmen, and not with each other. We could talk about the future: our course schedules, our majors, career goals, *et cetera, et cetera*. This must have been a real challenge for everyone else, but man, Sully. It saved my hide. I didn't have to answer questions about my family or why I was a twenty-year-old college freshman. Thanks to recruitment parameters, I was free to be whomever I pleased.

Annnnnnd I'm just realizing that is the very reason such a rule exists. Wow.

Is this what it was like for you to write your novel, Sully? Did you figure out *all* the things? Because that would definitely explain why you're ahead of me in the wisdom game these days.

On Friday night, Dan, Braden, Ben, Drew, and I listed Sigma Phi Beta as our house of preference. Turns out all five of us topped their list as well, and for the first time in a long time, I felt like I was part of something bigger than myself. For an only child – an *orphaned* only child – having ninety-nine new brothers was everything I never knew I wanted.

Saturday – bid day – was one of the best days of my life thus far.

You can feel the *but* coming, can't you? Ah, Sully. You know me well.

Fast-forward to Sunday morning when I woke up to an imaginary elephant sitting on my chest. My mind roared, skipping through possibilities. Starting Monday – the first day of freshman orientation – my past would become my currency, just like everybody else. But how could I talk about my past when I'd spent the greater part of the previous year running away from it all?

By breakfast, I'd compartmentalized my fear long enough to plan a fun day with my new brothers. I chauffeured the guys all over Portland, then over to the Columbia River Gorge. We putzed around all day, hiking and whatnot, then somehow ended up at a local festival along the riverbank. Despite my nerves about Monday, I was having fun.

Right up until I spotted a food truck.

An eerie calm overtook me. Because when I saw that food truck, I remembered that my seventh-grade English teacher was absent for a week after she went to a food truck festival with a blind date. And yes, I know that telling students about your love life is a no-no in the teacherly world, but you're missing my point, Sully: Miss Freiburg was siiiiiiiiick. Like green at the gills even after she survived two ER visits and a week hugging the porcelain throne.

Hallelujah! A *faux* case of food-truck-itis was my ticket out of Highgate's orientation.

"Dudes," I chuckled, backhanding Dan on the arm. "I bet you twenty bucks *each* that I can eat six of those tacos."

Dan craned his neck, eyeing the workers inside the truck. "They're not even wearing gloves, Russell. What if you get *e coli* or Hepatitis C? Or both? You'd miss orientation."

Why yes, Daniel. I *would*.

Braden grunted in agreement, but Drew's eyes got that look – like he'd just learned a secret hack for mining bitcoins. Next stop: the Ferrari dealership (or whatever materialistic nonsense one buys with bitcoins).

"Fifty bucks says you can't eat more than three," he blurted. "No wait. A hundred bucks."

If I'd known then what I know now – that Sutton's mom had died way too young, that he'd worked for years at your restaurant to build up his savings and earned a full-ride academic scholarship so his grandparents didn't have to carry his burden – I never would've taken that bet. But he was watching me so smugly in that moment that I had to take him down.

So I ate *four* tacos, enough to wipe the smug off Sutton's face. A couple of bites into the third one, I started to set the scene – a little show of discomfort here, a little bit of pushing-through-to-win-this-bet-but-man-something-is-off-with-this-food there. I could see in Sutton's face that he was both disgusted and impressed that he'd just lost a hundred bucks on such an easy bet while also realizing that something had definitely gone wrong.

Braden was the first to speak up. "Cut that out, Russell," he said as I swallowed a mouthful of the fourth taco. "You've already cleaned out Sutton's wallet. Now let's get out of here before your lunch comes back up to say hello."

"Sutton never quantified that I had to keep them down," I smirked, holding my side as I shot Sutton a triumphant grin. "Hand over the Benjamin, bro."

"I don't have the money *with* me," he pouted. "It's back at the dorm."

"Well, then." I belched really loudly, frowned at the taco truck, then belched again. "I suggest we head back to campus right now, because I intend to collect on my winnings before our next stop: the play-all-day-for-ten-bucks arcade. My treat."

"An arcade?" Ben asked. "Where?"

"Five minutes from campus. Come on, I'll show you." I fake-winced, which didn't escape anyone's notice, and then took off toward the car, the other four trailing nervously behind.

When we reached the parking lot, I sort of punched Dan on the arm while the other three were busy joking around, and handed him my keys. Dan's eyes widened a bit, but he nodded. When we were settled inside, Sutton asked the obvious question.

"What the... Russell, you're letting *him* drive your brand new car?"

Dan looked over his shoulder. "Sorry, bro. I can't help that I'm the superior friend."

"You guys are idiots," he grunted, the pout in his voice loud and clear.

"Ah." Dan breathed in deeply, dragging the gear into reverse. "Gotta love that scent: fresh Eau de Charcoal Gray Range Rover."

"It's not gonna be so fresh if we don't get Russell back to the dorms," Ben said, sniffing the air, then leaning toward me to sniff a second time. "Dude, is there a sewer around here, or is that coming from Russell's backside?"

I'll spare you the next thirty minutes of post-adolescent potty humor, because I respect you, Sully. But suffice it to say that while your buddy Sutton hyperbolized the number of gastric explosions he heard coming from the seat in front of him, the scene was set for what came next.

Namely this well-kept secret: I know how to puke on demand.

HATLEY HALL

It's Tuesday afternoon as I write this letter. Just a little over twenty-four hours after I started this exercise, and you know what? I do feel slightly better. Color me shocked, but I really dig telling you stories. I sort of wish I'd told them to you before now.

I wonder if "cognitive exercise" is just a synonym for "dealing with your old baggage?" Hmm. That Keating fella's a trickster.

One of my favorite qualities about the twenty-first century is that with a little ingenuity, you can convince anyone that you are where they *think* you are. Before I left the dorm Sunday night, I told Dan I'd be at Gigi's. When I got in my car, I called Gigi to tell her Sigma Phi Beta was taking us on a brothers' retreat. Her response? "Have fun, Peter. And be safe."

Oh, I *was* safe. Safe and sound, tucked away inside a tiny beachfront cabin in Oceanside.

You've seen those cabins, right – thirty-ish miles north of Lincoln City, by the haystack rocks? For a thousand bucks cash, you can hide out there for a week without anyone asking your business. No maid service. No internet. No cell phone signal.

Bonus: the Pacific Ocean is just outside your front door.

The sky dumped buckets that week, so I lay on the floor of the cabin listening to the rain patter against the roof, letting minutes and hours pass me by.

I didn't read. There was no Wi-Fi to distract me. If the rain stopped, I would stand up, open the door, and walk across the sand to the surf. But the second the sky opened up again, I returned to my spot on the floor and stared up again at the ceiling, emptying my mind of everything but the steady *thunk, thunk, thunk* all around me.

On Sunday morning, I drove back to Portland via Lincoln City. My mission: to follow through on my mom's request and ask the Sullivan's hostess for her number.

(Surprised? Yeah, I bet. I flat out lied to you when I claimed I'd only visited Lincoln City three times. I just couldn't admit the fourth.)

Sunday brunch at Sullivan's Restaurant was remarkably chaotic that day. I sat there for a couple of hours, hoping to catch a glimpse of the tall girl with the auburn hair. I finally struck up the courage to ask my waitress if she knew where you were. "Sorry," she said, chomping her gum. "Just started here yesterday, and the owners are up in Seattle this weekend. But if you come back tomorrow, you can ask them yourself."

Um, no thanks, Violet Beauregarde. Don't let that gum turn you into a giant blueberry.

Despite my mission failure, I headed back to campus that afternoon with a week's worth of stubble on my face and a renewed sense of purpose. I may not have tracked down the leggy hostess, but it didn't matter. When I walked in the dorm room, Dan gave me a rundown of everything I missed at orientation, and by that night, my weeklong freak-out felt like fake news.

The next morning, I zoomed to French Composition 3301 half an hour in advance. Why? Because you and I both know wherever you sit on the first day of college determines your success for the next four years. Too far back? Slacker. Too close? Well, in that case, you're a different kind of loser – the kind who shows off what they *think* they know without realizing everything they *don't*. But hey, I don't need to sell *you* on the merits of that optimal middle seat, do I?

Because thirty seconds after I'd settled into my desk, you walked through that door with stars in your eyes and your jaw set for victory.

Right up until you spotted me in the exact seat you'd been dreaming about all summer.

I couldn't believe it when I lifted my eyes, Sully. It was *you*. The Sullivan's hostess. The very redhead I'd driven to Lincoln City to find less than twenty-four hours prior.

"Um, pardon?" you asked demurely. *"C'est le cours de composition 3301?"*

Okay, so I'm going to brag on you here a little bit, missy. You always talk about my accent and my grammar like I'm some sort of academic genius, but in my opinion, none of those skills reflect upon *me*. I simply lived in France during the age range where kids' brains are developing their language center.

It's science, Sully. Look it up.

But you? Dude, you started French as a teenager. Your pronunciation skills were perfected by sheer tenacity and discipline, not to mention how hard you rock French grammar and spelling.

Everything I know, I learned by proxy – Liz Russell practiced her best classroom materials on me back in the day. You didn't live with a French teacher, therefore you and your work ethic deserve full credit for your success.

Okay, bragging rant over. Let's get back to the story.

On our first day of college, when you walked into Hatley Hall 207, you were wearing a green Sullivan's shirt – possibly the one you wore the night of our car accident. Only this time, instead of shorts, you had on a jean mini-skirt. And instead of a ponytail, your hair was straight, long, and glossy. Like you were headed to Milan to walk the Dolce & Gabbana runway.

Your arms hugged a Moleskine notebook to your chest, and in your left hand, you held a turquoise rolling ball pen. I wanted to check the bridge of your nose for freckles, but your face went blotchy as your gray eyes narrowed in my direction.

I lowered my gaze to my textbook because… *dude.*

I. Could. Not. Believe. My. Eyes.

In what sick universe would the redheaded hostess from Sullivan's Restaurant choose the same college as me? No wait – not just the same college. The same exact French course down to the same specific section, even though the catalog listed two other choices?

But the very worst thing? It was clear you did *not* recognize me. And Sully, I'm gonna be honest: that *hurt.*

A wave of confusion rushed through me in that moment as you sped past my desk without a second glance. After the accident, you'd become a bit of a saint in my mind. Yes, I found you attractive, but that's not why I'd driven to Lincoln City twenty-four hours earlier.

I went to Sullivan's that Sunday because I'd convinced myself we had a metaphysical connection – you'd *saved* me, right? *You.* The redheaded hostess. And I believed with all my heart that if you ever laid eyes on me again, we'd have a *moment.*

Except that moment didn't happen. You simply walked past me and took the seat behind me.

So I went rogue.

"Lincoln City? Are you serious?" I scoffed, wheeling around to face you. "I freaking *hate* that dump."

The second your face crumpled, I knew I'd taken things too far. Was it your fault I'd concocted an elaborate cosmic backstory between us? Uh, no. You absolutely did not deserve my sarcasm.

Luckily for both of us, Dan Thomas walked in a few seconds later, chiding me for letting him oversleep on the first day of school. After class, I took my sweet time gathering up all of my things, and by the time Dan and I finally exited the building, you were a couple hundred yards ahead of us on the sidewalk. And guess who was scurrying toward you like a little puppy? Drew Sutton, who skidded to a halt in front of you.

In two seconds flat, he had you giggling. "Dude," Dan chuckled. "We need to get Sutton to teach us his rock star ways. Did you see the way that ginger's face lit up just now?"

Yes, Daniel. I did. Thanks for the confirmation.

I studied Sutton for a moment, then looked down at myself: grungy cargo pants, oversized Sigma Phi Beta jersey, FLIP FLOPS. And then I remembered my wild hair and scruffy cheeks.

No wonder you blew me off that morning, Sully. As far as you knew, I was a yeti half-breed who slept in a backwoods yurt and ate a steady diet of goji berries and chia seed pudding.

Don't lie, sister. You know that was your first impression. You told me so yourself once upon a time.

That evening, after our first official Sigma Phi chapter meeting, every recruit was sequestered in mandatory study hall. Sutton chose the seat next to me, and for the first hour, we scribbled dutifully side by side, like good little freshmen recruits.

But I wasn't studying, Sully. I was concocting a plan. Because despite my rudeness that morning – despite the left side of my brain insisting you were a stuck-up little goody two shoes – my inner detective couldn't let it go. Especially once I saw you with Surf Boy Sutton on the quad.

Just before eight o'clock, the study hall monitor stood up and announced we could take a five-minute break. I followed Sutton to the kitchen, and pounced.

"How was orientation last week?" I asked nonchalantly. "Did I miss anything fun?"

"Dude," he replied with half a cookie in his mouth. "It was awesome. Too bad you got sick off those tacos."

"Yeah, too bad." I filled a mug with decaf coffee, then filled one for him. "So, about that that hundred bucks you owe me…"

He snorted. "Come on, man. You can't be serious right now."

I took a slow sip of my coffee, my eyes locked on his. "A bet is a bet, Sutton. Especially among brothers."

"Whatever, Russell," he snorted. "We both know that you flaked on the bet when you puked out the window of your own car. I don't owe you a dime."

"Fine. If that's how you want to play things, how about this option: give me the ginger's number, and I'll never mention the money again."

"Which ginger?"

Which ginger? Who did he think he was, Sully? A British boy-bander?

"Come on, man," I laughed. "You *know* which ginger – the one you met at Hatley Hall today after French class."

"Meredith?" He frowned. "But how –"

"Relax, bro." I clapped him on the shoulder. "It's no big deal. Dan Thomas and I just want to get to know the smartest person in our French class a little better. Befriend the competition, level out the stakes. You know the drill."

And without another word, I walked back to study hall and resumed my work.

I wish you could have seen your hometown buddy squirm the rest of that night. Even though I never lifted my eyes from my homework, I could feel the wheels turning inside his brain. What a shock, right? When Mister Perfect decided to join you at Highgate, I bet he never dreamed his favorite goldfish would break free and thrive in the big pond.

A few minutes before nine, the study hall monitor stepped briefly out of the room. So I scribbled the following onto a ripped out page from my spiral and slapped it onto his history book.

YOUR MONEY
YOUR GINGER
YOUR CALL

Sutton sat there, face forward, for at least a minute – long enough for the monitor to return. Then he scribbled something down on the back of my note, dug into his pocket, and slipped a crisp hundred dollar bill inside the fold before he slammed it down on the table beside me.

THE GINGER IS OFF-LIMITS.
PERIOD.

Ginger Spice

For the first month of school, Drew Sutton waited for you after French class every Monday, Wednesday, and Friday. Sometimes he brought you coffee. Sometimes he took your messenger bag and carried it to your next class. But always – one hundred percent of the time – he brought a smile to your face that no one else could manage. Heart eyes for days. *Le sigh.*

Hold up – make that *le PUKE*.

When Sutton sent me his little warning that night in study hall, I just figured he wanted to remind me that in a fraternity, you never step in on a brother's prospects. Even without that note, I could see that the two of you had a history. And if anyone understood the stakes of a lifelong male-female friendship, it was me. (*Cough* BROOKS. *Cough* DARBY.)

But then, at the Panhellenic mixer in early October, I saw your boy Sutton making out with a buxom brunette. And a week later, I caught him pressed up against a tiny blonde in the library stacks. So when he showed up to French class the next day with the same starry eyes he'd used on those two ladies, I began to question whether his motive in protecting you had less to do with *you* and more to do with Sutton keeping every option available at all times.

So I decided to call his bluff.

You probably don't remember this, but for several days in a row, right around mid-terms, you and I left French class together. I'd follow you out the door with questions about the previous day's reading that I already knew the answer to, or I'd mention the study group Dan and I were organizing for the midterm – anything to keep you talking long enough for your boy Sutton to notice us together on our way out of Hatley Hall.

That Saturday, I invited our mutual friend to shoot hoops over at the outdoor intramural court. The pair of us walked chummily across campus like we'd known each other for decades, and despite the chill in the air, Sutton was as cheerful as I'd ever seen him.

After I let him win HORSE a couple of times, we switched off shooting free throws for a while. And once my so-called brother got nice and comfortable, I set my trap.

"You've been busy this semester, Sutton," I said, dribbling to set up my shot.

"Busy?" He bounced the ball off the backboard, then held it to his chest. "With school?"

"With the ladies. I guess you've got a date lined up for the Halloween party?"

"Still weighing the possibilities." He stole the ball away from me and dunking a perfect shot. "You jealous, Russell?"

"Wow. Can't sneak anything past you, Andrew. You pegged me for sure."

Drew circled me, then slammed a rim shot. "Who are you taking next Saturday? That Alpha Chi who keeps texting you?"

"Alpha Chi?"

"Come on, man. Don't play dumb. Dan said you've been chatting up some girl named Rebekah or something. No wait, Mary? Jezebel? I don't know. Some biblical name."

There was no Alpha Chi texting me, Sully. But I kept up the ruse because Dan had obviously sold Sutton on this little white lie. This is one of my favorite Dan Thomas qualities: he always has my back while playing players at their own games.

"Oh," I fake chuckled. "You mean Rachel?"

"Yes! Rachel! That's the one." He high-fived me right there in the middle of the court. "Nice one, Russell. You're taking *her* to the party? Dude. That chick is smokin'."

Chick? Smokin'? Was he for real? Didn't he realize we'd crossed into the twenty-first century?

"Meh, I *guess*. If you're into aspiring YouTube makeup tutorial wannabes," I shrugged. "Actually, I've almost convinced Dan we should ask these two girls from our French class. Adrienne White and Meredith Sullivan. You know Meredith, right?"

Dribble, dribble. Dribble, dribble. That was all I heard, because Sutton had just grabbed the ball from me and was now pounding the pavement with it. Then he turned on me, eyes blazing. "I told you Meredith was off-limits, Russell. That was only a few weeks ago. Don't act like you've forgotten."

"Whoa, whoa, whoa," I laughed, lifting my hands in mock surrender. "Take it easy, Andrew. There's no reason to give yourself an ulcer about it. We both know I'm a gentleman."

"I'm not fooling around, man. Don't hit on my friend."

"Who said anything about hitting on her?" I leveled my best smirk at him. "I'm just a guy asking a girl to hang out on Halloween. What's so scandalous about that?"

Sutton glared at me for a full ten seconds. Then he scooped up the same ball he'd chunked at me and headed off toward the dorm. I followed behind him from a safe distance, because I knew I'd accomplished my goal. He couldn't even stick to a straight path, he was so unhinged. And when we got within earshot of Peyton Hall, he wheeled around and sprinted back to meet me.

"I paid you the hundred bucks," he seethed. "We settled our bet, and you promised to stay away from her. You *promised*, Russell. No take-backs. A deal's a deal."

"Take a breath, son." I clapped him on the shoulder, then pretended to pick a piece of lint from his sleeve. "As I recall, you paid me off instead of giving me Meredith's number, but I never agreed to any deal. This is college, bro. Ginger Spice can hang out with whomever she pleases."

He blinked at me for a long time. Maybe it was because I'd just used *whomever* correctly, but I choose to believe it was the first time ever someone had challenged Drew where you were concerned.

I didn't say another word. I just watched him watching me.

Maybe I scared the Lincoln City out of him. Because with all his might, your boy Andrew chucked the basketball at my chest, then skulked off in the direction of the parking garage.

DEAR SULLY

GILBERT BLYTHE

For six months, I was the epitome of fraternal loyalty. Right up until Tommy Harding threw his *Famous Gingers and their Friends* party.

"Thanks for driving me all over Portland yesterday," Adrienne White smiled at you in class one day that April. "I never realized thrift shops would still have so many Eighties clothes."

"I know, right?" You beamed. "I think you and Jacob will be the perfect Duckie and Andie. That auburn bob wig transforms you into Molly Ringwald's twin."

"It's amazing! But I'm sorry you've had such a hard time finding costumes for you and Drew. Can't you guys pick another couple? Anne and Gilbert are so old-fashioned."

You dug in your bag for a pen. "Yeah, well, this is one of those times it's a liability to go on a date with someone who's known you your whole life. Drew insists we dress up as Anne and Gilbert because they're my favorite book characters. Besides, he wants to win the originality prize, and he doesn't think anyone else has heard of them."

"Is he crazy?" Adrienne gaped. "Everyone knows who Anne and Gilbert are."

"I know. The books are huge all over the world. Not to mention the movies and the new TV show. In Japan, they even built a replica of Green Gables itself!"

In Sutton's defense, he was not entirely wrong about the general public's lack of awareness re: your favorite couple. Until that day, I had never heard of *Anne of Green Gables*. So imagine my shock when I pulled out my phone to google "Anne and Gilbert," and 43 million hits popped up on my screen.

While you and Adrienne brainstormed where to find Drew some knickers, I downloaded L.M. Montgomery's books to my Kindle app. That weekend, I read the entire series. Then I formulated a plan.

Dan and I had volunteered to serve as sober drivers at Tommy's party, because while it wasn't an official Sigma Phi Beta event, the officers always made sure they were covered in case of liability. Therefore, neither of us had a date that night. But that didn't stop us from dressing up.

Dan went as Ed Sheeran. (Duh. They share that beautiful voice.)

And I picked Gilbert Blythe.

Yes, that's right. I *did* copy Drew, but I had a good reason, Miss Shirley: did it ever occur to you that I actually *am* Gilbert Blythe?

I'm older than the rest of our class.

I may, from time to time, overdo it with the nicknames.

I'm in love with the girl who broke a metaphorical slate over my head for my insulting behavior, in a classroom, on the first day of school.

I even have curly brown hair.

Are you freaking kidding me, Carrots? I'm the dude you've been looking for your whole life! So you can forgive me for trying to even the playing field with your charlatan of a best friend.

That night at Tommy's party, I was standing on the back porch when you followed a blundering Sutton down to the river dock. I knew he had feelings for you. Everyone in our pledge class knew. Scratch that – everyone at *Highgate* knew. So the second your feet hit the planks of that dock, forty brotherly heads turned toward the water. Like a herd of meerkats, we stood at attention, waiting for the predator to (finally) pounce.

It was no surprise that liquid courage had emboldened our brother Sutton.

The real plot twist was *your* response.

Oh, man, Sully. You shoved Drew away so hard that I thought he might fly into the water. Your hand flew to your lips, and when you looked down at your fingers, you stared and stared, like they held physical proof of your broken heart.

And then… Sutton puked.

I asked Dan to drive you back to the dorms that night. Maybe I should have swooped in to save the day, but I didn't want you associating me with whatever you felt after that disaster.

You looked like you'd just lost your best friend.

Now that I think about it, maybe you *did*. Because a couple of days later, I saw Drew making out with your roommate, Lindsay. Next thing I knew, he'd stopped meeting you after French class.

So I watched, Sully. And I waited. And maybe I never said anything, but by the spring of freshman year, I had definitely caught a *really* bad case of the feels for you. Not just because you're beautiful and quick-witted and hard-working and very, *very* kind.

All of that is true. But the quality I love most? It's your courage. When life snatches away someone you love, you never run for the hills. Someone like you would never hole up in a tiny cabin or stuff your face with Ben and Jerry's Chubby Hubby.

No way. Not Meredith Sullivan! When life goes haywire, you dig in. You take your pain and use it to fuel your dreams.

Every. Single. Time.

Which is why I'm sitting here, writing this letter, wondering how I ever let you go.

THE SULLY SWAGGER

It's Wednesday now. I've been writing you these letters for, like, thirty-six hours. My hand keeps cramping up, and to be blunt, I'm ready to quit this nonsense. It's not like you'll ever read them, you know? Why am I doing this to myself?

Oh, yeah. Because I promised Dr. Keating. So I forced myself to sit in the window of the upstairs loft in that oversized Starbucks on Boulevard Saint-Michel.

That's right – wrap me up in an American flag and call me basic.

Don't judge, okay? I need *something* to feel normal in my life. My first choice was a pint of Chubby Hubby, but apparently, it doesn't exist in Paris (believe me, I've asked everywhere). So my next best coping mechanism is a Venti Samoa Frappuccino. Extra whip, extra mocha, extra caramel sauce, extra coconut chips.

Merci, madame la barista. The name's spelled P-I-E-R-R-E.

Um, yes – Girl Scout cookie Frappuccinos *do* exist. Go ahead and fact-check me if you like. They're on the secret menu.

I may be a flake, but I would never lie about coffee.

Now listen, this letter's on the serious side, which probably explains my foul mood today. But I'm going to write it anyway, despite my crampy hand, because this story feels important. Why else would I have made an outline beforehand?

What? I know how to outline papers. I learned it from you.

Okay, you ready? Here we go.

As you know, my Pops died suddenly that summer between our first and second year at Highgate. Maybe someday you and I can talk more about him, but for now, I'll keep it short.

My grandfather was the best guy I ever knew. He loved my grandmother with his whole heart, yet he somehow managed to love my mom, my dad, and me with his whole heart too.

Peter Beckett lived a full life. He served in Vietnam, then flew all over the world for his job with the airlines. He loved fly fishing and camping with his grandson. He loved his daughter so much that when she died, it shaved twenty years off his own life.

I think about him often, especially in Paris. I never asked him what it was like to come here after the Naval Academy to study at Addison. And more importantly, I wish I knew his side of the Gigi + Pops epic Parisian love story. That's not the sort of question a teenage boy would ask his granddad. Lucky for me, Gigi told me her version of things before she died.

To be honest, I don't remember much about the months following Pops' sudden death. Sophomore year, I lived at Gigi's and spent as little time on campus as possible, which basically meant I showed up for class and fraternity duties and then disappeared before anyone detected my presence.

Because of my family situation and the years I'd spent living in Paris as a kid, Dr. Sweeney kindly waived my credits for our next French course – *Communication 3601*. Maybe you didn't notice my absence that semester, but trust me, I wasn't there. I bet we didn't see each other more than a couple of times that fall.

You've always walked with what Dan calls the Sully Swagger – head high, shoulders back, hips swaying ever so slightly like you own the ground you walk on. I used to think you did it on purpose – that you strutted like that to drive us menfolk mad. But after spending time with you in Paris, I realized you're unaware of this secret weapon. Totally and completely oblivious.

That first day back in January, I was fifty feet behind you on the path to Hatley Hall. You'd pulled your hair into a messy knot and your shoulders were hunched forward. Your gait was so slow that I could've easily overtaken you, but I hung back and observed. Because something about your energy felt... off. The Sully Swagger had morphed into a leave-me-alone lope.

The sun was shining that day, and the air was unseasonably warm. So when you reached the steps leading up to building, you stopped to peel off your coat and scarf. For a long moment, you stood tall, eyes closed, breathing in the abnormally spring-like air.

I could not take my eyes off you. Not because you'd just sent my hormones flying. No, the sight of your ribs poking through the thin cotton sweater you were wearing stopped me dead in my tracks. My first instinct was to sprint over, wrap my arms around your waist, and hug you tight.

Instead, I trotted past you to open the door. After the briefest of side-eyes, you grabbed your stuff and scurried past me, head down, eyes on the floor.

It freaked me the whole way out.

In the years since, I've filled in the blanks on your life sophomore year. I know you and Lindsay Foster were super tight freshman year, so it must have been double the punch when she started dating your childhood best friend. And look, I know Sutton has turned the corner now that he's on his way to legal fame and fortune, but back in the day? He had the self-awareness of a gnat. The Sutton I knew back then paraded his on-again-off-again love life right in front of you, all day every day. And I, for one, don't understand how you forgave him.

No wonder you moved into the singleton dorms that year. And no wonder you dropped twenty pounds without trying. Maybe you should take up my Chubby Hubby and Samoa Frappuccino addiction the next time some loser distracts you from your dreams.

(You can't see me, but I'm pointing at myself right now.)

That spring semester, you were a woman obsessed. We all knew the stakes: we either won a Beckett Scholarship for Paris, or we spent the summer in Tours. And even though Tours is the opposite of shabby, that summer program didn't seem to be an option for you. *Paris or bust.*

On the Friday of our qualifying exam, I picked Dan up from the Sigma Phi Beta house two hours before the test started. All week, we'd planned to eat a full breakfast at Ruby's Diner, and to be honest, it was the best decision I made all year.

DEAR SULLY

Maybe it was nerves, or maybe it was just being at a place I knew so well, but Dan and I laughed so hard that morning that my lungs felt clean.

And then you and Sutton walked in for your standing Friday morning breakfast date.

The two of you took a seat in a booth close enough that I could hear you, but neither you nor Sutton noticed us sitting in the corner. From the moment you walked in, Sutton never shut up, shoveling his mouth full of food and chirping so loudly that I didn't even have to strain to hear the subject: Lindsay Foster. She'd just broken up with him again the night before, and he was telling you in no uncertain terms that this was it. "I'm done playing her games," he barked, stretching himself wide across the booth. "Hold me accountable, Fee. And not just for the rest of the semester – I'm talking all summer, all next year, and forevermore. You're the only person I'll obey."

On and on, he droned. And while he chattered away, your fingers clutched a notebook. For every three seconds you looked at Drew, you spent four staring hard at the notes on the page. *One last review*, your eyes seemed to say. *If I could only read these once more, I'd be grand.*

You were a bird inside a cage, trapped between hope and despair, wishing someone would set you free from the overgrown toddler heckling you nearby.

Later that morning in the exam room, the desks filled up steadily until only one seat remained – in the very back, off to the side. When you walked in the room, you'd somehow transformed into a ginger Audrey Hepburn – black jacket, black pants, hair pulled back in a high ponytail like this test was just a pit stop on your way to the *Sabrina* movie set. Watch out, Humphrey Bogart. Sabrina Fairchild 2.0 is ready to rumble.

But after scanning the room, your face fell. You *hate* the back row.

I couldn't take it, Sully. I stood up. "Here you go, McMeredith," I smiled and bowed. "I was just keeping this seat warm for you."

"Are you trying to psych me out, Russell?" You narrowed your eyes. "Because it's not going to work, you know. Not this time. I'm getting one of these scholarships today. You and your little mind games won't stop me."

Dan shot me a look from behind you, shaking his head slightly in warning. So I slinked back into my desk and willed myself not to turn around as you skulked to the back row with only seconds to spare before Dr. Sweeney took his place at the lectern.

For whatever reason that day, I had no problem filling out the exam – grammar questions, syntax problems, *whatever*. Blowing off steam with Dan that morning had cleared my brain. For once, I wasn't burdened by the wreckage in my life.

For once, it was just me against the Blue Book.

You blitzed out of Room 207 before time was called, which might not have seemed like a big deal to anyone else, except you sniffled as you walked by my desk. My eyes followed you up to Dr. Sweeney's desk, which means I saw your hands trembling as you handed in your work. I also saw you stumble on your high heels as you hurried into the hallway.

A few moments later, Dr. Sweeney called time. I was the first guy out the door, immediately followed by Dan. The two of us stood there together, staring down the hallway at you huddled on the floor, arms around your knees, attempting to hide behind a bench.

DEAR SULLY

You were crying, Sully – sobbing so hard that I could see your body heaving from fifty yards away.

I guess we stood there too long, because you lifted your head and turned your face toward us, dark mascara lines blazing trails down your cheeks. And because I was the very last person on the planet you wanted to see, you lowered your forehead back to your knees.

Dan gave me a pointed look. Then he turn left and walked to the nearest exit while I sped down the hallway toward you. It wasn't that I wanted to speak to you – I'd read your raccoon eyes loud and clear, after all. But our classmates had begun spilling out into the hallway. If I didn't hurry, someone else might disturb your privacy.

Without a sound, I sauntered toward you, picking up one of the recycling bins from the center of the hallway. Once I reached your hiding place, I lowered the bin silently to the ground on the far side of the bench so that no one would spot you from the exam room.

Dan had circled around the building, so when I stepped through the side doors, he was waiting. We walked to the frat house in silence, like a tiny squadron on a mission. Once inside, we found Drew shooting pool in the game room, as blithe and carefree as ever.

"Hey, Sutton," I barked from the doorway.

He glanced up. "Yeah?"

"I need to talk to you."

Drew looked at Dan, then at me, and back at Dan. But time was ticking, so I stormed outside and waited on the steps. A couple of minutes later, he finally moseyed through the door.

"What's up, Russell?"

"A lot, actually. Are you still friends with Meredith Sullivan?"

I scoured his expression for any sign he'd seen Dan and me that morning at Ruby's, but his face was as neutral as ever. "Of course I am," he said with a glib smile. "What's it to you?"

"Nothing. I just thought you should know she seemed a little… upset after our test."

"Test?" He lifted both eyebrows. "What test?"

"Dude, does it matter? My point is that your *friend* looked visibly shaken. Shouldn't you go check on her?"

Sutton pulled his phone out of his pocket and pressed the button to light up the home screen. "She hasn't texted," he shrugged. "She's probably in the library. She's *always* in the library."

I took a step toward him. "You're not hearing me, man. Your girl was a wreck."

"She's not *my* girl," he retorted. "Well, not yet anyway. Besides, you obviously don't know her very well if you think a test would rattle her nerves. Meredith handles stress better than Congress, the Supreme Court, and the President combined. Trust me. She's fine."

How I kept from decking him in the jaw, I have no idea, because in that moment, I wanted to wipe that self-satisfied grin right off his face. Instead, I took a deep breath, lifted my hands in surrender, and walked away.

All the way back to Hatley Hall.

You weren't there, of course. So I hurried over to the sophomore quad. Then to the library and even the cafeteria. No, no, and no.

And then, because I had no idea what else to do, I swung back by Hatley Hall again, circling around it until I found you hiding in that tiny alcove on the north side. There you were, still hugging your knees, only this time, you were sitting *on* a bench instead of beside it.

DEAR SULLY

So maybe now you understand why I freaked out when Dr. Sweeney called me to his office later that afternoon to announce that I'd placed third on the Centre Lafayette placement exam, right behind Dan Thomas and Marshall Freeman. Because as much as I wanted to spend junior year in Paris, I had this sickening sense that if you *didn't* go, your entire world might implode.

I spent all weekend asking myself how those rankings might be different if Drew hadn't shanghaied you beforehand. Every time, the answer came back the same: you would have beaten me, fair and square. In fact, you might have outranked both Marshall and Dan. Because on a good day, your brain is a beautiful sight to behold, Miss Sullivan. And on a bad day, on arguably the worst day of that semester, you still got a 94.5.

You deserved the Beckett Scholarship, Sully. Never question that again. I mean it.

Chalk up that one-point difference between our scores to your clueless breakfast companion, and let it slip into the ether like it never happened at all.

BEGIN AGAIN

You know that Taylor Swift song about the tall girl who's reflecting back on some guy who didn't appreciate all the little details about her that she happens to love about herself? Taylor called it *Begin Again,* and if I didn't know better, I would swear she wrote that song about the Russell-Sullivan-Sutton love triangle of junior year.

She did set her video in all of our favorite parts of Paris *and* dressed all retro like a certain redhead I know. I'm just saying.

I was all set to spend my summer in Tours with the rest of the Beckett Scholarship rejects when Gigi told me about her cancer later that spring. And even though she severely downplayed her prognosis, I still refused – flat out *refused* – to go to Tours.

"I don't need the practice and I definitely don't need the credits," I argued, my eyes flooding with tears. "Please, Gigi. Don't make me leave you here alone. I don't want to regret missing time with you."

And because my grandmother could never stand to see me cry, she caved. Temporarily.

Here's a little tidbit I bet you never realized about the free flights included in the Beckett Endowment scholarship: you can thank Pops' never-ending cache of air miles from his piloting days. Every year, we booked the scholarship students' airfare out of those miles, but that summer, the usual ticketing agent – a.k.a. Gigi – was in a fight for her life. So her dashingly handsome grandson booked the flights for Marshall Freeman, Meredith Sullivan, and Dan Thomas.

Your original seatmate was Dan, by the way. You can thank Marshall's kale obsession for my humanitarian benevolence there.

The thing is, helping Gigi sent me down a Meredith-shaped rabbit hole of personal information which led to no good. For example, the résumé you'd provided to the scholarship committee listed a place called Treble Jig as your longtime dance studio. Which helped me find about thirty competition videos on YouTube, including your Oregon state championship dance to *Gangnam Style*.

That's right. I only pretended to be surprised that night you danced for me in Doolin.

Anyway, I could terrify you for several more pages with all the ways I stalked you that summer, but here's the real point: Gigi was onto me. Over and over again.

Now look, I realize there are more humiliating things that a grandmother could catch you looking at on the internet than Irish dance competitions, but I swear, every time I typed your name into Google, Gigi would walk into my room. And every time, I would jump sky high, eyes wide, looking guilty as a raccoon caught digging through a restaurant trash can.

I don't know when exactly that summer she decided to force Dr. Sweeney to bend the rules, but force him she did. Like, whoa.

On the first Friday of the school year, after a full day of fraternity recruitment, I was sitting in the kitchen, eating cereal in my Sigma Phi Beta jersey when Gigi walked in and sat down beside me.

"Why are you wearing a suit?" I asked.

"Don't speak with your mouth full of food, Peter." She undid the top button on her jacket and began to fan herself. "Where is your passport?"

"I don't know. In the safe upstairs, I guess? I haven't used it in a couple of years."

She took out a piece of paper and a pen from her pocket and began scribbling down notes. "I spoke to your friend Daniel today. He's agreed to leave for Paris tomorrow so you can take his spot on the flight this Sunday."

"What? Hold on a second –"

"Luckily, my contact in the rewards department was able to find a first-class seat for him from Portland to LAX and then another first-class seat to Paris. I figured it was the least I could do on such short notice. But… oh, dear. I'll need to e-mail the concierge at the Guénégaud apartment to let her know Dan will arrive early. I hope she's available to let him in."

"Gigi! Rewind ten sentences. Did you just say I'm moving to Paris?"

"Yes, I did. I went to Dr. Sweeney's office yesterday afternoon and accused him of subverting my authority by giving away your scholarship to that Sullivan girl. Today I spoke to the registrar, who has removed you from all of your classes on the Highgate campus. You will spend this year in Paris, no arguments allowed."

DEAR SULLY

"But you can't punish Meredith like that!" Sweat slid down the small of my back. "Dr. Sweeney didn't give anything away. That was *my* decision, not his!"

"I know that, darling, and I agree: Meredith deserves her scholarship. But so do you, which is why *four* of you will go to Paris instead of three. So you can stop running your fingers through those messy curls like I've just stolen your puppy or something. Oh, and speaking of your curls, you *will* visit the barber first thing tomorrow morning. And not just for a haircut. Your beard collects crumbs, and I don't want to hurt your feelings, but the average woman doesn't find unkempt facial hair attractive."

I touched my beard, and she was right – some cornflakes fell onto my jersey. "What's this all about, Geeg?"

"It's not *what*, it's *who*. You, my darling boy, are in love with a lovely redhead named Meredith, and I insist that you spend this year exploring Paris by her side."

"What? I'm not in –"

"Yes, you are, and I will not allow you stay in Portland pining for her while you watch from afar. You've suffered enough in your young life already, and now it's time for you to live."

I could feel the tears lining my eyes, but I couldn't say a word, Sully. I just sat there, staring at Gigi, hoping she'd somehow developed ESP during chemo.

And maybe she had, because she said, "You're welcome, darling. Now then, let's make a list of all the things you will need this year because you're not coming home any time soon. I fully plan to spend Christmas in Paris this year, and I'm not hauling a second suitcase over the ocean for you simply because you failed to be organized on the front end."

And that, dear Sully, is the real reason Gigi forced me to Paris. I'm sure there were other factors, like the fact that she didn't want me to watch her die. But the truth is, Gigi got tired of me mooning around over you all summer, so she kickstarted my life into gear.

Saturday morning first thing, I drove to the barber. The bottom half of my face looked so pale after he shaved me that I looked like I'd gone skiing across Antarctica with only the top half of a balaclava. And then, snip, snip, snip… bye bye, curls. My hair was so short that when I walked into the Sigma Phi house Sunday morning to retrieve my mother's classroom flags, even Sutton noticed the change.

"Whoo! Fancy!" He whistled. "Where are you off to this time, Russell? Lunch with the dean?"

"Paris," I barked over my shoulder. "See you around, Sutton."

Maybe you know this, but the Sigma Phi Beta fraternity house was built in the fifties, which means the floors are creaky, rendering it impossible to tail somebody without their knowledge. I knew Sutton was following me – down the stairs to the basement storage while I looked for the flags, up three flights to explain my situation to the president in his room, and back downstairs again through the living room.

He followed me all the way outside to my car without saying a word. And when I finally turned around to confront him, Sutton's face was so white it appeared gray.

"You're… are you seriously going to Paris?"

"Yes." I crossed my arms. "My flight leaves in three hours, Sutton. Did you need something? Or can I leave?"

Oh, Sully. I actually felt sorry for the kid for a moment. I don't know if it was my new-and-improved hygiene or my sudden resolve, but I could see that Sutton finally accepted me as his competition. It might've made me laugh if it hadn't also hurt my feelings.

Really, Sutton? I thought. *I visit the barber and* now *you're scared?*

"I told you a million times, Russell," he growled, the color returning to his face. "Stay away from her. Or else."

I willed my expression to neutral. "I don't know who you're talking about, but whoever she is, does it matter? Because I'm pretty sure I saw Lindsay Foster attached to your face Thursday night. Or did I imagine that?"

"I mean it, Russell! Keep away from Meredith!" He shouted so loudly that some guys appeared at the window of the frat house. "She's not some shiny new toy for you to play with."

"No, she's not," I retorted. "How about you turn that accusatory finger back on yourself? Last time I checked, it was bad form to string along more than one woman at a time. You've already got your hands full with Lindsay. So don't worry; I'll watch over the ginger for you."

I turned around to leave, but he grabbed my elbow and turned me back to face him. "Meredith and I have a history! We have inside jokes that you know nothing about. Go ahead and ask her yourself."

"Sutton, I don't really have time to talk about your little hometown Hallmark movie right now."

"It's not *little*!" His voice went sky high. "You ask her, man. Ask her what she promised me on the lake a couple of weeks ago. Ask her why I said not to settle for anything less than a marquis. Because if you ask, her answer will prove why you can't have her. What we have is *sacred*."

I don't know what it was about his protest that emboldened me. But I smiled, I climbed in my car, and I left Drew Sutton behind.

The original plan was to ask you about the marquis nonsense on the plane, but the truth is, Sully, I could see I annoyed you that day. So I tucked the clue away, and waited.

A week later, on the bus to Normandy, you saw Lindsay wearing Drew's lavaliere. And when you didn't punch me that night at karaoke – when you actually seemed *grateful* at my attempt to cheer you up – I could feel my doubt lifting. So at the cemetery the next day, I finally scrounged up enough courage to ask.

"Sutton asked me to remind you not to settle for anything less than a marquis," I blurted out of the blue. "What did he mean?"

Your entire body went pink, which I might have taken as proof of a schoolgirl crush. Except you seemed… I don't know, is ashamed too strong a word?

"It's nothing," you said, waving me off. "Drew thinks it's funny to pretend I'll meet an aristocrat while I'm here. Like that will ever happen."

Um… what? I thought. *Does he even know this girl? She doesn't care about money. She could spend years in an aristocrat's orbit and never once notice.*

I know you felt terrible about the Romanov jokes after you realized my parents were dead, but I'm secretly glad you roasted me that day. Because when I flipped your joke about the Grand Duke of St. Petersburg on its head, you turned bright, scorching crimson.

Maybe it *was* proof of a schoolgirl crush. Only this time, the object of your crush was me. Except you had no idea the world had rotated backward on its axis.

DEAR SULLY

EDITH DE NANTES

It's now Thursday morning, June 28th. When Dr. Keating gave me this assignment, I wondered how I would write a single letter, and now, three days later, I've already written eight. And you know what? I don't hate the process. Probably because it feels like I'm talking to you.

The Parisian sky is spitting rain this morning, so I'm sitting at our favorite table at *La Rotonde* café near school. I'm even drinking Irish Breakfast tea. Why? Because the waitress *remembered* me, Sully. She just delivered a full pot to my table, asking where *La Rousse* was. At first, I thought she was asking if I had a dictionary, because *Larousse*, right? But then I realized she meant *you,* and for the first time in a very long time, I started to laugh. Like, belly laughing, so hard that my stomach muscles are going to ache for the next couple of days.

What an obvious nickname that I never once considered giving my favorite ginger wordsmith. *Larousse:* the dictionary. *La Rousse:* the redhead.

Genius.

Remember all those September afternoons we spent here junior year – you, me, Anne, Dan – pretending to study but flirting instead? I visit those days a lot in my mind whenever I feel nostalgic for happier, simpler times. For a few moments, I let my pathetic brain recall the filtered light streaming through the window, dancing along your hair like the sunbeams drawn to your fire. The tiny flecks of gold in your gray-blue eyes when you'd tilt your head just right.

You told me once that you imagined us as Hemingway and Hadley, and Dan and Anne as F. Scott Fitzgerald and Zelda. You should have known better than to associate us with those poor train wrecks, but still, I love your starry-eyed dreams. It's nice to view life through your eyes.

Back to *La Rotonde.*

One Tuesday afternoon – I think it was the last week of September – I was standing in line at the sandwich shop across the street from *La Rotonde* when I spotted you sitting alone at our usual table by the window. Ever since that day at the Normandy cemetery, I'd been trying to steal another moment alone with you. So I took a chance, ditched the sandwich line, and hurried across the street.

Rain drops pelted the boulevard that afternoon, and even though it was less than a month into the school year, the air smelled like winter. You were wearing an emerald green sweater and your hair was pulled into a knot on top of your head. I'd watched you that morning in the *Grande Salle* reconfiguring said topknot seven different ways before leaving it alone.

DEAR SULLY

You've made an art out of looking effortlessly cool, Sully. I don't even think you're aware.

The café was uncharacteristically empty that afternoon, which is why it shocked me that you failed to register my oafish presence hovering so close behind you. Like, horror-movie-villain close. Yet there you remained, laser-focused, shifting and re-shifting your tea pot and mug among the pens, index cards, and spiral full of history notes you'd already splayed across the table. On the left side of your spiral were twenty-six lines full of notes, and on the right side? A full-page drawing of a diner waitress in all her big-haired, small-town glory.

"Who's the Betty?" I said, startling you as I plopped into the chair to your right.

You flipped the notebook shut. "Oh, hi," you said, a slight flush creeping into your earlobes. "Um, nobody. I'm just studying for our history test tomorrow."

"We have a history test tomorrow?" I deadpanned. "What's it over?"

You jerked to grab your spiral notebook from the table, but I grabbed it first, hugging it to my chest.

"Give that back, Pete."

"Don't worry, I will," I smirked, curving myself slightly away from you. "But first I'm gonna need to hear an explanation for this waitress you sketched, and then we'll negotiate the ransom terms."

The look of bewilderment on your face in that moment nearly convinced me to give up the game. "Fine," you sighed. "The waitress is named Edith."

"For real? Why?"

"You know why!" Your brows knotted together. "Oh, come on. Seriously? It's Edith of Nantes! The lady Monsieur Ludovic spent forty minutes talking about last Wednesday in class?"

I blinked at you for a long moment. "Are you pulling my leg right now, Sullivan?"

"What? No." You grabbed back the notebook that had gone limp in my grasp. "Look, you probably think my little doodling habit makes me childish, but it serves an actual purpose, okay? Sketching helps focus my mind, and last Wednesday, Monsieur Ludovic was speaking so quickly that he lost me a time or two." Your frown deepened. "Okay, he lost me for a full twenty minutes. Which is why I'm here right now instead of at the movies with the Addison girls."

"Movies? On a Tuesday?"

"Well, yes. Kelly insists we make time for girls' night every week. So she scours *Pariscope* magazine to find the cheapest acceptable movie in town. For example: today, they're taking the bus up to some indie theater in Montmartre showing *Amélie*. I freaking love that movie, yet here I am, all alone, facing down hours of research on this Edith of Nantes lady."

"Alone?" I waved my hand back and forth in front of your face. "Am I invisible?"

You swatted my hand away. "Look, I can't afford to fail this test. Do you want Monsieur Ludovic telling the faculty what a backwards bumpkin I am? Next thing you know, Madame Beauchamp will call me into her office to tell me thanks but no thanks, my fourth of the Beckett Scholarship money's been revoked. Then she'll book me in steerage on the first cargo ship headed across the Atlantic, and I'll have to hitchhike my way westward across America from wherever the sailors dump me in Newark."

DEAR SULLY

"Relax," I said, plucking the spiral out of your fingers yet again. "I've already studied for the test. If you want, we can go over your notes together. It'll be fun."

Your face was a kaleidoscope for the next few seconds, shifting from doubt to desperation, then settling on acceptance. I choose to believe that in that moment, you genuinely wanted my help for the first time in your life.

You gave a tiny sigh, pulling the pen off your cap as you slid your index cards closer. "Okay, I'm in. But let's make it snappy, okay? I've still got fifty pages of art history to read before tomorrow."

"Right. Let's see what you've got here." I opened your notebook again, skimming your notes on the left-hand side of the page. "Hold up, do you write your notes on the back side of the page so your left hand doesn't have to battle the spiral binding? Genius! That drives me –"

"Pete!"

"Sorry, sorry," I pretended to wince. "Okay. Well, first of all, no one named Edith will appear on our test tomorrow, so let's start there."

"What are you talking about? It's right here in my notes – Edith of Nantes! A Protestant who married some guy named Hugh Guennot. Or maybe Hugues. I missed whatever Monsieur Ludovic said about Henry the Fourth and the island of St. Barth's. That's why Edith is standing on an island balancing a bottle of rum – to remind me to look it up later."

"Huh. Well, that's… something." I bit the inside of my cheek so I didn't laugh. "I mean, we *could* look it up. But I think Monsieur Ludovic was talking about the Edict of Nantes. *L'Édit,* not *Édith.* It was a law signed by Henri IV which gave the Huguenots the right to worship as Protestants in Catholic France. Sort of like a peace offering, you know? Thousands of Huguenots were slaughtered a couple of decades earlier at the St. Bartholomew's Day Massacre. At least I think that's correct. I'm not so great with the actual dates."

Your face drained of color for a second, and then it went all splotchy, like some invisible swarm of mosquitos had just attacked you in the blink of an eye. You covered your mouth for a long moment, staring at me like I'd just slapped you right across the face. And then, just as I opened my mouth to apologize… you began to laugh.

No, wait. Not laugh.

Guffaw.

Cackle.

Chortle.

You were laughing so hard that you could not breathe, like a silent scream into the universe. And then you grabbed my forearm and squeezed so hard that I thought you might be stroking out.

"Meredith? You okay?" My eyes searched yours. "Wrap your hands around your throat if you're choking."

You shoved me in the chest with your free hand. "No, I'm not *choking*, you lunatic. I'm just… I can't… I can't breathe, and I can't believe… why aren't you horrified?"

"Horrified? By what?"

"I drew a WAITRESS, Pete! A waitress named Edith. Why? Because I'm an idiot who needs her scholarship revoked and – oh my *word*." You poked your finger at your notebook. "Hugh! Guennot!"

Hysterical giggles overtook you just then, and oh, man, Sully – I finally lost it. The two of us made such a scene that people on the *outside* of the window started laughing. The waitress appeared with the check and stole your teapot and cup from the table, like, *get out of here, you crazy Americans,* which only made me laugh so hard that I'm pretty sure I pulled a muscle loose from my ribs.

The rain had paused for a moment, so I snagged your check off the table and left your waitress fifteen euros while you gathered all of your stuff and shoved it into your messenger bag. The two of us hustled back to school, still laughing our heads off like we were the only two people in the world.

That afternoon, you huddled up next to me in one of the study rooms behind the *Grande Salle* while I retaught everything you'd missed in class. For those two hours, I felt like we were filming montage scenes for some cheesy rom-com movie, because WHAT THE *WHAT?* I'd never seen you so soft. Like, ever.

You know what I learned that day? That the girl who'd spent two years side-eyeing me for no apparent reason finally trusted me enough to let me inside her fortress of solitude. Instead of covering up your error, you let me see it. Even then, I recognized what a huge step we'd taken, because let's face it: you do not like to be wrong. The fact that you didn't push me away that afternoon meant more to me than I could have imagined.

You gave me hope, Sully. And hope was exactly what I needed that year.

DAN THE MAN

For the next couple of weeks, I'm not ashamed to admit I walked around in a bit of a Sully-induced haze. On the day of *La Nuit Blanche*, Dan finally called me out.

We were cleaning the apartment a few hours before you and the Addison girls were meant to arrive, and I guess my head was totally in the clouds because four times in a row, Dan asked me to take out the trash, and four times in a row, I thought he said to empty the vacuum filter.

"You've already done that," he said, taking the vacuum from my hand and replacing it with a black plastic trash bag. "Dude. Are you feeling okay?"

"Of course," I said, dropping the trash all over the floor just as I opened the front door. By the time I'd cleaned up the mess and delivered the trash to the bin, Dan had settled into his usual chair at the breakfast table.

"Sit," he commanded, sliding a glass of water my way. I felt like a suspect on one of those crime series they show in perpetual reruns on cable TV.

I lifted the glass to my lips. "What's up?"

"You know what's up." Detective Dan crossed his arms over his chest. "Stop acting nervous, man. You and I both know she's totally into you."

My stomach flipped. "Who's into me?"

"Don't be cute, Russell. You know I'm talking about Meredith."

"Sullivan?"

"I told you not to be cute. This is me you're talking to. And if you're going to pretend you haven't spent every second since orientation trying to win over our favorite ginger, I'll call you out in front of her *and* the Addison girls tonight. You know I'll do it. Do not tempt me."

This may surprise you, but Dan and I had never talked about any girl in this way before. Sure, we'd given each other a hard time about making out with our formal dates in the back of the party bus (sorry, sorry…TMI). And yeah, we may have had an understanding about who sat by whom at *La Rotonde* (sorry again). But an actual conversation about *feelings*?

Um, no thank you. *Never*. Nope. N-to-the-NOOOOOO.

I took another sip of my water, then crossed my own arms over my chest. "What makes you think Meredith's into me? Like, what *specifically* has she done to give you that impression?"

Dan rolled his eyes. "Look, I know you think you're charming, and in general that must be true, because you never have a shortage of ladies hanging around at any given time. But Meredith Sullivan has never given you two seconds' worth of attention in the whole time we've known her." His cheeks tugged up in a grin. "Not until this semester, that is."

"Are you messing with me right now?"

"Dude." He fixed me with a look. "She laughed at your Monsieur Dufresne imitation in class this morning. And it is *terrible*. Instead of a half-blind octogenarian, you look like a turtle."

"Maybe Meredith has a more refined sense of humor than you."

"Oh, she absolutely does. Which is how I know she's into you, because she would never laugh at something so ridiculous if she were in her right mind."

He was correct, you know. I can't think of a single time you laughed at me before Paris. On a good day, you'd tolerated me, but laughter? This was unprecedented. And the weirdest part was that your attitude had shifted with very little effort on my part.

"What about Sutton?" I asked, finally.

"What about him?"

"You know what I'm asking. Isn't he Meredith's soul mate or something?"

Dan looked around the apartment, under the table, then looked back at me. "Is he here?"

"No. But –"

"But nothing. Sutton's MIA, Pete. And even if he weren't, he's had his whole life to lock down that soul mate thing. If you ask me, he's only got himself to blame if Meredith's over his games. Plus, we're in *Paris*. City of Love, blah-dee-blah-blah. So take a chance and ask her out already. What's the worst that can happen?"

"Oh, I don't know. That I'd be breaking Sigma Phi bro code?"

"Since when do you care about that? No one is *less* involved in the fraternity than you are, Russell. I'm sorry. I know you'd like to believe you're a card-carrying member, but even when you're there, you're not *there*."

That stung a little bit, I'm not going to lie. And even though I knew Dan was right – that I'd never quite lived up to my fraternal responsibilities – I do care about loyalty.

Sutton was your first love, Sully. And even though he was thousands of miles away, I still wasn't certain your heart was free.

WHITE (K)NIGHT

Back in the day, Dan used to call you Emma Woodhouse – just like the beloved Jane Austen heroine known for her matchmaking fiascos. But here's a weird twist – some scholars believe that in the original manuscript, the main character was a man.

Emmett Woodhouse, Esquire.

Okay, okay. You know Jane Austen would *never* have named a guy Emmett! Pffft. That's ridiculous. But I think I'll call Dan "Emmett" from now on because he's one hundred percent the matchmaker that you aspire to be. And I'm about to prove it.

Maybe you didn't notice it at the time, but Dan spent the first half of *La Nuit Blanche* in your orbit. Keep in mind that this was only a couple of hours after his pep talk.

Sutton's MIA, bro! We're in the City of Love! Ask that ginger out already! Cue Donny Osmond singing I'll Make A Man Out Of You!

Dear Sully

At the time, I remember thinking Dan should be a life coach or a motivational speaker or something. Who in their right mind would ignore such an impassioned, LOGICAL call to action?

You can't see me right now, but I'm the literal personification of the raise-your-hand emoji.

Real talk here: I chickened out the second you and Anne walked through the door to my apartment that night. By the time Kelly and Harper arrived, I'm pretty sure Dan wondered if an alien had invaded my body because I started talking about – wait for it – *prepositional nuances.*

"Sorry we're late," Harper said, hanging her coat on one of the hooks by the door.

"Yeah, sorry," Kelly seconded. "We just ran into Marshall and that Élodie girl down the street. Did you guys know they're dating?"

"Oh, yeah. That's old news," I replied, grabbing Kelly's coat to hang it next to Harper's. "Marshall spilled the beans to Dan yesterday after class. Speaking of which, have you ever noticed," I blurted, "that in French you say you've been dating *since* six months instead of *for* six months? Or days, or years, or whatever. The amount of time isn't my point. It's that the prepositions of the world are the very thing that will peg us as a non-native speaker if we're not careful. BAHAHAHAHA WHY IS FRENCH SO WEIRD, YOU GUYS?!"

Please tell me you heard me vomiting words all over your friends that night, Sully. Because Dan definitely did. He gave me side-eye for a full minute after that, and when I saw him join you in the kitchen, I imagine he muttered, "Run, Meredith. Run for your life."

Now listen, I love Dan Thomas like a brother. And if I had been in my right mind that night, I wouldn't have even noticed that Dan was hovering around you at all.

But the night of October 8th wasn't normal. It was the Paris all-nighter – the *White Night.* It was also the night of the brightest moon in four hundred years. So when Dan sat beside you at dinner, I didn't see my roommate distracting my redheaded crush while my brain malfunctioned.

I saw a con artist who had been playing me for a fool all day.

And when he hung back to talk to you as we all strolled over to Notre Dame, I didn't see a heartsick dude who was asking his friend how to win over a certain curly-haired Anne.

No. I saw a narcissist who had spent his life gaslighting me.

And when the two of you started shaking your fists at the moon, laughing and snorting so hard that you ruined the *Magic Flute* cathedral light show for all two hundred people in attendance?

WELL. I freaked the heck out, didn't I? Which is, by the way, what Emmett Woodhouse, Esquire had planned from the get go.

You see, Dan knew all along that his pep talk would never work. He knew I would never ask you out unless I felt the flames of terror licking my feet.

So I followed you to the Big Band concert that night. And I think Dan might have been onto something with that brightest moon nonsense because Sully, you did *not* seem sorry I was there. Not when I followed you, not when I convinced you to dance with me, and not when we were sitting alone by the fountain together.

Did you realize you were catching the feels for me? Because when I swept you onto the dance floor to the opening notes of *Begin the Beguine,* you were into it, sister. If I hadn't been so completely freaked out, I might have let myself believe that the size of your pupils had everything to do with your heart shifting and nothing to do with the twinkle lights overhead.

DEAR SULLY

And when the music ended – when you were still in my arms, staring into my eyes like you were seeing me for the very first time in your life – whoa. I have no idea how my rational brain kept my lips from touching yours in that moment.

Good thing I didn't risk that kiss, though. Because a half-second later, the drummer began that familiar opening riff to *Sing, Sing, Sing*, and lindy-hopping with you that night is one of my best memories of all time. Do you know how lucky we are?

Nobody has that kind of instant chemistry on the dance floor, Meredith. *Nobody*.

I, for one, was *petrified*. Over the years, I probably convinced myself that someone had cursed me at Stanford orientation. *There's no way this girl is into me*, I kept telling myself the whole time we talked at the fountain. And even later, alongside the river, when I surprised myself by inviting you to hop on a train to nowhere with me, I never believed you would go.

But you would have, wouldn't you? I can see that now. You would have met me at the *Gare du Nord*, and all would have been right with the world. By Thanksgiving, we would have fallen in love. You would have been my rock all year while Gigi's life withered away. You would have made me laugh when I wanted to cry. You would have held my hand when I tried to run away.

Except none of that happened. Because Drew Sutton appeared later that morning at the Centre Lafayette. And from that day forward, you and I swerved far, far off that course.

THE EIGHT

When I saw Sutton arguing with that taxi driver later that morning, I couldn't quite believe my eyes. Because seriously, *what*? At the time, I would have sworn that kid had your phone tapped, or at the very least, that he'd paid Marshall Freeman handsomely for Russell/Sullivan intel, because come on, man! How else could he have known we were *this* close to ruining his fun?

So when my phone rang and I saw it was Gigi, I walked away without another word.

"Good morning," she chirped. "How's my favorite grandson?"

"Fine, fine," I lied, zooming into the Centre Lafayette. "I mean, I'm a little tired. My friends and I stayed out all night for that *Nuit Blanche* celebration I told you about last week."

"Did you?" I could hear the smile in her voice. "Well, that's nice. I hope you made some good memories together."

Oh, Gigi, I thought. *If only you knew.*

"We did," I said out loud. "And how are you? It's a little past your bedtime, isn't it?"

It was nine a.m. Paris time. Technically, midnight might not be too late for someone as active as my grandmother, but that was before she got sick. We rarely talked about her energy levels, because Margaret Beckett was from the Whiney-Butts Are Losers™ generation, but I knew the drill. Chemotherapy makes you tired. Which is why I should have known that call would take a bad turn, because cancer is a friend to no one. Especially superheroes like Gigi.

"I'll get straight to the point, Peter. I had an appointment today, and the doctor let me know they've discovered two new tumors."

"What? Wait, hold on a minute, Geeg. How is that possible? You promised me your team would use the most aggressive treatment available. You said –"

"I know what I said." Her voice sounded brittle, like it might crack at any moment. "Everything I told you was true, but you know there's never a guarantee. Ever."

"What does that mean?"

She paused for a long moment, then cleared her throat. "Listen, darling, there's no point in sugarcoating this news. The doctor says we can try a few experimental treatments to sustain my quality of life, but the best-case scenario is that I've got nine months to live."

Let me just say here that I'm thankful for whoever invented aviator sunglasses, because I slid mine on and walked to the back of the courtyard as tears I didn't even know I still had flooded down my cheeks. "I'm coming home," I told her through gritted teeth. "Release whatever restrictions you've got on the airline mileage account, Gigi, because I want to be with you."

"No," she retorted. "You're staying in Paris, Peter. It's been years since I've heard you as happy as you've been the past month, and whatever magic you've found there, you need to hold onto it. Now more than ever."

"But –"

"We can talk more frequently if that would make you feel better. I'll even try to learn that video chat thingamajig you're so fond of, but I refuse to let you take more time away from your future, okay? You are twenty-two years old, and you have a full life ahead of you. The last thing I need when I arrive at the Pearly Gates is to find your grandfather and your parents with their arms crossed in disapproval."

Gigi rattled off a few factoids about the experimental drugs the doctors had proposed. She told me she'd already booked herself a flight so we could spend Christmas together in Paris. When she hung up, I sat there willing myself to pull it together before I joined you guys in class.

Except I never pulled myself together. So I never joined you.

When you saw me after class, I was on the phone with Vick Darby – Brooks' dad. I was begging him to grant me power of attorney over Gigi so I could fly home and help her, but Gigi had already cut me off at the pass. For every question I lobbed his way, Vick lobbed an answer right back – one my very wily grandmother had already provided. So when you and Sutton suddenly appeared on the other side of those glass panels in the entry hall, I hung up the phone and slipped inside a nearby classroom until the coast was clear.

The very last thing I needed that morning was another smug grin from Drew.

Sixteen hours and at least two liters of boo-hoo baby tears later, I hopped the first train headed out of the *Gare de Lyon*. I had no agenda, really – I just needed a change of scenery, preferably of the mountainous kind. So imagine my surprise when Meg Green and the entire New York contingency spilled into the club car while I was drinking my third cup of espresso.

Dan told me once that thanks to Facebook's tagging mechanism, you were under the (mistaken) impression that I spent that weekend holed up in the hot tub of a fancy Swiss chalet with the ice queen of the Upper West Side. I have to laugh every time I think about that, because really, Sully? Could your imagination be any more clichéd? I'm not a male bimbo.

Here's a fact: in another life, you would have been friends with every single one of the Hudson College crew, including Meg and the girls you call her minions. The second they saw me on the train, all eight of them took me in like I was an honorary part of their squad. They even started calling me the ninth member of The Eight.

That's what they called themselves: The Eight. Some of them even got *VIII* tattoos that year. Why didn't we get tattoos? Arrows are way cooler than Roman numerals.

All weekend, I hung out with the Hudson guys – Dylan, Mark, and Jared. The best part was that those guys didn't care who I was. No one asked me what it felt like to be an orphan at age eighteen. None of them knew I was about to lose the only family member I had left. And even though they must've noticed that I drank soda every time they drank beer, not one guy ever mentioned it. All we really did that weekend was play tourist together.

On Sunday morning, hours before we headed back to Paris, we took a cogwheel train up to the top of Rigi-Kulm. The summit is exactly what you imagine the Swiss Alps should be: jagged peaks, snow glinting in the midday sun. The nine of us took a billion pictures up there and had an all-out snowball war. Maybe it was the pure mountain air, but I started to feel like I could breathe again.

At the train stop halfway down, you can take a horse-drawn carriage ride in freshly fallen snow. Every member of The Eight clambered up the steps onto one enormous carriage just as the horse took off around the snowy village path.

Everyone, that is, except Meg and me.

A smaller carriage idled nearby– a two-seater pulled by a donkey and an old man who weighed ninety pounds soaking wet. Meg took one glance at the set-up, then looked up at me.

"On a scale of one to Nora Ephron, how badly do you want to have this sleigh ride experience right now?"

"Uh… zero?"

"Good. Because I am literally freezing my butt off out here, and I think that coffee shop over there is a wiser decision. I predict that donkey will keel over dead in the next ten minutes. Possibly in the next five."

I laughed. So did she. And then we strolled through the snow to the café.

We took a seat near the window, and while Meg texted her friends our location, I ordered two hot chocolates. After a bit of small talk, she gave me some serious side-eye.

"Why are you here, Pete?"

"Uh… you mean here on the planet?"

"No. I mean *here* here." She scowled, gesturing around us. "You and that Meredith girl have been joined at the hip ever since school started. Then on Friday, I saw her walking around the Centre Lafayette with Malibu Ken's twin brother."

I'd never thought of it before, but she was right. Sutton *does* look like Malibu Ken, minus the androgynous zones and the plasticine skin, of course.

"Oh, *that* guy?" I attempted to smile. "Yeah, that's Drew Sutton. The Dawson to Meredith's Joey. Soul mates, party of two."

"You've seen *Dawson's Creek?*"

"Only the first season."

"Interesting." Meg surveyed me over the rim of her cup. "Um, not to spoil seasons two through six for you, but Joey and Dawson don't end up together."

"Really? But they were so perfect for each other."

She shook her head. "Were you even paying attention? Joey and Pacey had chemistry for days. Even in the first season."

"They did?"

"Yep. Plot twist." She bumped the home button on her phone to check the time, which was when I noticed her lock screen photo. It looked like that *Hey, Girl* actor. What's his name? You know, the one from *The Notebook*? Ryan something... Reynolds? No, wait. Ryan Gosling. Yes, that's him, and this guy could have been his twin. He even had that same straight nose.

I gestured toward her phone. "Who's the fella?"

The tiniest smile danced at the corner of her mouth. "Oh, you know. Just my high school boyfriend."

"Yeah?" I cocked my head to one side. "Does he have a name?"

"Devon. He's studying Spanish in Argentina this year."

"Wow. Good for him." I paused for a moment, studying her face. "Are you guys... together?"

"We are. Well, we *were*." She turned her phone over, screen face down. "It's complicated."

"Ah. Got it." I rapped my knuckles on the table. "No further explanation necessary."

Meg's mouth shifted into a straight line, and for several seconds, she didn't look at me. And I don't know why, Sully, but just like that, I realized Meg and I were in exactly the same boat. She was pining, I was pining. So I reached over and squeezed her hand.

And to my surprise, Meg squeezed back.

So that's how we got started. Meg missed Devon, I missed you, and at first, all we really did was find comfort in each other's company. We were like… you know those tiny blankets kids carry around with them? The ones with a stuffed animal toy head sewn on to them? That's how I saw Meg.

Well, okay. She's a little prettier than a blanket or a stuffed animal. But you get my point.

When I got back home that night from Lucerne, Dan was already asleep. But when I got to my bedroom, I found a hastily scribbled note on my pillow.

"I'm going to cut you some slack because your grandmother is sick," Dan's scrawl said. *"But I thought you should know that two of the three Addison girls wish you would've forced Drew Sutton on the next flight home to Portland instead of running away on a train. (Don't be mad at Kelly. She thinks Sutton is hot.) Hope your little stunt this weekend was worth it, loser, because Sutton or no Sutton, you've tanked your chances with Meredith. Welcome home."*

THIRTY THOUSAND STEPS

After Sutton went back to Portland – after you two went Facebook official – I removed myself from your orbit. At the time, it felt like the noble thing to do. Sutton was still my fraternity brother, and you were… well, you mattered to me, Meredith. You always have.

Step aside, I told myself that first Monday back in class. *Let her breathe. Think of what Drew Sutton would do, and then do the opposite. Be the better man.*

But I'm not sure I really *was* the better man, Sully.

The truth is my ego got walloped the same day Gigi told me she was dying, and once again, I handled my pain in the only way I knew how: by avoiding it at all costs. So I hung out with the Hudson College crew, and with the exception of the week your brother came to visit, I steered clear of Marie-France's house as often as I could.

By the way, Marie-France was on to me from the very beginning. Why do you think she pulled that mistletoe trick the night of your birthday junior year? Or that surprise reunion in your *chambre de bonne* last Friday? She knew (then and now) that my heart belongs to you.

I think Ian figured me out too the night we had his birthday dinner in Marie-France's apartment. He spent more time talking to me than he did to the Addison girls or Dan combined. And yeah, maybe it's because we had a lot in common, but every time he glanced between you and me, I couldn't help but wonder if Ian noticed the spark between us.

It's always been there, hasn't it? Even now, after all these years, I still feel the pull.

"You guys should come out and visit us in Lincoln City sometime," Ian said to Dan and me while we rinsed Marie-France's dishes that night. "I mean, not at Christmas, of course. The coast is just as dreary as Portland in the winter … drearier, maybe."

Dan gave me a (not subtle) look, then smiled at Ian. "That sounds awesome. Thanks for the invite, man."

"Absolutely. We've got plenty of room. And hey, aren't you both in Drew's fraternity? Maybe one of you could stay at his place. His grandparents would love it. Drew never brings anyone home but my sister."

Dan cleared his throat, and the fancy plate in my hand narrowly escaped its demise on Marie-France's floor. I guess your brother noticed, because his cheeks went splotchy, just like yours do, and then he started rambling on about your Prague itinerary in such detail that I could have stalked you every step of the way had I been so inclined.

Who knows? Maybe that's what he wanted. I never got a chance to ask him.

After that night, I went cold turkey where you were concerned. It just hurt too much to be around you. So every time I heard Dan making plans with you and the Addison girls, I would text Meg to see if she wanted to hang out. Watching football with her at Le Galway pub morphed into Saturday nights at the movies, and within three weeks, I was eating dinner with her host family several nights a week.

But it didn't work. Every time I thought I had my feelings for you under control, you'd show up to class with a rosy flush in your cheeks, and instead of glowering at me like you had back at home, you would always wave hi and smile.

Sometimes I even let myself imagine a wistful look in your eyes. One that meant you missed me.

And then your birthday happened. I spent all day with you – all freaking day – and everything between us felt so right, so *perfect* that I couldn't sleep afterward. Sometime around two a.m., I pulled on my jeans and a sweater, shrugged on my coat, and headed out into the night, final destination unknown.

But I guess I wasn't as stealth as I'd hoped, because I hadn't even made it to the end of the rue Guénégaud before Dependable Dan was by my side.

"It's not safe to roam around the big city by yourself in the middle of the night, old sport," he said, worry lines wrinkling his forehead. "Didn't you hear that Bucknell dude at school yesterday? He got sucker-punched outside his own building Saturday night."

"I heard him," I said, zipping up my coat. "He'd also imbibed half a flask of whiskey beforehand."

"Yeah, that probably didn't help." Dan wrapped a scarf around his neck. "Anyway, let me join you, okay? I need to walk off some of Meredith's birthday dinner. Marie-France has gotten good at the American-style mashed potatoes, but she puts something in there that congeals them into a lump in my stomach, you know what I mean?"

Dan is such a liar. But he's also a really good friend.

We made it all the way to the Eiffel Tower before either of us said another word. Just the swish, swish, swish of our jeans against our coats.

I turned around to start back home (because three miles one way equals six miles round trip equals stupidity on a cold December night). But when my eyes met Dan's, I stopped in place, shoving my hands in my coat pockets.

"My grandmother's going to die," I said, the words forming white puffs that disappeared into the sky. "And the only girl I've ever truly cared about is in love with an idiot."

Dan held my gaze for a minute, then reached out to squeeze my shoulder. "I'm sorry about Gigi. I really am."

"Thanks, man." I kicked at a rock on the pavement as the silence stretched between us for a long moment. "And the other thing?"

"The idiot thing?" He sniffed. "Oh, I couldn't agree more – Meredith *is* in love with an idiot. The king of the idiots, if you ask me. The kind of lunatic who strolls around Paris in the middle of the freaking night."

And just like that, Dan strode off in the direction of the apartment, walking at such a fast clip that I had to jog to catch up with him.

"Hold up, hold up," I wheezed. "What was that supposed to mean?"

DEAR SULLY

"It means *you're* the idiot, Russell. What is the matter with you? For weeks, you've been making out in broom closets with the Bachelorette while simultaneously composing Meredith's secret birthday scrapbook with Anne. Nice touch putting that double-paged shot of her and Sutton on the centermost page. I bet you threw Meredith totally off your scent with *that* trick."

Blood roared in my ears. "I think you've made your point."

"Have I?" He stretched his arms wide, then turned in a circle. "Meredith is *here*, man. Every day, she sits right in front of you in every single class, and for whatever reason, you refuse to tell her how you feel. Instead, you're killing time with some other girl you may never see again after this year. A *nice* girl whose feelings for you have morphed way beyond casual. Tell me how you're any different than Drew Sutton, and I promise to stand corrected."

Here's the thing about Dan, Sully: I doubt he's ever had to do this with you, but whenever one of his friends goes rogue, he becomes like that bull statue on Wall Street. You're not getting past him. Like, ever. Not even if you're that tiny little girl statue with her hands on her hips.

Dan glared at me for a handful of seconds, then when it became clear my only response was to blink, he turned back toward the apartment and headed home. I may have fifty pounds of muscle on the guy, but on the night of your birthday that year, I felt like a ten-year-old boy walking in the shadow of his older and wiser big brother.

When we arrived back at the apartment, Dan took the stairs two at a time, and nearly crossed the threshold to his bedroom before I closed the front door behind me.

"Hey," I said quietly. "Can you give me five minutes? I'd like to answer the charge you just tossed at my feet back there."

Dan turned around to face me. For a full minute, he scoured my expression for any latent signs of clownery. Once he was satisfied that I meant business, he abruptly dropped himself into the nearby arm chair. "Go ahead. I'm listening."

Hesitantly, I crossed the room and took a seat on the couch. "Look, I'm sorry, man. I can see that you're disappointed in me, but I promise, I haven't been gaming Meg on purpose."

"No? Then what have you been doing?"

I breathed in and out for a moment, then lifted my eyes to his. "You're not wrong about my feelings for Meredith. But I like Meg too. Until tonight, I hadn't realized how bad my behavior appears to the outside world, but you make a valid point. It's definitely something to think about."

"Mmm hmm," he muttered, removing his glasses to clean them on his shirt. "It's five in the morning, Russell. You want to tell me the real reason we just clocked twenty-five thousand steps? Because I'm pretty sure I know, but I want to make sure you've figured it out, too."

"Okay." I took a deep, steadying breath. "The thing is, all day today it felt like… like maybe Meredith missed me. That she wasn't sure she picked the right guy."

Dan's face softened, and he leaned forward on his elbows. "So what are you going to do about it?"

"Right now? Not one thing." I stood up from the couch, stretching my arms to the sky. "Like you said, we've got an exam in five hours, and I don't know about you, but I can't afford to fail it."

"Russell –"

I walked to the door of my room, still stretching as I went. "By the way," I said over my shoulder, "it's more like thirty thousand steps from here to the Eiffel Tower and back. So, hey, gold stars all around."

He laughed, shaking his head. "You're a piece of work. You know that, right?"

I turned to face him, bowed mockingly, then bumped the door open with my butt. "Hey, you had your choice of where to live, my friend. I warned you that Marshall Freeman's a less complicated cohabitant than that Russell wackadoodle."

"That's for sure. But in the battle between you and a year filled with kale farts, I chose you. Remember me in your will someday, would you?"

"Absolutely." I saluted him from across the living room, then pulled my door shut.

JOYEUX NOEL

Gigi had called off the experimental drug treatments just before Christmas, but her body stayed strong the entire three weeks she stayed in France. Every morning, we visited a different museum. Every afternoon, we walked a different neighborhood. And despite the constant ache in my heart, it was also sort of beautiful too.

Not everyone gets to experience their grandmother's own Paris.

At night, Gigi was too tired to go out, so we'd order in and watch old movies together in the Guénégaud apartment. And every night, when I wasn't dodging Meg's calls, I was stalking social media, convinced it was only a matter of time before you and Sutton split up.

Can I ask why you didn't break up with him that Christmas? Because I know you and I had a moment on your birthday. In fact, we had an entire day filled with moments.

I was there, Sully. I saw your face in the elevator when I nearly kissed you.

DEAR SULLY

Sutton had always been the over-sharing type, but that Christmas, he flooded his feed every hour on the hour. I was fine with the two-headed selfie you took after running together on the beach. I also didn't mind the shot of you and Ian singing *Bohemian Rhapsody* during your families' shared Christmas.

No, the one that finally got me was the drone shot of you two cuddled together in a tiny dinghy decorated with twinkle lights. Honestly, Sully, did you have to pose with that *Merry Christmas from us to you!* sign in your adorable, doodly handwriting? I wanted to throw my phone in the toilet.

That particular night, Gigi finally took pity on me. "This movie is terrible," she said. "Let's make cookies instead."

"Huh?"

"Cookies, Peter," she repeated, clicking off the TV. "Hop up and help your grandmother navigate your pantry, would you?"

"Uh, Gigi, if you think Dan and I have cookie mix sitting in the pantry, you're nuts."

She rolled her eyes. "We don't need a mix, darling. When you've been baking for decades, certain recipes stick in your mind. All we really need is a little elbow grease."

And to my surprise, she was right. We had flour. We had baking powder *and* baking soda. Sugar. Salt. Butter. Milk. Vanilla extract and food coloring from some previous tenants which were somehow unexpired. And the weirdest thing of all? Powdered sugar.

Yeah, I have no idea where that came from, either. Maybe Dan was running a high-end fondant operation out of our apartment? No clue. But our mystery powdered sugar stash was useful all the same.

For the next couple of hours, we made the dough and baked the cookies. The next morning, we decorated side by side until we ran out of icing. And would you believe I actually had fun? Drawing funny faces on snowmen erased ninety percent of my angst.

"Hey Gigi?" I said as I grabbed the red icing from her side of the table. "I'm sorry I went all sullen earlier. I don't have any excuse for my misbehavior, especially since I'm dating Meg, no matter how unofficially. But for the record, I do know cyberstalking is wrong, no matter how harmless my intention may be."

"This is true. Cyberstalking is a serious crime in several US states. Is it illegal yet in France?"

"Um… I don't know. Maybe?"

"Hmm." She bit her lip as she outlined a mitten-shaped cookie with green icing. "Well, Peter, I applaud your resolve. You should always stay on the right side of the law. But for the record, if smart phones had existed when I was falling in love with your grandfather, I would have made you look like an amateur."

I laughed. "Come on, Geeg. You're just trying to make me feel better."

"I most certainly am not! But in the future, you should know it's better to educate yourself about people by social engineering their friends rather than scouring their online presence for clues. Everyone knows the internet is a web of lies."

"Good point. Hey, quick question: what's social engineering?"

"Do I know something you don't?" She feigned horror. "Well, Peter, social engineering is the act of manipulating other people into sharing details that can help you achieve your goals. But I don't like the term 'manipulation.' I prefer 'persuasion.'"

I couldn't help but smile. "And how exactly do you know about this strategy?"

Dear Sully

"Oh, darling, I'm an expert! For example, do you think I've befriended Brooks Darby out of the kindness of my heart? No, no, no. It's because she keeps me informed on all of the tomfoolery you never see fit to share with me. Or rather, she tries. According to Brooks, you've become quite the ninja since you moved back to France."

Now listen, Gigi was kidding about Brooks. She adored having her own personal twenty-something sidekick, and not for spying. But despite her sarcasm, she wasn't wrong. You really can find out a lot about a person from their friends if you play your cards right.

"So is that how you and Pops fell in love? You social-engineered him away from that nice Kansas girl back home?"

"A nice *Missouri* girl," Gigi corrected. "And not just any girl, either. She was Miss Kansas City at some point, according to my former intel sources."

"Wow, Geeg. You stole Pops away from a beauty queen?"

She fixed me with a look. "You cannot steal a person away when they're actually in love with someone else. And yes, I did my research. Marcus, the other Naval Academy graduate in our Addison class, wasn't nearly as intelligent as your grandfather. After a couple of martinis, he would have given me his bank account number if I'd asked nicely. This isn't exactly high-level spying, you know. Anyone who watches a James Bond film can figure out these tricks."

"Aha. The honeypot calls the kettle black!"

"Honeypot is a terrible term, Peter." She filled in the center of the mitten cookie. "As for my younger self, she was perfectly within her rights to *listen* while a classmate spilled the beans on his friend."

"Uh huh. Sure you were."

"Is it my fault Marcus told me that Lydia nagged your grandfather in her letters? Goodness, what a fool she was. Everyone knows you should never badger a grown man. Which is why I made sure your grandfather saw me as a sensible, easygoing alternative."

"Gigi, I love you, but you are far from easygoing."

"Oh, shush yourself," she grinned, pressing so hard on the icing bag that a blob exploded onto her cookie. "You didn't know me when I was twenty-three. In those days, I was – well I believe the word you use nowadays is *chill*. I just treated Pete Beckett with the respect he deserved, and poof! After Christmas break, Marcus let it slip that Pete and Lydia had broken up."

"Interesting. All because you treated Pops with respect, Lady Margaret the Chill?"

"Well, no. Not exclusively." A sly expression crossed her face. "He might have appreciated the dress I wore at the Addison Christmas party. It was this lovely green velvet number, cut very low in the –"

"La la la la la!" I screamed, covering my ears. "Stop that right now, GRANDMOTHER."

I'm not going to lie to you, Sully. Gigi laughed so hard she started to cough uncontrollably. Which should have worried me, but instead it made me laugh too. And in those days, between my heartache over you and the cancer countdown, I was hanging on to my sanity by a literal thread. As the seconds ticked forward, the weight of everything snowballed down on me out of the blue. And just like that, my laughter turned to sobs.

Gigi got to her feet faster than she had in months and wrapped her arms around me, cradling my head in both hands. "Shh," she whispered. "Don't cry, Peter. My whole point in telling you that story was to remind you that feelings change. Someday your lady troubles will be nothing but a memory. I have a good feeling about this little redhead of yours. She sees the real you."

"I'm not… this isn't about her. It's about *you*." A giant sob shook me hard. "What am I supposed to do without you, Gigi? Who will I talk to when I need help? Who will call me out on my nonsense? You're my best friend in the world."

I felt her abdomen tense up and release against me as she took three deep breaths. "Correction," she finally said. "I am *one* of your best friends. When I'm gone, you will still have Dan. You'll still have James and Brooks. And if you are very lucky, you'll have the love of a hard-working Irish girl named Meredith Sullivan. And if not, well, that she's an idiot and I want my money back."

Snot ran down my nose as I sucked in a laugh. "You're awfully sassy for a dying lady, Margaret Beckett."

"Yes, I am," she replied, voice shaking. "Listen to me, darling. You cannot give up on life after I'm gone. If you've learned anything from these past few years, let it be that you must keep choosing reasons to live. Your friends need you. This world needs you. Your heart is too beautiful to stop beating just because life is unfair."

I stood up and hugged her so hard that I was worried I might break her ribs. In that moment, I swore to myself never to let her down again. That I would stand up and fight, just like Gigi had asked.

How long did it take me to fail her? Fifteen weeks? Sixteen?

Reading back through this letter, I'm pretty sure Gigi knew where I'd end up – running, running, running away. And that makes my heart ache so badly I can't breathe.

OBJECTIVELY

Objectively speaking, January, February, and March of junior year were a Dumpster fire. My grandmother was dying. My other best friend spent most of his free time avoiding my new girlfriend by hanging out *chez* Marie-France with you and Anne. And Meg, who knew next to nothing about Gigi's illness, quickly grew weary of brooding, surly Pete.

Your dad had a heart attack. Gigi died. Spring break in Italy got canceled.

See? Dumpster fire.

But there's one memory from the days before Gigi died that I revisit on the regular: the night you and I watched my Ducky Shincrackers' highlights reel together. Because that night, despite all the sadness bracketing both our lives, I caught you staring at my younger self on the screen like he was your childhood idol.

Don't try to deny it, missy. I still have photographic evidence somewhere on my phone.

"Dude," I said, bumping your arm with my elbow. "Stop checking Baby Pete out. You are way too old for him."

"I don't understand." You stole the remote control from my hand and pressed pause. "If we met at Sullivan's the night of your accident, why didn't I recognize you the first day of school?"

"Aw, Sully," I laughed, still not following you. "It's fine. I've got a forgettable face."

"No. You don't." You stared at the screen for a long moment. The boy frozen in close-up had a very Gilbert Blythe-ish air about him: dark, curly hair with laughing brown eyes, plus a body in that epic stage between boy and man, with bulging lean muscles under his clothes.

Not to mention swagger for days. High School Pete's confidence had never suffered a single blow. Every time he put forth minimal effort, he won – in the classroom, on the soccer field, and *definitely* out on the dance floor among his lady friends.

The kid staring back at you from my TV screen had no clue what was about to hit him. And just like that, I realized with horror why you didn't recognize me on the first day of school.

Freshman Year Pete didn't hold a candle to his bright-and-shiny former self.

True fact: pity discomfits me, and in that moment, your pity was rolling off you in waves. And because I have done everything in my power to avoid the bad feels, I started to laugh. Quietly at first, like church giggles, and then gut-shakingly LOUD. Which made you blush. Hard.

"Stop that," you hissed, turning even darker red. "I'm just appreciating God's handiwork here. Hasn't anyone ever taught you that beauty can be objectively quantified?"

"Um, no," I said, biting the inside of my cheek to calm my hysteria. "I was taught not to objectify people, Miss Sullivan. Especially not in God's name."

"You're hilarious."

"I like to think so," I grinned. "Fine, Sully. If we're talking about basic physical attributes, then yes, I can admit that some people are more eye-catching than others. Let's take Kelly James, for example. The first time we met, I may have noticed that her hips are proportionate to her upper body. Objectively speaking, of course."

Dude. You *scowled* at me. "Is that your way of saying she's hot?"

"I don't need to say it. According to you, we can quantify her hotness with objective data. Actually, for the record, all three of the Addison girls rank high on the hotness scale."

You slammed a cushion against me with more righteous indignation than I'd seen in a long time, my friend. But then you must have wondered if Gigi's couch was expensive, because you brushed your fingers gently over the cushion, then laid it nicely back in place.

"Okay, fine," you said, clasping your hands in your lap. "If we're trading objective data, Kelly James thinks Dan has kissable lips."

Wow, Sully. You went right for the jugular. "Kelly? Or Anne?"

"Kelly," you replied with a slight quirk of your eyebrow. "When we got back to the hotel in Rouen after karaoke last September, she collapsed into a chair and sighed. 'We gotta watch ourselves around Eagle Scouts like Dan Thomas. Maybe it was his Jagger moves or that

DEAR SULLY

Ed Sheeran voice, but something tells me Dan's pouty bottom lip is *definitely* worth exploring.'"

"Wow. And how'd you respond?"

"Ha!" You crossed your arms over your chest. "Wouldn't *you* like to know?"

Listen, sister, *you knew* you were making me jealous right that second. You knew it, and you did it anyway, which was my final clue that something had shifted between us.

You'd never done that before – provoking me to jealousy. At least not on purpose. And I realized as I unpacked your words that there was a good reason you'd swiped at me.

For the first time ever, you saw the Addison girls as competition. And hey, after months and years of orbiting your world, my inner fanboy felt vindicated. So I reset my flabbergasted face into my most charming smile, and tested a boundary.

"You know what, Sully? Maybe you should test Kelly's theory about Dan's lips."

"You know what, *Russell*? Maybe I will."

"Good." I crossed my own arms over my chest. "Here's an insider tip: skinny margaritas on the rocks are Dan's personal kryptonite. He's *very* friendly on Cinco de Mayo. Not to mention health-conscious. How else do you think he got those Jagger moves?"

You huffed a little bit, Sully, and I thought I might have pushed you too far. But when I pushed play to restart my senior year highlight reel, the blooper reel queued up instead. And even though you'd just silenced me with one flip of your hair, the next minute you were laughing so hard that you could not breathe, which made me want to explore the pout of *your* bottom lip.

I love your laugh, Sully. And the younger Pete inside me – the one who first saw you that day at Sullivan's – was giving me internal high fives every time you giggled at his on-screen shenanigans. In that moment, he wanted me to lock it down with you so we could spend every night bantering for the rest of our very long lives.

But you weren't free yet. And neither was I, for that matter.

Still… you gotta wonder how many times I've screwed up our chances. For example, if I'd admitted I still love you last Saturday in my apartment, what would you have said?

Would you have stayed in Paris? Or would you still have run home to Irish Jack?

I know, Sully. I know. There's no point in *what if.*

But that doesn't stop me from remembering your face when I said Kelly is hot. It's my memory, and I'll go full-on only child with anyone who tries to alter that moment in my mind. Because objectively speaking, you are most beautiful when I surprise you.

Or maybe when you laugh.

DETENTE

A couple of days after my grandmother died, I called the Sigma Phi Beta president to request a meeting. I'd already decided to deactivate my membership, but not before I cast my vote for Drew Sutton in the upcoming officer election.

Drew was always meant to be president. He was the only one from our pledge class who genuinely loved Greek life. That's the sort of person you want representing your organization, you know? A guy who can see the experience's value despite the everyday nonsense?

Before I left the house, I hauled my plastic bins up from the basement, one by one. I was loading them in the back of my car when Sutton walked by on his way home from class.

"Oh. Hello." He adjusted his backpack straps for a couple of seconds. "Listen, man, I'm really sorry about your grandmother. I know she's... um, what I mean is..."

He stopped himself mid-sentence, and as I watched his face shift from one emotion to the next, I actually felt sorry for the kid. No doubt he understood that the last thing you want to hear when you're grieving is some throwaway phrase about a life well lived or the end of someone's suffering.

Which is why I didn't punch him when he suddenly (and very awkwardly) closed the distance between us to give me a hug.

Oh, yeah. I know. It was next-level weird. Believe me.

When he stepped away from me, Sutton cleared his throat. "Hey, um… listen, I've been meaning to thank you for picking me up from the bar the other night to bring me to the hospital. I was in no shape to drive, and it goes without saying that I needed to be with the Sullivans."

I leaned back against my car. "Yeah, no problem, man. I was only trying to help."

"I know you were. Which makes me feel a little sick, actually, because you should have spent those couple of hours with your grandmother instead of babysitting me. And for that, I'm truly sorry."

My stomach knotted. "Don't worry about it, Sutton. Gigi was already in bed by the time I came to find you. You didn't cost me anything but a couple hours' sleep."

"Okay, then. Allow me to be sorry for extending your jet lag." He smiled, but for once, he didn't smirk. "Speaking of my bad behavior, has anyone told you yet that Meredith and I broke up?"

"Uh… no." I couldn't stop blinking, Sully. "Gosh, man. I don't even know what to say. I mean, I'm –"

"Don't say it." His eyes were lined with silver. "Don't you dare say you're sorry, Russell. You and I both know I never deserved

Meredith's friendship, let alone her love. Apparently she reserves that privilege for better men. Looks like Molly and Jamie raised her right."

On a normal day, I might have called him out on his self-pitying word bait, but that day was far from normal. Because that day, for the first time ever, I no longer viewed Sutton as competition. No, in that moment, I only saw Drew Sutton as the boy who loved you first.

And that, my friend, changed my paradigm forever.

"Hey Sutton?" I said after a very long pause where we both stared at our feet. "Do you ever wonder how things might have gone down if your Girl Friday had gone to Harvard instead of Highgate?"

He squinted at me. "What are you talking about?"

"Well, hypothetically speaking, what if we had only ever been Drew and Pete, Sigma Phi Beta pledge brothers? If that Sullivan girl had gone to Harvard, would we be friends now?"

He watched me for a moment as he replayed the past through a new lens. Then he smiled. "You know what, Russell? One hundred percent, I think we would. We started out that way, didn't we?"

"We did." I reached my hand out toward him. "Maybe when I get back from Paris this summer, we could start back at the beginning? I know I'd like that."

He eyed me strangely, as though I'd said some magical combination of words he'd never expected to hear. "Yeah, man," he said as he took my hand and shook it firmly. "I think I'd like that too. You game to find some non-lethal food-truck tacos?"

I laughed, and Drew shook my hand again. But instead of shaking it a third time, he punched me in the shoulder, turned on his heel, and walked into the Sigma Phi Beta house without another word.

PROMENADE DES ANGLAIS

I almost kissed you three times junior year.

The first (and most obvious) time was that night we were dancing at the Tuileries. But I knew it was wayyyyy too soon for that level of old-school Hollywood nonsense, so I refrained.

The second time was in Marie-France's elevator on your birthday. When that pulley jerked to a halt and you pitched forward into my chest... well, let's just say you have no idea how close I came to risking two black eyes. (One from Sutton, one from Meg. And maybe one from you as well.)

The third time was in my bedroom the day of Gigi's wake. The third time is charming, right? Uh, no. Not when a certain overprotective big brother ruins the mood.

I know you've heard these three stories, but I wanted to remind you that despite my many foibles, I do recognize the sacred nature of what's happened between us. You mean more to me than some random kiss. That's the point of these letters, right? To tell the truth.

And the truth is, I didn't plan to kiss you that day on the boardwalk in Nice. I didn't plan it, because I was legit convinced I might lose you the second I admitted how I felt.

It was May 10th – more than two months after you'd broken things off with Sutton, and four weeks after I'd broken up with Meg for good. When I'd confessed I was single again that morning at the perfume factory, the air between us felt light again. Like you'd finally given up a battle with your own heart, and I was somehow the victor.

"For the love of everything good and holy, would you just kiss her already?" Dan groaned two hours later, shoving me playfully into a hydrangea bush on our way to the arcade. "March yourself back to that boardwalk, put your lips on hers, and move on to Happily-Ever-After Land already."

"But –"

"No buts, Russell. I can't keep watching the two of you *yearning* for each other until the end of time. Do something now, or I'll tell her about the night of the twenty-five thousand steps."

"It was thirty thousand and you know it, Danny," I shouted over my shoulder as I took off sprinting down the hill.

I spotted you *way* before you noticed me. Your copper hair was shining like a beacon from a thousand meters away, and every few seconds you glanced out to sea. But your eyes never met mine.

Frenetic energy flooded my veins. I began to pace from side to side, weaving in and out of tourists like a stray dog. *Calm down*, I told myself. *Calm. The. Heck. Down.*

And just like that, you were standing before me, your hands on your hips. "I thought you guys went to the arcade?"

Okay, Russell, I thought. *Just be yourself. If she wasn't into you, she would never have started that @vertismes Twitter account.*

Deep breaths, man. Come on. Do NOT pass out now.

"Arcade?" I answered, trying not to hyperventilate. "Uh, yeah. Dan went there. But I, um… I guess I came to find you."

You relaxed against the boardwalk wall and asked me some question, which I absolutely don't remember, because I was too focused on your lips and the sudden flush in your cheeks as I brushed a rogue hair behind your ear.

When my fingers touched your skin, your entire body stiffened for the briefest of moments. If it had been a week earlier, I might have stepped backward and made some slapstick comment to put you at ease. But this wasn't a week earlier, or a month earlier. This was *it*. I couldn't wait any longer. And as I stepped closer, pressing my hand against your cheek, you immediately relaxed into my touch.

Maybe you didn't want to wait either. Because when I kissed you, you kissed me back.

Did you surprise yourself that day? Because everything you said afterward sounded like nonsensical gibberish to me, and it took everything inside me not to laugh, because *dude*. *THE* MEREDITH SULLIVAN kissed ME.

You kissed me, Sully. And if anyone had told me that day that I'd be running away from you two months later, I would have punched them in both eyeballs. Twice.

THE NORTH STATION

Despite all appearances to the contrary, I'm an old-fashioned guy. The last thing I wanted to do once I'd finally found the *cohones* to show you my true feelings was to squander my chances at an epic first date. So on the bus back from Nice to Paris, I made my move.

"Hey," I said quietly, looping my index finger around your pinky. "What are you doing next Saturday?"

You looked at me funny. "Saturday day, or Saturday night?"

"Uh, both, I guess. You busy?"

Your eyes shifted back and forth between mine, then you grinned. "Well, I'll have to check my planner when we get back to Paris, but I think I'm free."

"Good. Would you go out with me? On a date, I mean. Like, officially or whatever."

"Sure." You flashed me a flirty smile. "Gosh, it's a good thing you asked me six days in advance. Because wow, does my social calendar fill up *fast*."

Har-dee-har-har, sister. Thanks for drawing attention to my overly eager request.

Speaking of overly eager syndrome, the following Saturday at six a.m., I found a model-esque redhead *slash* former Irish dance champion waiting for me outside Marie-France's building dressed in jeans, comfortable shoes, a thin sweater layered over another top, a crossbody bag, and a rain jacket. Just in case.

No one should look that effortlessly gorgeous, okay? Especially not while they're carrying a rain jacket.

We hopped on the *Métro* at Saint-Sulpice and took the 4 line north to the *Gare du Nord*. A few steps into the station, you tugged at my hand to stop me. "What are we doing here?"

I lifted your hand and nodded toward your charm bracelet. "If you arrive home with any blank spaces, you will totally offend your brother. So I thought I'd help you out a little today."

Your eyes widened. "Wait, what? Where are we going?"

"Look, Ginger Spice, when I asked you to run away with me last October, you ditched me the next morning for some West Coast surfer dude. So I figured we should hop the first train to anywhere and start over where we got sidetracked. See what I did there? Some train imagery for my bookish girl who digs that sort of thing."

You laughed, Sully. Then you kissed me right there in the middle of everyone. "You're a romantic," you whispered against my lips. "You do *not* give that impression, my friend."

Dear Sully

"Maybe you just need glasses," I whispered back. But you were right, Sully. I've never been romantic in my entire life. I've never *wanted* to be until I fell in love with you.

Here's a little fun fact you never knew until now, Miss Smarty Pants: I timed every single second that morning to arrive at the *Gare du Nord* exactly at 6:43 a.m. I knew in advance that we'd take the *Thalys* high-speed train to Brussels at 7:32 – First Class, baby. I'd researched Saturday morning *Métro* schedules between Saint-Sulpice and the train station. I'd even low-key calculated how long it would take our matching strides to carry us toward the departures board in the main hall.

I used my *left brain*. Can you believe it? Dude, I even did a test run on the subway before class on Friday morning. Because when I plan a perfect first date for my favorite girl, I don't want to leave any detail unattended.

So what you took as serendipity that morning was simply my evil plan to remind you of where we left off in the fall. Cupid can always use a bit of organizational help.

Brussels was magical, wasn't it? You indulged my inner twelve-year-old and took a selfie with me at the *Mannekin-Pis*. You made me split a *gaufre* with you (like anyone needs cajoling to eat a waffle smothered in Nutella). You proved you'd paid attention in your art history class when you played tour guide in the *Musée des Beaux-Arts*. I've never found Flemish art so fascinating in my entire life.

You are amazing, Meredith Sullivan. And the most amazing part about you is that you have no freaking idea how amazing you are.

We found a dinky little tourist shop that had about ten silver charms, and when I insisted you let me buy every one that would make you remember this day, you *let* me. The second we walked outside, you slid your fingers into my hair. "You're my favorite, Pete Russell. I hope you know that."

Oh, man. I did *not* know that. And the second you said it, my heart filled with dread that you might change your mind if you ever knew the real me.

Dr. Keating and I have spent a lot of time this week talking about fear. He claims that losing my family has created a trust vacuum in my heart. That ever since an event beyond my control claimed my parents' lives, I try to control *all* the things. Like the way I'd choreographed the whole day trip to Brussels so that you'd think I was spontaneous and whimsical when in reality, I'd scheduled every minute to showcase what I hoped were my best qualities.

But taking you First Class on the fancy train didn't impress you whatsoever. The following Monday at lunch when you told our friends about our "spontaneous" trip to Brussels, you never mentioned the fancy leather seats or the waitress who served us *café au lait* in porcelain tea cups.

Nah. You were too busy gushing over the three-euro-apiece dinky silver charms I bought.

For whatever reason, you find my sentimental side adorable. In fact, I bet if I asked you to make a list of my best qualities, not *one* thing on that list would be something I control.

Write me that list someday, Sully. Because if there's one thing this notebook is teaching me, it's that the only Pete I respect is the Pete *you* love.

DEAR SULLY

ENNISTYMON

It's six in the morning on Saturday now, and I'm sitting in my living room staring at the muted light outside my apartment's wall of windows. The rue Guénégaud is always so quiet, despite its proximity to the river, and most days, that's a selling point for this apartment.

Today, it's a liability.

I woke up early this morning, which is not my usual habit on a Saturday, but nothing about today is normal. Two years ago today, on June 30th, we flew home from Ireland with Ian, and even before my eyes opened, I knew I would hate every minute of the day ahead of me. It's an anniversary I managed to ignore last year, but this year, I don't have that luxury.

I loved your brother, Sully. I've never met anyone with a bigger heart than Ian Sullivan, and from the second I met him, I believed we'd be best friends someday. Some people suck the life from a room, but Ian? He was like sunshine personified. And watching you lose him was the last nail in my broken heart's coffin.

I've never told you about the following conversation – not because I had something to hide, but because I never thought anyone (including you) would believe me. But when I woke up today, I knew I needed to write this story down for you. Because when Ian died, he took a lot of unfulfilled dreams with him. And if I feel that way, I know you must feel it too.

Remember my twenty-third birthday? We'd just spent two weeks with your brother and Kate in your Nana's tiny cottage in Doolin, and it wasn't going well. At least not when the four of us were together. Kate drove me crazy, mostly because she drove *you* crazy. So when Ian asked me to help him drive your Nana's things to some charity shop, I hopped at the chance for a break.

The two of us loaded up the Irish equivalent of a U-Haul truck and headed south down the tiny coastal highway. Somewhere near that hub town called Ennistymon, we got stuck behind a herd of sheep with no shepherd in sight. Your brother cursed in Gaelic (!!) and promptly shut off the ignition. It was so postcard-worthy and stereotypically Irish that I couldn't help but grin.

But it didn't take long to realize Ian wasn't grinning with me. He was just staring ahead, eyes fixed on nothing in particular, like his soul had left the vehicle. Then he turned to me, eyes still unfocused. "Sorry, mate. Did you say something?"

"Dude, are you okay?" I punched him on the arm. "Do we need to stop and get you some food or something? You look a little pale."

"Oh." He huffed out a joyless laugh. "No. I'm just… thinking."

"About?"

He glanced my way one more time, then shook his head. "It's nothing, really. I just have so few memories of living here when I was a lad. I mean, I know I was only six when we moved to the States, but isn't six old enough to have a solid anchor to this place?"

If I'd known your brother better, I probably would've figured out a way to make him laugh. You know how skittish I get when things get dicey, but in that moment, I couldn't think of anything to make him snap out of his weirdness.

The herd of sheep started to walk off to the side of the road, loping their way along the rushing stream beside us. One by one, they hoofed it off the roadway, and as Ian turned the key in the ignition, he asked, "Did Meredith ever show you photos from when we lived here before?"

"Not yet. Actually, now that you mention it, she hasn't told me much at all about the past."

"Don't take it personally." Ian's eyes narrowed a bit as he put the truck in gear. "Meredith doesn't like to make a fuss – she's been this way her whole life, even in the womb. Mum used to let me lay my head against her pregnant belly, and I would talk *at* Meredith until finally, she'd kick the spot right next to my face. Like she'd heard enough, and I needed to stop messing about."

"I bet she rolled her eyes at you, too. You just couldn't see her."

"Exactly. My dad always says the first time he held her, she gave him major side-eye, like he'd forced her to make an appearance three days early. He insists that she frowned, like, 'Hey, mister! The doctor said I'm due December *sixteenth*. Just like Jane Austen. Why aren't you following orders?'"

We both laughed that time, because seriously, Sully – that is so you. Stubborn to the core. Always on time. My favorite little rule follower. "If she did that to your dad, what'd she do when she saw you? Kick you for real?"

"No. She just looked up at me with those strange baby eyes and I could not stop staring. The first thing I did was touch her hair to see if it was real, because I'd never seen anything like it. She was born with a full head of dark copper hair. Did you know that?"

"No."

"Well, she was. I should have known then it was just the fire in her soul making itself visible, daring the world to mess with Meredith Fiona Sullivan."

Oh, man, Sully. Ian had you pegged.

"Here's some trivia for you, Mr. Russell. Did you know that red hair and gray eyes is the rarest combination in human genetics?"

"No."

"Well, it's true, apparently. Meredith did a research project on it in high school biology."

"I believe it. She's the only person I know with that combo."

"Me too. And I've been around." Ian glanced across the truck's cab at me. "Suffice it to say, my sister is different. She always has been, which is why I never understood her fascination with Drew Sutton, because Drew is… well, I believe the word kids say nowadays is *basic*."

If anyone else had called Sutton 'basic,' I might have laughed. But when it came from Ian, it didn't sound funny; it sounded a lot like disappointment. I could see clear as day that Ian loved Drew, that your family's connection with the Suttons went way deeper than I'd ever dreamed. And something about that revelation made my stomach flip.

But just as my thoughts began to spiral downward, Ian did something I will never forget: he reached across the truck and clapped me on the shoulder, then squeezed. It lasted less than half a second, and on a different day, I might have found it borderline weird. But for whatever reason, in that moment, I read between the lines and understood.

Yes, Ian loved Sutton like a brother. But that day, when it was just the two of us alone in the truck cab, your brother's gesture made me believe he had room in his heart for me as well. The note he gave me in the Portland airport a few days later confirmed it.

You see the best in Fee, which makes me think you're alright.

When Dr. Keating asked me to write letters in this journal, I figured I'd humor him for a couple of days. Shrinks are always asking people to jump through one hoop or another, you know? How else would they get us to pay them a hundred euros an hour, over and over again?

But now, six days and a hundred handwritten pages later, I can see Dr. Keating's exercise has worked. I've just read back through my own words, and guess what I learned?

You and I are not over.

Not by a long shot.

If these letters have taught me anything, it's that I have a million things left to say to you. Except now, it's time to move past the pages of this notebook.

Now I need to say them to your face.

Gotta go, Sully. I've got a bag to pack and a couple of planes to catch if I want to make it to Dún Aonghasa by tomorrow morning.

I'm ninety-nine percent certain that's where you'll be.

Saturday, October 21ˢᵗ, 10:33 pm

Dear Pete,

I'm ignoring your instructions – that we're only allowed to communicate by snail mail about these letters – by texting you a picture of this note. That's right, I *am* breaking a rule, but only because your rule is insane. What were you thinking? Why would you ask to wait an entire week for my response to these letters just so you could get some snail mail?

You've lost your mind completely. And according to these letters, you've severely underestimated my appreciation for your beautiful soul.

As requested, here are a few of my favorite Pete Russell things:

- The way your eyes twinkle;
- Your curls – thanks for growing them back out for me;
- Your laugh, especially the one from your belly that makes your eyes water;

- Your sentimental side;
- Dr. Keating's right – your handwriting is the actual coolest;
- The way you are better than me at E V E R Y T H I N G but you don't even know it;
- The way you hug me so long that the world fades away;
- When you love someone, you love them *big*… which probably explains all that running away you do when your heart gets broken;
- Your butt in jeans (don't even try to pretend you didn't know);
- The way you wrote me twenty letters in a journal without even knowing if I would read it. But please tell me you'll explain what happened at Dún Aonghasa this summer in the so-called October journal (which, by the way, was sitting on my parents' kitchen counter when I got home this evening). HELLO, CLIFFHANGER. (!!)
- You really *are* Gilbert Blythe. Like, WHOA. Now that I've seen it, I can never un-see it. I guess this is why you're the academic and I'm just a storyteller. (For the record, you'd look hot in a newsboy cap. Let's buy you one soon.)

love,

Sully

PS – Don't worry, I'll mail you the original of this list. I expect to see it up on your fridge the next time I'm in Paris.

PSS – Ian loved you too. And you would have been best friends.

OCTOBER

TUESDAY, OCTOBER 16TH

DEAR SULLY,

AS PROMISED HERE'S MY SECOND
JOURNAL FULL OF LETTERS FOR
YOU. i FILLED THIS ONE UP LAST
WEEK AFTER i READ NIGHT AND DAY,
AND THIS MORNING ON MY WAY TO THE
CENTRE LAFAYETTE, i PLAN TO MAIL IT
TO THE JUNIPER HOUSE BEFORE i
CHICKEN OUT.

IT WON'T TAKE YOU LONG TO SEE
WHY i THOUGHT YOU SHOULD READ
THIS ONE AT HOME INSTEAD OF ON A
PLANE (YOU KNOW, JUST IN CASE YOU
NEED TO THROW IT AT SOMETHING).

LOVE,
PETE

TAKE TWO

I bet you're wondering if I made it to Ireland in July.

Why, YES, I did. I landed in Shannon late on June 30th, and on the morning of July 1st, I boarded the tiniest plane known to mankind and flew to Inishmore, where I took a shuttle out to Dún Aonghasa.

Guess what I found there? The girl I love sitting on the edge of the world, tangled up in the arms of some hipster I seriously hope was Jack.

That *was* Jack, right? Because even though my rational brain tells me that the jumble of his arms plus your legs was just your final goodbye, my heart's a little terrified that you've fallen for a second swoony Irishman. One who is ridiculously good-looking, by the way.

Even now, three months later, I'm still not certain.

Anyway, after my eyes blew out of their sockets that Sunday morning, I somehow made it back to Paris in one piece by noon on Monday. But instead of going home to wallow in a pint of ice cream,

I took the train from Charles de Gaulle airport and walked straight to Dr. Keating's office – with my luggage, by the way – and waited outside his office until he had an opening.

I waited four hours. Here's a sampling of the accusations I lobbed his way that afternoon:

You're a hack.

I made an idiot of myself this weekend and it's all your fault.

Where exactly did *you study, and why don't you have any diplomas on your walls?*

Why yes, I *am* a gem. Thank you for noticing.

To his credit, Dr. Keating listened to me without interrupting, and when I finished ranting about all the ways he had failed me, do you know what he did? He came to stand beside me, and with something even worse than sadness in his eyes, he laid one hand on my shoulder.

"I'm sorry, Peter," he said with a gentle, paternal squeeze. "I should have warned you not to speak to Meredith yet. We still have a lot to do before you're ready for that step. So please don't disappear on me, lad. It would be a shame to undo all the hard work you've done this past week. And if it will make you feel better, I'll put up my diplomas first thing tomorrow morning."

Tears were already spilling down my cheeks by the time he uttered my name, but that last statement made me laugh. And then, because I am a complete wackadoodle, I hugged him like he was family, which I'm pretty sure violates several doctor-patient laws.

But he hugged me back, Sully. And when I left his office that afternoon, I promised to come back again the following day.

"Tell me," he said the next afternoon once we'd settled into our respective chairs. "Why did you buy a one-way ticket when you came to Paris this summer?"

"Who told you I did that?"

He simply smiled. "If your goal is to understand the motivation behind your behavior, you might as well be honest with me. Isn't that the point of our visits? For us to suss out the truth?"

I shifted uncomfortably in my seat. "Well, I guess the official reason I came to Paris on a one-way ticket is that I needed to update my apartment, and there was no way to guess how long it might take."

"Mmm hmm. And the unofficial reason?"

I rolled my eyes. "Are you seriously going to make me say this out loud?"

"Yes. I am."

Even though I was seated, I shoved my hands in my pockets. "Look, I'm not a jerk, Dr. Keating. I know I left my quote/unquote relationship in limbo when I jetted off to Paris without warning. But if Brooks were here, she'd assure you my disappearing act came as zero surprise. I've done this same thing plenty of times before."

"I know that, Peter. I've been listening to every word this past week. But weren't you and Brooks friends for years before she became your partner?"

"Partner?" I scoffed. "I'm not even sure Brooks would call herself my *girlfriend*, sir. Labels like that are so... I don't know. High school, I guess. The last few weeks I was home, we barely even hung out. We weren't planning a future together or anything. We're both too busy with our respective lives."

"I see. So when you found Meredith in the arms of another man this weekend in Ireland, what *label* did your mind produce? Neighbors? Leprechauns? Please enlighten me. I'm dying to know."

Dude. He totally called me out. I would have knocked knuckles with him on any other day, because *touché,* Keating. The guy knew his way around my double-speak. But I was too busy trying to hide underneath my own chair to congratulate him on clenching the championship round.

"Here's your next challenge, Peter: why don't you fly home to Portland for a few days? Make eye contact with Brooks. Give her a proper goodbye, and while you're at it, a proper apology."

"But I don't have to fly home to do either of those things, sir. Wouldn't it be easier to break up with her over the phone?"

"Of course it would be easier. But just because something's easy doesn't make it the better choice. It would be *easier* for you to keep running away from your inner pain for the rest of your life, but you're trying to curb that behavior, are you not?"

"I am." My stomach flipped as I shifted once again in my chair. "But isn't the point of therapy to learn from our own mistakes? I already know I've hurt Brooks, and not just by running away. She must know she's played second fiddle to Meredith this whole time. I don't want to rub it in her face with an apology just to accomplish a therapeutic leap on my end."

Oh, man. The *scowl.* "You can be certain Brooks knows *exactly* how you feel about her, with or without your apology. And you are wise to recognize that it will hurt both of you to admit out loud what you've done. But it's important to end things properly, and not just for Brooks."

"What do you mean?"

DEAR SULLY

He steepled his fingers. "On our first meeting, you told me that Meredith fled your apartment last Saturday. If I remember correctly, you were on the phone with Brooks at the time. You also mentioned that Meredith flew home to Ireland immediately, even though she was meant to spend the weekend here with friends she hadn't seen in ages. Why do you think she took such extreme measures?"

"Um, because things got weird?"

"Weird, or confusing?" His eyebrow hitched up even further. "Tell me, son – did it ever occur to you that Meredith knows your game better than anyone? That maybe she noticed you pulling the same disappearing act on another woman that you pulled on her? That it hurt *Meredith* to see you treating Brooks with the same flippant disregard that you'd shown her in the past?"

If he'd called me a malignant narcissist, it might have stung less. Was he right, Sully? Is that why you left Paris that day in June? I don't want to believe him, but I have a sneaky feeling that I'm not the only person Dr. Keating understands in this world.

The above conversation took place on July 3rd. Today is October 8th. Three whole months have passed, and I still haven't found the courage to contact you. Every time I look up your number in my contacts, I nearly pass out from my blood pressure spiking.

But then Dan overnighted me his copy of *Night and Day*. And as I read your words, I couldn't help but notice how mysterious your Luke Jameson character reads, especially when it comes to his past. So this time, I decided to fill up a second notebook with everything I'm terrified to tell you. Everything you probably wonder but you're too proud (or afraid) to ask.

I've got eight days to write you the rest of the story. And this time, *you* might be the one who runs away. Because this time, the stories I write might change your mind about me forever.

Meredith Sullivan, I present to you the updated history of my past six years. Once more with feeling, bad decisions and all.

RUBY'S DINER

After our accident in Lincoln City that summer, I never stepped foot in my family's house in Sherwood again. Vick Darby handled the sale while neighbors and friends packed up our things and put them in a storage unit. By late September, our gray-with-black-trim cottage was under contract, and by Halloween, another family occupied our white-picket-fence life in the 'burbs.

Good-hearted people executed the tiny details on my behalf, and I let them. Because I couldn't do it, Sully. I couldn't face my own life.

So Pops and Gigi set up camp for me in their ground floor guest room. It was much less practical than the upstairs bedroom you saw.

Big fluffy white bed. Plush towels. A full-sized fridge, a microwave, plus its own private entrance from the garage.

Kind of like the hotel I lived in this past year. Treat that heartbroken kid like a king, right? Make all his troubles disappear.

In the months following the accident, my life consisted of three things: physical therapy, food, and sleep. No TV. No video games. No mindless hours scrolling social media.

Are you kidding me? The very last thing I needed was a reminder of the life I'd never have.

One afternoon in early November, on our way home from physical therapy, Gigi pulled into Ruby's Diner right across the street from the Highgate campus.

Yes, that's right. The diner you and Sutton used to visit every Friday morning.

While I fiddled with the jukebox, Gigi ordered cheese fries and two sodas, which the server delivered minutes later. The two of us sat there in chummy silence, filling our guts with junk food and bobbing our heads in unison to Gloria Gaynor. By that point, my leg was out of its cast. My stitches were scars. My bruises had faded.

All the physical bruises, at least.

"Your grandfather spoke to Stanford's dean of admissions this week," Gigi said quietly, folding her hands primly in her lap. "Dr. Urbanek told him she'd spoken to you sometime last month. That you'd requested deferred matriculation. Is that true, Peter? Did you speak to her without telling us?"

"Uh…" I took a sip of my soda and willed my insides to calm the heck down. "I mean, yeah. She told me deferred matriculation is standard protocol under the circumstances."

"Mmmhmm." Gigi's eyes flickered back and forth between mine. "Listen, Peter – Pops and I are not your parents, and we don't want to treat you like a child."

"I appreciate that."

"Yes, well, don't misunderstand what I'm saying here, young man. As much as we've loved having you as our guest, I'm afraid you can't hide out in our house forever."

"I know that." I pulled the straw out of my drink, gnawing on the ends as I looked *anywhere* but her face. "Look, Geeg, I don't want to sound like a complete brat here, but I'm not sure I really *want* to go to Stanford. Nothing against the school itself, you know? It's just…"

Tears pricked at my eyes in that moment, and even though it wouldn't have been the first time I devolved into a sniveling mess in front of my grandmother that fall, I'd grown tired of the way those feelings always smacked me right in the face when I wasn't looking. I threw my straw down and dropped my head into my hands. A couple of seconds later, I felt Gigi's fingers pressing gently against my curls.

"I know, darling. Stanford reminds you of Liz and Jim," she murmured, her voice crackling with grief. "It represents an entire timeline of memories that will never come to pass. I understand. So you don't have to go to Stanford. Not next semester. Not ever."

I lifted my head. "I don't?"

"No, Peter. You don't even have to go to college. But you do have to *live*. It's what your mom and dad would want you to do."

I looked into her eyes – *really* looked. Gigi was always straight with me, and something about her words felt like she'd just unlocked a prison cell from which I never believed I'd escape. So I stared at her hard, letting the truth sink in. Gigi meant what she was saying. I didn't have to pick up the pieces of my old life and cobble together some shabby existence just to keep up appearances. Instead, my future was mine alone to choose.

I pushed myself upright so fast that my head sort of spun, because man, Sully. The wheels of change were upon me, and just like that, I had a plan.

"So, Geeg, you know how James Logan calls me every Sunday night?"

She tilted her head to one side. "Of course I do. Why do you ask?"

"Well, the last time he called, James mentioned that traffic always picks up at the Restoration Initiative during the winter months. Dropping temperatures plus a lack of food, water, and shelter means more people in need. Makes sense, right?"

"Of course. Even in Portland, the homeless shelters are filled to capacity during the winter months. With China's population, I imagine the situation is dire."

"Exactly." I clasped my hands in front of me on the table. "So what if I spent a few months in Shanghai after Christmas? Assuming I can get a visa and the doctors think I'm ready, of course."

Gigi's eyes blazed all of a sudden. "Oh, Peter. I don't think that's a wise decision."

"But I'd be making a difference in other people's lives! That must be a hundred times wiser than staring at the ceiling all day. Besides, I thought you loved James."

"This isn't about James, darling. I know you want to skip the hard part of losing your parents, but if you don't face down your grief, it will grow and grow until one day, it will cripple you when you least expect it. You can trust me on this. I know from experience."

"But how am I supposed to heal *here*? I can't walk five feet inside your house without seeing a picture of my parents. We drive past St. Francis Prep ninety times a day. Dude, my tear ducts exploded in the cereal aisle at the grocery store last week. Who does that?"

She stifled a grin. "I'd bet a lot of people cry in the cereal aisle. High fructose corn syrup wields a very powerful magic."

"Come on, Geeg. Be serious." I took a deep breath, then released it. "I need a change of scenery. Just for a little while. You've already admitted you get that, so why the resistance?"

"Billions of people process their grief perfectly well in their own hometown, Peter. You're acting rather privileged at the moment."

"Fine." I lifted my hands in surrender. "I'm willing to admit that's true. I'm the brattiest of all the spoiled brats on the planet. So how about I use my privilege to make a difference in someone else's life? Isn't that the point? If I went to live at the Initiative, not only would I have to do laundry and clean, I'd learn some carpentry skills. It's a win-win: I could serve others *and* get my body back in shape."

"Yes, but –"

"But nothing, Geeg – you know it's a brilliant idea! And I bet James would let me teach the guys English in a formal classroom setting. How cool would *that* look on my résumé?"

"Oh, Peter." Gigi's eyes looked weary. "We both know you will set yourself back if you move to China. Your mind will be too busy taking in new stimuli and adjusting to a new language and culture to deal with anything *real*. How many times must I tell you? The road must be walked."

She was right, Sully. I knew she was right. But in that moment, I just didn't want to listen. So I rubbed my fists against my eye sockets and took another deep breath.

"I have to get out of here, Gigi. I don't care where you send me, just get out of your guest room, okay? Because I've already read every novel on the bookshelves, and if I turn on the TV, I'll start watching the home improvement channel, and then the zombie apocalypse will happen, and –"

"Rewind just a moment," she said, spiraling a finger in the air. "What was that about home improvement?"

"Uh… that I don't want to start down that dark path to hell?" I watched her eyes brighten. "Oh, no, Gigi. Please don't tell me you have plans to redecorate the dining room in some godawful brocade."

"My dining room? No. Absolutely not. It doesn't get enough light for brocade," she winked. "But maybe I could persuade your grandfather to let you spearhead the Guénégaud apartment renovations."

"But… I don't know anything about decorating."

"I know you don't. But Brooks Darby does, and you know French. You'd be the perfect team for this project."

Oh, Sully. My grandmother appeared so kind and gentle, didn't she? Yeah, well, she was also shrewd and conniving, and without my realizing it, she'd just dangled the one carrot guaranteed to wreak havoc on all my Shanghai dreams.

Because earlier that fall, unbeknownst to me, Gigi had offered Brooks a rent-free gig at our Paris apartment while she learned to make marzipan and *macarons* at some fancy Left Bank *pâtisserie* school run by an American blogger. In return, young Brooks would update the apartment to modern standards. But as my grandmother filled me in on her plans, the only detail my nineteen-year-old boy brain absorbed was *Brooks, Brooks, Brooks.*

I know, Sully. I've always been your worst nightmare come true. I just tricked you temporarily with all of that lindy-hopping back in the day.

CAVEAU DE LA HUCHETTE

By early December, Gigi was so thrilled with my *seven* college applications across the United States that she allowed me leave for Paris on New Year's Day, one whole week earlier than Brooks. She thought I might need time to sort through my feelings once I'd settled back into our family's flat. So many memories, so much to haunt me.

The silver lining? I'd get to buy a *galette des rois* (or four) before Epiphany on January 6th.

See, the bakery down the street from the Guénégaud apartment has these awesome ceramic garden gnome *fèves* that they bake inside their cakes. If you're the only one eating the cake, you have a one hundred percent chance of finding that super cool gnome collectible.

You saw my collection of mini gnomes the day you were up in my apartment in June. You just didn't realize at the time just how dorky that collection makes me.

Garden gnomes notwithstanding, wise old Gigi was correct: staying in that apartment those first few days was *trippy*. Despite the passage of time, everything still felt the same. I kept expecting my mom to burst through the door with a baguette under one arm or my dad to walk into the kitchen with his glasses propped on top of his head, asking me for the billionth time what the country code was for the United States.

But then my guest arrived, and everything felt new again. According to Brooks, our first job was to move any outdated furniture to the living room. By the next morning, when the charity truck came, every room but the kitchen was empty. We painted every wall, then applied one more coat for good measure, and while our brains were high on paint fumes, we pulled out Gigi's credit card, went online, and restocked the whole apartment, right down to the coffee table coasters.

All day that Friday, delivery trucks dropped by with new furniture and accessories. By six p.m., the apartment looked like an Anthropologie catalog. Which was sort of the point, wasn't it? How else was Gigi going to attract the junior-year-abroad renters of the world?

That evening, Brooks suggested we walk over to the Latin Quarter to grab crêpes and explore. As we strolled, we found a place called *Caveau de la Huchette* just a stone's throw from Shakespeare and Company.

Why yes, that *is* the place you asked me to take you swing dancing about a million times after we started dating.

Guess what, Sully? You're about to learn why I refused.

It was late by the time we walked inside the *Caveau*. People were decked out from head to toe in their best forties gear: women in bright red dresses that hugged their curves, men in doo-wop shoes with their hair slicked back. The atmosphere was electric.

And don't forget, Brooks was the captain of the Ducky Shincrackers her senior year. Two former swing dance team captains in a place like that? We boogied our hearts out for at least an hour, even though I was still healing from the car accident. Pffft. You think that stopped me? Please. I was a nineteen-year-old dude. I laughed in the face of pain. Especially when there was a girl involved.

When the band finally took a break, Brooks dragged me to a table back in the darkest corner of the room. She ordered lemon drop shots and a carafe of water, but when the waiter returned, he'd brought six shots instead of two – "from the band," he said, "for the lovely American couple."

"Look at you, Captain Fancy Pants," Brooks grinned, clinking her shot glass against mine. "Even with that bum leg, you still looked better than half the professionals on that dance floor."

I didn't respond. I just tipped my head back and swallowed the first shot whole.

This was before I'd quit drinking, of course, and the hour spent dancing had creaked its way into my bones. So I took a second shot, just to speed the pain relief along. Which only sent Brooks into hysterics.

"Well, this should be interesting," she muttered under her breath. Then she took two shots herself.

Vodka snaked its way through my veins, my heart thumping so wildly I thought it might burst out of my chest. So I poured us both some water. Then I fixed Brooks with a knowing smirk. "How's that loser Charlie you used to date?"

"I'm sure he's fine," she said flatly, taking a small sip from her water glass. "Last time I saw him, the day before finals, he'd moved on to his fifth new girl of the semester."

"Classy." I watched her over the rim of my water glass. "Do you miss him?"

Brooks didn't answer. Instead, she picked up both of our third shots and slid a little closer to me on the banquette, her eyes suddenly glued to my lips. "To the future, Russell."

"To the future," I repeated, clinking my glass to hers. And down the hatch those lemon drops slid.

Listen, I know you've never experienced my intoxicated inner frat boy, but let's get real – *no one* makes wise choices after three shots in ten minutes. And sadly for me, I've never been one to black out, so I remember every second of what happened next.

I slid my arm behind her along the back of the banquette, and to my surprise, Brooks didn't flinch. In fact, a couple of seconds later, she took up residence in the space between my chest and my bicep. When she finally lifted her eyes to mine, I could see something was… well, different. At least on her end, it was. Except with that much vodka in my system, all I could do was laugh.

"Come on, Brooksie. You can't mess with me. We've known each other too long to bother playing games."

She shot me a sexy grin. "You don't like games?"

"Well, I suppose that depends." I tilted my head down until our eyes were level. "What'd you have in mind?"

And just like that, she grabbed my shirt and tugged me toward her. We might have morphed into a jumble of legs and fingers in hair… except the waiter picked that instant to return and plunked down a bill for all six shots.

"Sorry," he said in heavily accented French. "I'm afraid ze lemon drop shots were meant for a *different* American couple."

Well, that killed the mood.

At first, Brooks tried to sweet-talk him out of the charges, and judging by the cool expression plastered across her face, I could tell this wasn't the first time she'd used her beauty to her own advantage. Now that I think about it, it wasn't even the first time that *night*.

But the *serveur* wasn't having it. In hoity-toity, aristocratic French (not English this time), he backtracked, admitting that he'd only brought us those shots to capture Brooks' attention. "But if you prefer wasting your time with an infant like this boy, I don't see why I should foot the bill. Besides," he added. "You have big teeth, *mademoiselle*. Very straight, but enormous. Like a horse."

Dear waiters of the world: this is why you should never assume Americans only speak English. Because some of us understand you fluently. Especially when you call us a *bébé*.

"What'd he say?" She asked after he stomped away.

"Oh, you know. Just that he hates Americans," I lied. "Guess why?"

She thought for a second, then scrunched up her nose. "Because our teeth are too straight?"

I pointed at her like she'd won the jackpot. And suddenly we were double-high-fiving and laughing so hard that the patrons around us started to give us judgy looks.

Brooks slung her purse across her body. "Let's get out of here."

"Without paying? No way!"

She touched her fingers to my lips to shush me. "Go! Now! Before that loser comes back."

She certainly was persuasive; at least, I thought so in that moment with her fingers against my lips. So I got up and stumbled up the staircase up to the ground level, narrowly avoiding a full wipeout at the top while Brooks zoomed past me out into the street.

A lot of things could have happened next. But I'm telling you this story right now because I want you to know from the horses' mouth ... er, ball-point pen ... what exactly *did* happen.

Ten feet outside the club, in the cold, damp January night, Brooks spewed the contents of her stomach onto the rue de la Huchette. And being the loyal gentleman that I am, I employed my hidden talent and followed suit. After all, I couldn't let my dream girl Brooksie barf in a medieval Parisian gutter all by herself.

The thing about synchronized street puking is that it tends to throw a wet blanket on any vodka-induced hormonal fires. Somehow, we staggered the half-mile back to the rue Guénégaud and up three flights of stairs to the apartment before Brooks took up residence in her bathroom for the rest of the night, and I passed out on the floor in mine.

SHANGHAIED

For as long as I can remember, I've wanted to *be* James Logan. He's the same age difference from me as Ian was from you, and for an only child with no cousins, having a close family friend like James was the next best thing. I can't even tell you how many holidays the Logans spent with us in Portland, especially since Becky's parents lived down the street from Gigi. And even though James was older, he always found ways to befriend me, whether that meant taking me to see the latest sci-fi movie on Christmas Day or playing soccer with me in the backyard while our parents caught up over coffee.

You know those people who just love *people*? James is one of them. He doesn't care who you are or where you come from. "Everyone has a story," he used to tell me. "You find out a person's story and you're opening up a new portal to discover. We each have value, Pete. Sometimes we forget that, now that the world is both too big and too small at the same time."

So after proving myself in Paris, Gigi finally conceded: I could spend the rest of the school year in Shanghai, as long as I carried my weight around the Restoration Initiative and didn't cause James to regret his invitation.

By February, I was a temporary citizen of the second largest city in the world. Every Monday, Wednesday, and Friday, I got up before dawn to help the people lined up outside our building for laundry services. If James needed a courier, BOOM – I hopped on the Restoration Initiative's scooter and took off without a second's hesitation. If something in the building required attention, I YouTubed the heck out of that task and completed it myself before James even knew the problem existed.

My. Shanghai. Life. Was. Epic.

Meanwhile, in Paris, Brooks grew bored of that *pâtisserie* school. Turns out making marzipan piglets and multicolored *macarons* was the opposite of her life calling. So on a random Tuesday, with no notice whatsoever, she handed the apartment keys over to our building's *concierge*. Several weeks and several vagabonding adventures later, Brooks appeared in Shanghai.

As you know, Vick Darby, Becky Logan, and my mom grew up together, so for better or worse, James and Brooks and I have been friends our whole lives, despite our age difference. Back in the day, it didn't feel strange that Brooks just showed up out of the blue. In fact, it's not until I'm writing you this letter that I'm asking myself the important questions. Like how'd she get a visa so fast? Why would she ever flake on Paris after my grandmother gave her free rent? Those are some pretty obvious red flags. And yet, I was clueless.

On her first night in town, we met Brooks in her upscale hotel lobby. She was decked out – red lips, stiletto heels, and a yellow sundress that was better suited for the Hollywood Walk of Fame than the Restoration Initiative.

Looking back, I can see that Brooks was one hundred percent tone deaf to everything James stood for. And yet, at dinner, all I could do was watch in horror as she hung on his every word, her hazel eyes bright as stars.

I wanted to melt away and roll out the door, right into the Yangtze River.

After we walked Brooks back to her hotel, James and I sauntered back to the Initiative along the Bund. With the Pearl Tower glittering off to our right, James glanced over at me and smiled. "You know that was all a game, right?"

"What was a game?"

"Come on, man. The heart eyes? The over-the-top giggling?" He elbowed me hard in the gut. "Brooks is into you, kid. She only flirted with me to make you jealous."

"Don't be ridiculous," I grunted, shoving him into the railing. "That cougar's *way* too old for me."

James laughed and changed the subject, which was my goal. But that didn't stop hope from taking root in my young heart, and for the next few days, I decided to try an experiment.

Step one: continue to volunteer for every random task at the Initiative so I could say no when Brooks wanted a local tour guide.

Step two: when Brooks mentioned taking the overnight train up to see the Great Wall, activate my aforementioned vomit-on-demand skills and well, BYE BYE BEIJING.

The following Monday, I was folding laundry when I heard a familiar voice. "Hey, Pete."

I looked up. Instead of a sundress and stilettos, Brooks wore a Princess Leia "Rebel" t-shirt and jeans. Her hair was pulled back into a ponytail, and for the first time I could remember, her energy was dialed down from a ten to a three.

"Hey yourself," I replied, stacking towels into the laundry basket. "Nice t-shirt, fly girl."

She smiled but her eyes didn't quite meet mine. "Need some help?"

I nodded once and Brooks joined me on my side of the desk. For the next couple of hours, she copied my every move. When one dryer would go off, she'd pull out the clothes while I unloaded a washer to refill it. If a new person walked in needing help, she listened quietly as I gave my stock speech about our services – one of the only things I'd mastered in Mandarin by that point.

She was placid, Sully. Humbled.

When my shift was over, she looked up at me with those big hazel eyes and smiled. "Would you walk me back to my hotel? I mean, you know, if you're not busy or whatever."

I wasn't busy... so I went. We didn't talk much along the way, and even though the silence was deafening, I just couldn't bring myself to fill it. When we got to the river, Brooks touched my arm, then pointed to a bench. "Mind if we sit down? Just for a couple of minutes?"

The silence followed us to the bench. Brooks never looked at me; instead, she scooted so close that I could feel her lungs rise and contract against my bicep. When she finally did speak, her voice was so soft that the sound of the river almost swallowed her words. "Did your grandparents ever tell you I came to visit you in the hospital last summer?"

My heart thumped hard in my chest. "You did? When?"

"Every day you were in the ICU." She paused for a moment, wincing at that last word. "And every time, Margaret always let me sit with you by myself, no interruptions."

"I hope you weren't checking me out under the covers, Darby. Because I may be a man now, but that doesn't mean my body is your personal property."

Brooks huffed out a tiny laugh. I expected her to tell me to get over myself, but when her eyes met mine, her face crumpled. And to my shock, her eyes went shiny with tears.

"Hey." I laid my hand over hers and squeezed. "It's okay, Brooksie. I'm okay."

"I know you are," she sniffled. "But you weren't okay then. You could have died, Pete. *You could have died.*"

I wrapped an arm around her, pulling her as close to me as she'd ever been before. Brooks rested her head against my chest, so I cupped my hand around the back of her head and cradled her against me. My mind raced ahead of itself, strategizing all the ways I could keep *this* Brooks around for a little while. Because in that moment along the banks of the Yangtze, I believed it was the start of... well, I wasn't sure, but it definitely felt like the start of *something*.

You know where this story is going, don't you, Sully? Of course you do. The next morning, James got the following text:

> Change of plans, Jimmy. A friend just offered me the chance to spend summer – er, winter – working at a ski resort in Queenstown, New Zealand. Flight leaves at noon-ish. Tell Russell I'll see him around!

Freaking. Brooks. Darby.

I'd love to tell you that was the last time I let Brooks tug at my heart strings, but you already know I spent that entire summer on New Zealand's South Island.

I guess now you know the pathetic reason why.

You probably don't remember this, but on your twenty-first birthday, you said: "No wonder you were so weird freshman year, Pete. If I'd known you'd been living upside down and in the wrong season, I might have cut you a little more slack that first day."

You have no idea how badly I wanted to hug you for that small mercy. Because you and I have experienced the same dilemma: unrequited feelings for a childhood friend. Sub Brooks in for Sutton and a ditzy South African ski bum for Lindsay, and… yeah.

Same song, same verse, same whiney, wailing bridge.

They say to hate the game, not the player, but I say "they" are full of crap. In my opinion, all the players of the world can take a flying leap off the Burj Khalifa without a parachute. I spent years chasing Brooks while she scattered tiny breadcrumbs to keep me coming back for more. But on the flight home from New Zealand that August, I vowed never to fall for her shenanigans again.

Maybe now you understand why I took it personally when Sutton hurt you over and over and over again. That is, if you're not too busy calling me a hypocrite, because UGH. When it comes to mind games, Sutton and Brooks have nothing on me.

Keep reading, please. And feel free to throw this journal in the fire whenever you finish the last page. I endorse your wise choices.

FOUND AND LOST

I didn't see Brooks again for a really long time. But then one day after Pops died, she dropped by unannounced to deliver cheese fries to my grandmother. Gigi was so charmed by her irreverence that they struck up the unlikeliest friendship of all time.

While you and I studied in Paris, Brooks drove my grandmother to her doctor's appointments. And after Gigi's funeral, it was Brooks who made the detailed inventory that Hearth required for their rental properties. For days, she and I worked together in relative silence, organizing and cleaning and moving things into yet another storage unit. Somewhere along the way, we forged an ironclad truce.

When I left Lincoln City on the day of your brother's funeral, I definitely intended to return. I told you the truth that day – I *wanted* to face down the accident anniversary with you by my side, and then spend the rest of the summer figuring out how to move forward. Together.

But when I walked into Gigi's house alone that summer night, the emptiness swallowed me whole. I stumbled up the stairs to my room, curled into a ball, and drifted off to sleep. I didn't even lock the front door.

Thirty-six hours later on Monday morning, I opened my eyes to find Brooks standing over me. "Welcome home, loser," she sniffed. "Lucky for you, I've put off my murder spree until the weather cools down. Otherwise this would have been the easiest kill of my burgeoning assassin career."

I rolled over, facing the opposite wall. "Go away, Brooksie."

"I'd like to, but you see, my annoying neighbor has suddenly reappeared at his house, even though he's supposed to spend his summer out on the coast."

I shot a glance over my shoulder. "How'd you know I was here?"

"Remember? Hearth requested that we set up that motion-activated camera on the front porch to notify my phone of any intruders, just in case their precious celebrities were in danger. Lucky me, I get to watch every firefly in Multnomah County flutter past your front door on the regular."

I groaned. If Brooks had played back the front door footage, she knew that I'd walked through the front door with giant tears flooding my face. And as though she could read my mind, her eyes trailed from my disheveled clothes back up to my splotchy face.

"Look," she said softly. "I'm really sorry to barge in on your privacy, but you've been cooped up in this house for thirty-six hours. Alone. Someone needed to check your vitals."

It was the wrong expression – too close to ambulance-speak for my wobbly heart. The specter of my grief filled that room again with so much darkness that I couldn't even cry. I simply curled back into a ball, like it was the only choice I had left.

"Hey." I felt the bed dip behind me, then I felt a hand on my shoulder blade. "Hey, come on, Pete. You're scaring the crap out of me right now. What is going on?"

I lay there for a minute or two while she rubbed her thumb along my shoulder blade. Then I let out a shuddering breath. "Meredith's brother and his girlfriend died in a car accident Tuesday night near the Canadian border."

"Hold on a minute... *what*?"

"You heard me. And the worst part is that Meredith tried to convince them to stay here – at this house. She didn't want them driving to Canada in the middle of the night, which is perfectly sensible and wise. And instead of supporting her, do you know what I did? I told her to let them go." Covering my face with both arms, I muffled a sob. "See what happens when you share a life with me, Brooksie? The people you love die for no good reason at all. I am a living, breathing curse."

We sat there together in silence as she let my story settle in. I couldn't move, Sully. I just hid under my arms, curled into myself like a child, wishing God would show mercy upon me and let me fade away, once and for all.

I couldn't face you. I couldn't face your family. Not ever again.

But after what felt like an hour, Brooks squeezed my shoulder. "Get up," she said gently. "Come on, Russell. Take a shower, change your clothes, and meet me downstairs. You need to eat some breakfast. And don't forget to shave, okay? You look like a grizzly bear."

For some reason, my inner schoolboy kicked in and I did as I was told. When I walked into the kitchen half an hour later, Brooks was flipping omelets. While she worked, I filled her in on every detail we'd learned so far about Ian and Kate's accident, trying to ignore the mechanical quality of my own voice.

We ate the omelets and drank coffee together in silence, and when we were finished, we loaded the dishwasher and set it into motion. For several moments, Brooks and I stared into middle space, neither of us looking at the other. But then she stretched her hand out in my direction. "I have an idea," she smiled. "What's the one thing in life that makes everything else feel better?"

I froze in place. "I have a girlfriend, Brooks. I can't –"

"I'm not talking about *that,* you idiot," she interrupted, eyes narrowing. "Just follow me, okay? And lock the front door behind you. The last thing you need right now is a break-in you could have prevented."

Once upon a time, Gigi had crowned Brooks the Keeper of the Keys. She had full access to my car, the house, or any other item from the Beckett/Russell collection she might need access to during our absence. So as we pulled into the self-storage parking lot, I finally understood Brooks' comment about making life better.

That's right, Sully. Like your mother, Brooks Darby is a minimalist devotee.

First, we cordoned off the section around my three storage units as a staging area, like we were the co-hosts of some new reality show on HGTV. And while the sun blazed high in the sky, we dragged my belongings outside and then designated each of the three empty units with a new purpose: *to sell, to donate,* and *to keep.*

"You know the drill," she said. "You're allowed to keep anything that puts a genuine smile on your face. My job is to judge the sincerity of your smile. We have until five o'clock. And... go."

By noon, the "donate" unit was so full that we transformed the "sell" unit into a second donation hub.

By five, the "keep" pile contained two archival boxes of my dad's photos, two of my own, and another box holding my mom's classroom tchotchkes and my collection of tiny gnomes.

That's it. The end. My entire life condensed to five bankers boxes.

While Brooks arranged the boxes inside a small shipping crate, I closed out my accounts with the manager and paid him extra to arrange the donation pick-up for me. After a quick stop at a twenty-four-hour shipping store to send my crate to the concierge of the Guénégaud apartment, Brooks drove me back to Gigi's.

Even with my head turned away, I could feel her sidelong glance. "Having regrets?"

"Too many to name. But right now, I'm thinking about Wednesday."

"Right. Man, July's a really terrible month for you." She pulled her lip between her teeth. "Has it really been four years?"

"Yeah. And I promised Meredith I'd spend that day in Lincoln City, but maybe I should drive to Palo Alto instead. Spend the rest of the week with the Logans."

"Huh." She tapped her fingers against the steering wheel. "When will you be back?"

"I don't know. Whenever the idea of being in Oregon doesn't feel like a prison sentence?"

"Mmm." The tapping grew louder. "So basically, you're running away again?"

I ran my fingers through my hair and turned to face her. "Look, don't do that, okay? Don't make this personal. My entire family is gone, Brooks. You don't know how that feels."

"You know what? You're right. How dare I imagine myself in your shoes?" She laughed bitterly. "You're almost twenty-three years old; of *course* you know what's best for your life."

"Brooksie –"

"No, seriously, Russell – just go for it. Run away to California. No wait, why stop there? You could be in Bali forty-eight hours from now, no problem. Why stick around this continent? You've got nothing important to fight for here. Not your education, not your friends who love you, or that brand new girlfriend you're so crazy about. Nope. Nothing important whatsoever."

She gripped the steering wheel so tightly that her knuckles went white, but to her credit, Brooks never increased her speed. She drove all the way back to Gigi's house without saying another word… right up until she wheeled into the driveway and threw the car into park.

"Listen to me, you little jerk," she hissed. "If you think I haven't heard your phone buzzing all day long, you're delusional. This Meredith girl must be worried sick about you, especially considering what happened to her brother. You can't just ignore her. That is cruel. And you don't have a cruel bone in your body."

"Relax, okay? I'll call her tonight."

"Will you?" She lifted an eyebrow. "Because you know I will side with her if you're lying."

"Hey, you don't even *know* her."

"I don't care. Female solidarity dictates I side with Meredith whenever you go mental."

"Fine," I grumbled as I opened the passenger door. "I will call her tonight. I promise."

But we both know I didn't follow through on that promise. Purging those storage units had unleashed something dark inside me. And even though I knew I would hurt you, I couldn't spend another minute in Oregon. The hole in my heart gaped too wide.

For a long time after I moved back to Shanghai, I convinced myself that my intentions were honorable. *Meredith's better off without me,* I told myself. *I'm removing my bad luck from her orbit. Sacrificial love is noble, right?*

Wrong. By dropping off the face of the earth, I made you believe that you weren't important to me. That I wanted to be free of *you.*

Nothing could be further from the truth.

COMMENCEMENT

You might notice that I've ripped out a few pages here. That's because I've started and restarted this letter at least four times. And every time, I rip it out all over again.

I *really* don't want you to read this story.

But here I am, writing again, because you need to know what happened between Dan and me on your twenty-second birthday. Or, as you probably remember it, the day you and I broke up.

After you walked out of the Treehouse that day, I sat on that outdoor sofa for what felt like hours. In reality, it was only twenty minutes until Dan reappeared, half out of breath.

"Hey," he said, sitting down on one of the lounge chairs. "No dice, man. Meredith had already left the English department when I got there, and now she's not answering her phone."

"That's okay," I replied with a fake smile. "Thanks for trying."

"So, listen," he said, leaning forward on his elbows. "I don't mean to be nosy, but do you mind telling me why you're back in Portland out of the blue?"

"Oh, you mean my surprise guest star appearance?" A rueful laugh escaped me. "Yeah, funny story. Apparently, I'm graduating this afternoon."

The color drained from his face. "That's not funny, man."

"No, no. It's definitely not funny. But I am graduating. You're welcome to come if you'd like. I've got eight tickets and only six guests RSVP'd."

His eyes widened. "Why?"

"Why what? Why didn't they RSVP?"

"No. Why are you graduating?"

"Oh. Right. Well, you see, Daniel, in college you have these things called credit hours –"

"Don't be a jerk, Russell. You know what I'm asking. Why would you want to graduate early?"

"Well, I don't know if *want* is the word I'd use. It's more like a plot twist. You see, thanks to my high school AP credits and the Mandarin classes I've been taking in China, Highgate won't actually let me stick around another semester. Rude, but what can you do?"

"Plot twist?" Dan pushed his hair away from his face. "And you didn't see any reason to warn us that you were coming home?"

"*Warn* you? Well, no. Silly me, I thought my friends would be happy to see me."

His eyes narrowed. "Okay, Smart Mouth McGee, calm down. I'm just trying to understand the big picture here, like why you weren't surprised just now when I said I couldn't find Meredith."

"Well, that's simple enough to explain." I crossed my arms over my chest. "The reason I wasn't surprised, Officer Thomas, is because Meredith showed up right after you left earlier. In fact, we were sitting right here on this couch together, having a moment… but then I said some things she didn't like, so she left and drove home. Which probably explains why she's not up for a chat at the moment."

"You broke up with Meredith?" Dan gaped. "Why? You're totally crazy about her."

"Yes, I am. But since I'm moving to Shanghai for the foreseeable future, breaking up seemed like our only viable option."

Dan glared at me for a full minute. Then just like that, he stood up and walked away.

A million words ran through my brain as I sat there, frozen in place for the second time that day. For the life of me, I couldn't figure out why I'd gone so snarky all of a sudden. It's not like Dan had asked me something weird. If anything, he'd shown enormous restraint.

By the time I walked back inside the Treehouse, Dan was outside in the front loading up his car to drive home for Christmas break. When he saw me in the doorway, he didn't stop working. For a minute there, I thought he might leave me alone in the house and drive away home to Eugene. But eventually, he walked back inside and parked himself on an armchair across from where I sat on the couch.

"Here's the deal, Russell," he said, jaw set firmly. "I'm not down with this new and improved version of you. The defensive posture, the flippant attitude – why'd you even come home if you're going to push everyone away? That mission's long since accomplished. No one on this side of the Pacific needed a reminder that you don't live here anymore."

"I know. I'm sorry." I took a deep breath, then exhaled. "Look, I know you think I ran away this summer because I'm a coward –"

"I never said that."

"You didn't have to. I know you. And I know how this looks, so I'll tell you the same thing I told Meredith today: I cannot be here right now. Not in Oregon, not even in America."

"You miss your family. Everybody gets that, man, we really –"

"No, Dan. You really don't." My throat began to ache. "It was hard enough to stay here after my parents died, and losing Gigi and Pops nearly killed me all over again. And I know you think I flaked on Meredith, but Ian's death was... well, it finally tipped the scales."

"But she needs you, Pete. Don't you care that –"

"Of course I care!" I shouted. "What do you want from me, Dan? Am I supposed to suck it up and be a martyr for the rest of my life just to keep the rest of you happy?"

"No one's asking you to be a martyr. But you can't just –"

"I can't what? Tell me, please, in your infinite wisdom and experience, what is the perfect pathway to relieve my grief? Have you lost *every* member of your family in the span of four years? Or instead, will you spend the next month hanging out with them in fuzzy socks, eating popcorn balls and watching Christmas movies until you fall asleep from the overwhelming joy?"

Oh, Sully. I was on fire that day. I might as well have punched Dan's glasses off his face for the look he gave me. I don't think we've ever spoken to each other the way we did on your birthday. And things were about to get much, much worse.

"For three years, you were my best friend," he said as he stood up. "But when you left this summer, you crossed a line. I don't have to tell you that you've broken Meredith's heart worse than Drew

Sutton ever could. You know you crushed her this summer, you've come back and crushed her again, and if I'm being honest, I don't know how I will ever forgive you."

"Dan –"

"I'm not finished. The answer you seek is not in Shanghai, Pete. You can keep running for the rest of your life, but you'll never escape that hole in your heart because you refuse to get the help you need. And until you get help, I think it's best if we end this friendship."

"Whoa, whoa, whoa," a muffled laugh escaped my throat. "There's no need to be dramatic, okay? Let's just calm down for a minute and talk things over, man to man."

"We're done talking. I'd like you to leave my house. Now."

"*Your* house?" I stifled a laugh. "Look, I paid an entire year's rent for all four rooms in this place, so if it's anyone's house, it's mine. Now come on, man. Sit back down. I'm sorry things got heated, but you can't just kick me out. We haven't resolved anything yet."

Without another glance my way, Dan walked past me to the front door and stood with one hand on the door handle, the other on his hip. For several seconds, I thought about standing my ground. But I know better than to argue with Dan Thomas when he's made up his mind.

So I did what I was told. I left the Treehouse.

As he followed me out the front door, Dan didn't even say goodbye. He just locked the door behind us and walked to his car, driving away without another word.

LOCKDOWN

James and his parents stayed at his grandparents' house the night of my graduation, but somehow I ended up in the Darbys' pool house. To be fair, it's roughly the size of an average person's homestead. So I was suffering in style.

I don't know if it was the jetlag or my disaster of a graduation day, but when my brain decided to throw a rave in the middle of the night, I could NOT. SHUT. IT. DOWN. The temperature that night hovered right above freezing – it was mid-December after all – but that didn't stop me from heading outside. I grabbed a blanket, a coat, and your favorite *chullo* hat and parked myself in a two-person lounge chair, wondering just how long it takes to catch hypothermia and whether anyone would care if they found a Pete-shaped popsicle at dawn.

A few minutes later, I sensed a presence drifting toward me from the main house. When I looked up, there stood Brooks, smiling at me like she'd just found an escape artist from the mental ward. "Listen, loser, you've got to ditch this habit of tripping the local motion detectors. Lucky for you, I get the text alerts from the security company, not my dad. Otherwise, you might be staring down the barrel of a shotgun right now."

"Oh. Whoops. I'm sorry. I didn't even think about the cameras out here."

"You're forgiven. This time." She lowered herself onto the chair next to me, tugging the left side of my blanket to cover her legs. "Come on, bud. Tell your old pal Brooksie what brings you out to the pool this fine evening."

"Oh, you know, just checking off the mental list of things I was meant to accomplish while I was home." I began to count on my fingers. "Number one: graduate from college. Number two: break up with my amazing girlfriend. Number three: sell my own house right out from under my own two feet. And last but not least, number four: lose my best friend. Hey, look at that. I win. Quarter-life crisis accomplished two years in advance!"

"Yes, look at you go! Gold stars all around." She pretended to do a high kick under the blanket. "What's your next trick, Peter Pan?"

"Let me think." I closed my eyes and lifted my chin to the sky. "Hey, do you have one of those memory-erasing spells like Hermione used on her parents? Because I can think of two people who'd prefer never to remember me again."

"Only two?"

I opened my eyes and smiled. Brooks was schooling me at my own game, and in that moment, I sort of loved her for it. She'd finally learned never to lecture me over life plans she didn't agree with.

Pulling the blanket up to her neck, she scooted closer to me. "So, you know my devotion to the purge?"

"How could I forget? You stripped me of all my family belongings this summer."

"Turn that finger right back at yourself, mister." She pulled out her phone and opened up Facebook. "Now listen, it turns out you can declutter more than just your belongings; you can also declutter your social circle."

"Yeah? How so?"

"Well, it takes a little bit more nerve than throwing out your holey socks, but day by day over the last couple of months, I've whittled my online circle down to forty followers. And I've got to tell you, Pete – I haven't been this happy since I was twelve years old. What good does it do to watch the rest of the world curate the image they want us to have instead of actually living our own lives?"

She had a point there, Sully. In China, It was a hassle even to access those apps. I hadn't been active more than a handful of times since I'd moved away, so in reality, a purge like the one Brooks proposed would only make my life break official.

Over the following days, as I closed all the doors on my old life, I started on the outer circles and moved steadily inward until the only 'friends' who remained on my socials were the people who populated my daily life, plus Kathy Beauchamp, the Logans, and the Darbys.

And as I put each channel on lockdown, the clamor up inside my head simply – poof! – faded away.

You and Dan were the last people I deleted. You were also the only two I regretted.

FLOWER POWER

By the time you and Dan started classes in January, I was back at the Restoration Initiative. Traffic is always heaviest in the winter, so with James' blessing, I expanded our Monday-Wednesday-Friday soup kitchen and laundry services to seven days a week.

When winter turned to spring, James gave me a new job: travel assistant. Most of our residents were homeless because they'd arrived in Shanghai without the correct work papers from their home province. For six months, I organized logistics, booked train tickets, and accompanied residents to their hometown until we secured the requisite paperwork.

But I guess I did my job a little too well, because by September, we had no residents left; every single one had found a job and somewhere to live. In fact, we had so few visitors that month that James voluntold me to help the Sisters of the Holy Cross at their flower shop near the Bund. Which meant I spent a lot of time hanging out with his favorite nun, Sarah.

One Thursday in mid-September, the novitiate who was meant to help Sarah was too busy hugging the convent's toilet to join her (thank you, Influenza B). So she texted me, and fifteen minutes later, I was helping her arrange three hundred dozen tulips for some hotel shindig.

You read that right. I had to touch *thirty-six hundred tulips*. Your favorite flower.

"You're pitiful today," she said, handing me another dozen multi-colored tulips to trim. "Plus, that beard's gotten a bit too scraggly for my tastes."

"Doesn't your nun-ness disqualify you from having thoughts about a man's appearance?"

"An opinion is not a thought. Especially if it's my opinion, which is always fact."

"Well, there you go," I muttered, making a mental note to groom myself a little better in the future, because Sarah *was* correct. I looked like a yeti.

For hours, we worked side by side, with me trimming the ends of each tulip to a uniform length while Sarah arranged them in glass vases. Every ten minutes or so, I would feel Sarah's eyes on me, and to be honest, it felt kind of nice. Sarah wasn't in Shanghai yet my first time around, but this time, she'd become the big sister I'd always wanted.

"You want to tell me what's bugging you today?" She finally asked when we reached the halfway point with the tulips. "You've been a grumpy pants for weeks now, but today is extreme."

"I guess it's the tulips," I mumbled, snipping the stems. "Sorry. They remind me of someone, and now I just... I miss her. And it's my own fault, because I'm the one who left."

Sarah untied the smock from around her neck. "Okay, time for a snack break," she said, nodding her head toward the back of the store. "Do you mind locking the front door? I don't want someone to come in and steal our best work."

I did as I was told, and when I stepped into the back room, Sarah was pulling some cookies out of her bag – oatmeal cookies, to be exact. With butterscotch and chocolate chips.

Just like my mom used to make.

Grabbing two waters from the fridge, I followed Sarah to the back porch of the store, which has an oddly unobstructed view of the Yangtze River, and, despite its location in central Shanghai, that space feels like a calm oasis from the world.

"Here," she said, handing me the bag of cookies. "Please eat as many of those as you can. Sister Mary Elizabeth keeps baking them for us because they remind her of home, and I can't afford to gain another pound."

"Don't mind if I do," I smiled, taking three cookies. "You know what's funny? These are my favorite cookies. You nuns really do have a divine connection, huh?"

She didn't answer. She just stared out at the river for a long moment. "So, Pete, this person you're missing... she was someone you loved?"

"Not *loved*. Love, present tense. Will always love, future tense. It's just... complicated."

"Complicated. What a surprise." She chewed her cookie, then took a sip of water. "Did I ever tell you how I ended up in Shanghai?"

"Um, no. Sorry, I probably should have asked you, huh? I just assumed you got sent here by the church."

She smiled to herself. "People assume a lot of things about the sisterhood – that we had no childhood because we were promised to the order, and then, poof! We become nuns, just like that."

She wasn't wrong, Sully. I honestly had never wondered about Sarah's life *before*. I had no reason to wonder. Sarah was *Sarah*.

"I grew up in Ohio," she began, taking another bite of her cookie. "I was an average kid who made average grades, but my real love was painting. So I went to an average college, expecting an average life – husband, kids, a white picket fence. And then I met Cooper."

Cooper? I thought. *Who the heck is COOPER? And does the church know? Does James?!?*

My face must have betrayed my inner monologue because Sarah smiled. "You heard me correctly, Mister Grumpy Face. Cooper Phillips was a redheaded spitfire of a man who loved China with his whole heart. His grandparents had lived here as missionaries in the fifties, and he'd grown up traveling with them to the land that held their hearts."

I gaped. "Are you saying you fell in love with a dude who isn't Jesus? Does Jesus know?"

"He does," she smiled knowingly. "At least I hope so. When Coop and I got married, we took vows in His name."

My. Mind. Was. Blown. "You were *married*?"

"Yes, a week after college graduation," she smiled wistfully. "And we moved to China a few months later so Coop could improve his Mandarin. He came here on a student visa, and I somehow managed to get a job as an administrative assistant for an American study abroad consortium here in Shanghai. That's how we met James."

"Whoa, whoa, whoa... James knew your husband?" Suddenly, I realized the complexity of their relationship went beyond a do-gooder having the secret feels for a nun. "Were the two of them friends?"

"We all were. I met James first; he popped by the office one day to meet with my boss, the dean. A few weeks later, the faculty decided we should include a service component to the study abroad program. Dean Waterhouse put me in charge of logistics, so James and I started working together immediately. That was... gosh, ten years ago now."

I did the math in my head. Sarah was at least thirty-two. Ever since I'd known her, I'd assumed she was closer to my age, but actually, she was even older than James. Mind blown again.

"Once Coop heard about the Restoration Initiative, he wanted to help too," she continued. "Within a few weeks, we were helping James every weekend. Coop was really good with the residents, you know? He liked learning about their provinces and figuring out all the nuances of the different dialects. It was... well, it was a really sweet time in all our lives."

Without warning, Sarah's eyes filled with tears, and Sully, I had literally no idea what to do. You can't hug a nun, bro. You just can't. I didn't even know if I should touch her.

So I pulled my hoodie off and handed it to her, like some sort of overgrown handkerchief.

Which might have been weird enough on its own, but underneath, I was wearing a Sigma Phi Beta Crawfish Boil t-shirt that read PINCH MY TAIL in three-inch letters.

Not my finest moment. But it made her laugh, which gave me the courage to ask the question I knew she wanted to answer. "Sarah? What happened to Coop?"

"He was stabbed," she answered with only a tiny wobble in her voice. "In the middle of the day on a random Wednesday. He and James were at the train station inviting people to the soup kitchen and some homeless guy just pulled out a knife and stabbed Cooper. To this day, no one knows why, because the man stabbed himself immediately afterward."

"I'm... Sarah, I'm so sorry. I can't believe I've never heard this story. James never –"

"Do not be sorry," she commanded, her lips trembling. "You haven't heard it because James doesn't talk about it. He still carries enormous guilt for what happened, as if he could have prevented it. One time he even told me he wished he'd been the victim. Survivor's guilt is a real thing, you know. Well, I guess you do know, don't you?"

For several minutes, we sat outside, the breeze blowing past us. I never know what to say in those moments. I always imagine what I might like to hear if I were the person in pain, but then I remember I *am* a person in pain, one who gets really pissed when people feed him platitudes. So I just sat there, mute. But Sarah hadn't finished her story. She took in a deep breath and carried on.

"I left Shanghai immediately," she said. "I didn't pack anything except my passport, my clothes, and Coop's ashes to give to his parents. I have no idea who cleaned out our apartment or who ended up with our belongings. I didn't care. I just wanted to be away from here, no matter the consequences."

"So that's when you joined the order? When you got back to Ohio?"

"I didn't stay in Ohio. I moved to New York City. My creative brain wanted to paint. But I couldn't do that, because my logical brain was too busy working overtime ignoring my grief. So instead, I worked in a flower shop by day and got blackout drunk by night. I don't remember most of the first eighteen months after Coop died. And what I can remember, I don't want to remember. There are a million ways to make a bad decision, Pete, and I've made them all."

My stomach flipped. "Listen, Sarah, you don't have to tell me the rest. It doesn't matter, right? You're here now. You're doing your life's work –"

She chuckled. "What does that even mean, 'life's work'? All I really did was join a convent to reboot my life. And when they sent me back here, I just figured this assignment was my penance for all the dumb things I did in New York. Living and breathing in Shanghai – the place where I lost everything that matters – well, that's its own special kind of hell, isn't it?"

My mind flashed to my parents' accident, then to Ian. "But... how do you do it, Sarah? How do you face your grief every day?"

"I don't know, really. But sometimes, it feels like God's forging together the broken pieces of my life for some new purpose. Whenever something I do or say alters the path for somebody else, it feels like a tiny spark igniting a flame. And on those days, I feel peace." She smiled a little. "You must think I'm crazy."

"Uh, no. No, I really don't," I answered, too freaked out to admit a tiny spark had just ignited inside me too. "So I guess this means you don't regret living in your own personal hell?"

"I regret a lot of things, Pete," she said, her expression suddenly tense. "But how can I regret coming back here when God keeps sending beautiful people into my life? Like you, for example. The sisters in my convent. And James..."

If Sarah hadn't just thrown my whole life into question with her *special kind of hell* tangent, I might have called her out for that little James-induced starry-eyed smile on her face. But I wasn't thinking about James *or* Sarah right then, Sully. I was thinking about you. For the first time in a *very* long time, I began to imagine a future rather than a long to-do list to complete before I died.

And in that future, I saw you.

Maybe I wouldn't have verbalized it that day in September, but the spark, Sully. A spark ignited that day of the thirty-six hundred tulips, and it's never flickered since.

That's the day that set me back on track toward you.

And, because I know my favorite matchmaker will ask what happened next, here's the scoop.

Sometime last spring, while I was teaching in Portland and you were living in Galway, Sarah quietly stepped away from her vows and became a normal civilian once again.

Dean Waterhouse hired her back to the study abroad program.

James finally confessed his secret love. Then she confessed hers.

And next September 21st, in Palo Alto, California, those two living examples of mercy and grace will marry one another in front of their family and friends.

I'll be the best man. Wanna be my date?

Aw, come on, Sully. You wouldn't make me boogie by myself on the *twenty-first niiiiiight of Septembahhhh*, would you?

(Are you smiling? Good. Hold onto those happy feels, please. These next few stories won't be fun for you to read.)

SUBSTITUTION

For fourteen months after your brother died, I flouted my unfinished dreams – grad school, teaching, growing old with you. But that all changed after the day of the tulips. Suddenly, I was on a mission to salvage my lost dreams and find you again in the process.

So while my right brain untangled the Sully problem, my left brain tackled grad school applications.

Addison College.

Columbia.

Stanford.

University of Wisconsin at Madison.

Yale.

Boom. Operation Reboot commencing. Stage One complete.

One morning in early October last year, probably around the same time you were finishing your first draft of *Night and Day,* I was sitting at James' computer when Brooks' avatar popped up on his video chat. When her brain finally registered it was *me* on the screen, she actually blushed.

"Oh, um... hi. I didn't expect... uh, where's James?"

"I'm sorry. James can't come to the phone right now. Can I take a message, ma'am?"

Brooks smiled. "You know what, rewind. Hello, bearded grizzly man who is not James Logan. Is Pete Russell available?"

"He might be. What's up?"

"I'm not sure, really." She held up a stack of papers with Vick's signature on them. "Do grad school rec letters count as billable hours or has Vick gone soft in his old age?"

"Um... the second? Sorry to ruin your inheritance."

A smile crept into Brooks' face that I hadn't seen in a really long time. "Look at you, smarty pants. What prompted this decision?"

"Dunno," I shrugged. "Guess I missed having ink stains all the way up to my wrist."

"Lefty weirdo," Brooks smirked. "Okay, well, since you've just gifted me with some good news, I guess it's my turn: Amy Harrington's pregnant."

Amy Harrington was my mom's co-teacher the last couple of years before the accident. She was young, fun, and Liz Russell's favorite mentee. And when my mom died, she took over the French department at St. Francis Prep at the ripe old age of twenty-six.

"Wow," I grinned. "That's a trip! When's she due?"

"Christmas, give or take a few weeks."

"Well, that's exciting. So, what made you think to call me? Because I don't want to burst your bubble, Brooksie, but I know nothing about babies. I've never even changed a diaper."

"Like I needed you to clarify that for me," she scoffed. "No, what Amy needs is a qualified long-term sub. Preferably one with a native-level accent and geek-level knowledge of useless grammar rules. Know where I can find one of those?"

I don't need to tell you why Brooks' words sent liquid sunshine coursing through my veins that day. I loved Shanghai. I will *always* love the Restoration Initiative. But at that particular moment when I was already repositioning my inner compass, the chance to put my real expertise to use was too good to be true.

So I said yes to substitute teaching. And six weeks later, I headed home.

Dear Sully

SULLIVAN'S

You know that expression "you can never go home again?" Let's talk about that for a minute. See, vagabond types like me tend to forget that life back home carries on. While you're off living in your alternate universe, you mistakenly assume the people back home are stuck on pause. That when you return home, everything will be just the way you left it, like a time capsule waiting to be opened.

But nothing – not the songs on the radio, or the slang, or even the drink menu at Starbucks – looks familiar when you return. The people from your past have been living just fine without you. They share thousands of memories collectively, and *none* of them look like yours.

Amy Harrington was set to be induced on the fifth of December, but in her e-mail, she'd asked me to come shadow her at St. Francis

Prep for a full week beforehand. So I flew to San Francisco the Tuesday before Thanksgiving.

The plan? To win you back before I drove to Portland, no matter what, no matter what.

Scott and Becky Logan took me to trade in my Range Rover for something with good gas mileage that wouldn't tag me as a trust fund kid. An hour after Thanksgiving lunch at the Logans' house, I drove north toward Lincoln City in my certified pre-owned hybrid sedan.

The original plan was to arrive at your house at twilight with my heart in my hands, ready to offer it back to you for safekeeping. I'd dreamed about it for weeks: the perfect Hallmark holiday reunion, replete with sweeping anthems in the background and magical twinkle lights and mistletoe above your door.

Do not judge me, sister. You wrote a Hallmark-worthy *novel* about us. I've read it *and* I've seen the cover. (Cough cough, twinkle lights, cough cough, Eiffel Tower, cough cough, BRIDGE.)

However, by seven that evening, jet lag reared its ugly head. And since driving tired is the same as driving drunk, I picked some random motel off the interstate near Medford and dozed for ten hours straight.

And so it came to pass that on Black Friday last year, I drove into Lincoln City and found myself in midday gridlock traffic by the outlet mall on Highway 101. Which is why I didn't arrive to your house until two p.m. And when I knocked on the door... well, it wasn't you who answered.

Hello, tween girl. Who are you, and what have you done with my Sully?

Okay, I didn't say that. I said, "Oh! Hello. May I speak to Meredith, please?"

DEAR SULLY

Either that kid had no idea who I was talking about, or she was a pre-teen passive-aggressive freak. And I guess her mom and dad were down at the outlet mall saving fifty percent on big-screen TVs, because they weren't home either, according to the tiny gatekeeper.

Dear American Tweens: never tell a six-foot-three, two-hundred-pound man that you're home alone. Even if he *is* dressed up.

What is wrong with kids today, Sully? My word.

I must have driven up and down Neptune Lane fifty times trying to convince myself that I'd picked the wrong white house with black gables, but nope. That was the only one. So, I drove over to your restaurant. And hey, good news: I barely registered any PTSD aftershocks when I pulled into the parking lot because guess what? Sullivan's Restaurant looked like an arcade.

Do you know about this clownery? Instead of your parents' subtle signage written in a tastefully Gaelic font, there is an enormous shamrock on a sign twenty feet in the air. But wait, it gets better – the apostrophe in Sullivan's is now a *leprechaun*.

Inside the restaurant, the dark mahogany booths have been altered to look like a fun house ride. Someone has decoupaged a bazillion touristy stickers onto the wood, and the cushions are now upholstered green, white, and orange, like the Irish flag.

Are we even *allowed* to sit on flags? I thought that was against the law.

When I asked the gum-smacking hostess if I could speak to the manager, she scurried away, the green shamrocks on her headband bopping up and down with each step. A minute later, some guy named Tony appeared at the front desk.

"Can I help you?"

It took my eyes a few seconds to focus on his face, what with all the flair decorating his suspenders. But when they did focus, I fixed that dude with a *look*. "You're not Jamie Sullivan."

"Uh, no." His dark eyes blinked back at me. "Sorry, do you know Jamie?"

"Yes. Sort of. I mean, I went to college with his daughter."

"Oh!" Tony's rotund face lit up. "Follow me to my office. It's quieter back there."

So I did. And after a dozen questions or so, I had all the answers I never wanted. Because SPOILER ALERT: you and your parents had moved to Ireland MONTHS before that day. What?!

Tony couldn't remember what town your B&B was in or what it was called. All he really knew was that Jamie, Molly, and their daughter had blown this Popsicle stand for their Motherland.

My brain didn't register much after that, so I excused myself as politely as I could, and when I got to my car, I searched the Lincoln County Appraisal District website on my phone for Andrew Sutton, hoping Drew was named after his granddad like I was. Ten minutes later, I was standing in front of Sutton's grandmother, Maureen. "Drew is spending Thanksgiving with his girlfriend's family up in Seattle," she answered politely. "But I'll be sure to tell him you dropped by."

I was so shell-shocked, I didn't even think to ask her about you.

Somehow my car made it the mile or so west to Road's End Beach, where I grabbed a couple of sweatshirts from my suitcase and stumbled down to the sand. Laying one down on the ground and tugging the other over my head, I sat my butt on the first sweatshirt and watched the winter sun begin to set over the Pacific.

She's gone, I kept telling myself. *She's actually gone.*

DEAR SULLY

For the briefest moment, I considered ditching my substitute job for the next direct flight from the West Coast to Ireland. How hard could it be to track you down? I assumed you'd moved back to Doolin, and in a town that small, everyone knew everyone else's business. I could find your new place in no time at all.

But then I put myself in your shoes for a minute. Instead of moping around after I left, you'd chosen a new path, and you know what? In that moment, I had *mad* respect for you, Sully. My girl Meredith doesn't waste time on losers. Are you kidding? She makes her own destiny.

The thought of you marching into the future made me smile all of a sudden. The Sully Swagger – back in full effect. Cue the pyrotechnics, Beyoncé. There's a new queen in town.

When the sun dipped below the horizon, I jumped back in my car to drive east toward Portland. By the time I'd pulled into the driveway at Darby Manor, I'd decided to let you go.

At least, that's what I told myself. Over and over and over again.

HERITAGE

I'm not sure I can describe the way it felt to stand in my mom's old classroom, using her quirky earworm songs to help a bunch of adorkable freshmen learn their irregular verbs. It felt... full circle-ish. Like she was right there with me, beaming with pride, ready to take on this challenge with me from her place inside my heart.

Too schmaltzy? Ah. Just you wait, my friend. You're gonna need that schmaltz to read the rest of this story. Yes, you will.

On the second Friday in December, Brooks convinced me to take her to some new micro pub near the Highgate campus called Heritage. I figured I'd hate it, not only because I was a teetotaler, but also, just... come on. "Heritage"? Is there anything worse than using a subjective noun as your one and only title? It's so *pretentious*.

Brooks was reading me The Heritage Story from the inside cover of the menu – those posers grow their own hops in a rooftop greenhouse – when someone cast a shadow over our table.

Two someones, actually.

"Hey, Sutton?" Dan Thomas barked over the music. "What's the likelihood that the Cheshire Cat would show up in Portland on Friday the Thirteenth?"

"Slim-to-none." Drew flashed his best Ken doll grin at Brooks, then back at me. "But if this isn't Pete Russell, he's got a twin in the world with a very cute Girl Friday."

And just like that, three sets of eyes were on me: Dan's and Sutton's, because they couldn't believe I was there, and Brooks', because... well, I'm pretty sure I looked like an eggplant.

Dan narrowed his eyes at me long enough to send a chill up my spine, then turned to smile warmly at my date. "Hey, Brooks," he said, like they were jolly old pals. "You look nice tonight."

"Thanks, Daniel," she grinned back. "I haven't seen you in a while."

"No. I guess you haven't. It's been at least a couple of years."

"More like three. It was the day you guys stole Gigi's cheese fries off the kitchen counter and took off in Pete's car without so much as a thank you. You owe me ten bucks, Russell." She smirked at me, then gestured toward Drew. "Who's your other friend?"

"That's Drew Sutton," I interrupted before Dan could respond. "He also went to Highgate."

Drew lifted an eyebrow at me – *way to crunch that truth to its smallest denominator,* his look said – and offered Brooks his hand. "Nice to meet you. How do you know Pete?"

"School," she grinned. "We teach together at St. Francis Prep."

Guess who else knows how to downsize the truth? Brooks for the win. But while Sutton looked perfectly content to accept her version of our story, Dan knew enough about my complicated past with Brooks to interpret what was brewing right before his very eyes.

"Teaching?" He barked at me over the indie music blaring from the speakers above our heads – less of a question than an accusation. "Both of you *teach*? Since when?"

"Pete's a long-term sub for our French teacher," Brooks explained. "I teach Geometry."

"Geometry?" Dan frowned. "Really?"

"Oh, don't tell me. You assumed I studied art history in college since my mom's in the D.A.R.?" The knowing smile on her face drew thin. "I studied Math, Daniel. Just finished my Master's last spring."

"Huh. Good for you." Dan plastered on his best fraternity recruitment smile – warm yet distant. "So, listen, Brooks, would you mind if we borrow Pete for a minute?"

"It won't take long," Drew added, the Sutton charm oozing out his ears. "We just need to catch him up on some fraternity news. We wouldn't want to bore you with it."

"Oh." Brooks gave me a pained look across the table, like she knew she needed to save me and didn't know how. "Um… sure, go ahead. I can entertain myself, no problem."

And then, I kid you not, she pulled a book out of her purse. A *book*, Sully. Brooks Darby never had the patience to read a tweet, let alone a novel.

I'll give you three guesses what it was.

Okay, forget guessing. It was *Les* freaking *Misérables*.

What?! Who did she think she was fooling? Like, *oh, don't mind me over here brushing up on my Victor Hugo. Why yes, I did notice this book was nine hundred pages long. It's the unabridged version.*
WHO BRINGS VICTOR HUGO IN THEIR HANDBAG?

DEAR SULLY

A math teacher trying to impress a French teacher, that's who. But I didn't have time right then to unpack the subliminal implications because Dan + Drew + me equaled bigger fish to fry.

I followed the guys out the front door and up a side street. Dan was wound so tightly you could have used him to propel a rocket into space. Sutton, on the other hand, kept casting sidelong glances my way as we walked. Like I was an extra-terrestrial. Or a real life boy-band member he'd only seen on the small screen.

Halfway up the side street, Dan skidded to a halt. "Brooks Darby? Are you freaking kidding me right now?"

"Come on, man," I clapped him lightly on the arm. "Can't we at least bro-hug it out before you start jumping to conclusions? It's Christmas."

"Shut up, Russell." His glasses glinted in the moonlight. "I don't care what time of year it is. You do *not* get to pop in and out of people's lives without a single consequence."

I rolled my shoulders back. "Is that why we're standing outside? You want to give me a consequence?"

"Step back," Sutton commanded. "Both of you, take two steps back. Right now."

I don't know what that guy learned in his first semester of law school, Sully, but Dan and I both obeyed. And then we looked at each other, because holy crap, we'd just taken orders from Andrew Sutton, former douche extraordinaire.

Sutton took a deep breath, then placed his body between us. "Okay, let's start over." He turned to me. "Hi, Russell. Good to see you back on American soil. When'd you move home?"

My eyes drifted to Dan for a moment, then I shoved my hands in my pocket. "A couple of weeks ago. I came back around Thanksgiving."

I don't know what was worse – the Dan Thomas shouting at me moments before, or the one gaping at me in silence. Wait, yes I *do* know. It was the latter, because while I deserved to be called every four-letter word in the book, it was the hurt in Dan's eyes that nearly killed me. I knew why he was so steamed. I'd ghosted everyone who ever cared about me except James and Brooks. And for Dan, knowing that I'd been in the same city for so long without calling him was one step too far over the line.

Which is probably why he turned on his heel and stormed away.

After a long, painful minute during which we both stared at Dan's retreating form, Sutton cleared his throat. Then cleared it again. "Your, um, teacher friend seems nice."

"She's not *just* some friend, and you know it, Sutton." Stomach churning, I ran a hand through my hair. "Brooks and I have history. It's complicated."

"Complicated?" Drew quirked an eyebrow at me. "Yeah, I think I'm vaguely familiar with that concept."

Oh, Sutton was good. He was very, *very* good.

"Speaking of," he gestured for me to walk with him away from the large group of drunk cretins who'd just gathered ten feet away. "Meredith's not here anymore. In Oregon, I mean. Actually, she's not even in the States."

"No?" I could see by the look in his eyes that his grandmother hadn't told him I'd stopped by their house on Black Friday. "Everything okay?"

"Um… allegedly?" He attempted to smile. "Jamie and Molly bought some B&B back in their hometown last winter. Meredith followed them to Ireland right after finals last May."

"Wait a minute. The world's biggest school nerd skipped her college graduation?"

Something in Drew's eyes flickered. "Well, yeah. With Ian gone… I guess I don't need to tell you how that feels."

Guilt kicked at my gut from the inside, Sully. Of course I knew how it felt to graduate without your people there to witness. But then it dawned on me that Sutton also knew – that he'd lost his mom too. And the churning in my stomach settled itself into a hard knot.

Which one of your exes turned out to be the bigger jerk in the end? Not Drew Sutton, that's for sure. And there he was, looking at me so kindly that I wanted to hug him.

"You should call her, Russell," he said with a sad, faraway smile. "Her Skype address hasn't changed, and I know Fee would love to hear you're teaching."

Ugh. *Fee.* Do they teach reverse psychology that first semester of law school? Because he'd just shot me twice between the eyes, and I hadn't seen either bullet coming.

"I don't think that's such a good idea, man," I muttered. "What would I even say to her?"

"How about you start with *Happy Birthday*? Despite everything that's happened, I know she misses you, Russell. No doubt you miss her too."

Your birthday. It was your birthday, Sully, and here I was, on an unofficial date with a counterfeit Victor Hugo fan, shooting the breeze with Drew Sutton instead of you. Without trying, I'd shifted back to

Bizarro Pete's timeline. But I had literally no clue how to make things right.

I took in a ragged breath. "Is she happy? Tell me she's happy, Sutton."

He reached over and patted me once on the shoulder. "Call her. You can ask her yourself." Then he shoved his hands in his pockets, turned around, and walked away.

Later that night after I'd dropped Brooks off, I sat in front of my laptop, Skype on the screen, with my finger hovering over the track pad for what must have been three hours. I wanted to talk to you so badly that my heart actually ached. Like, my chest was literally sore for two days afterward, because I needed to know you were okay.

But the longer the night dragged on, the more I realized that if I'd hurt Dan badly enough to make him storm away, your reaction might be infinitely worse. In the end, I decided my heart couldn't take another blow. So I closed my laptop and walked away.

WAFFLES

In the Sullivanized version of Brooks+Pete, you probably imagine our couple story began by lindy-hopping down Gigi's street while Rogers and Hammerstein played in the background.

Nope. Not even close. With Brooks, there are no epic moments. You just ride the waves until she suddenly decides it's time to level up.

The Saturday before Christmas, I was sitting in my hotel suite grading finals. You read that right – I lived in a suite, which I know sounds ridiculous and extravagant, but hear me out for a second. That particular boutique hotel has a hard time booking their luxury suite more than a handful of times each year. The one-time cash price I negotiated for December through the summer was basically the amount they normally make on that room per year, plus a little extra, just to sweeten the deal.

In truth, renting a hotel suite long-term didn't cost me anymore than a luxury apartment would cost in that same amount of time. In fact, it was cheaper, considering I got free maid service, free room service, not to mention gym access, cable TV, and Wi-Fi.

I know. It's wasteful and irresponsible. Wait until you read the rest of this story.

So, earlier that week, the maid in charge of my floor told me that her boyfriend's family owned an AKC-certified English cream golden retriever, and that ten weeks earlier, their best female had given birth to five puppies.

"They have one left," she explained as we crossed paths in the hallway. "She's the runt, and she has an overbite, so no one really wants to buy her. Would you be interested?"

Now look, Sully, I may be a hot mess, but I am somewhat self-aware. That was just a few days after your birthday, so my hot-messiness was at an all-time, inferno-level high. A sweet little runt needed a home just as I needed unconditional love? Surely Waffles and I were meant for each other!

That's her name. Duchess Waffles Von Wartburg of Dunthorpe.

Don't laugh. The purebred pedigree police have very strict naming rules. I did my best.

Heidi (the cleaning lady) delivered Waffles to me on Friday after school, and by the time I was grading my tests on Saturday, I already had buyer's remorse. Yes, Waffles was sweet. Yes I loved hugging her and playing with her. I didn't even mind taking her outside forty thousand times an hour. But DUDE. The constant wailing! The razor-sharp, baby shark teeth! The non-stop destruction!

I couldn't take it anymore. And I had no idea what I should do.

DEAR SULLY

That Saturday afternoon, Waffles had just fallen asleep in her crate hidden in the very darkest corner of my very dark bedroom, when I heard a knock at my door.

Surprise, surprise. It was Brooks. The only friend I had left in Portland.

She looked... well, I believe *extra* is the right word. Her manicure was fresh, her hair was recently blown out, and her eyelashes were... um... you know those caterpillar-looking things Meg Green used to pay someone to add on top of her lashes? Extensions, I think they're called? Well, I guess someone told Brooks her eyelashes were lame, because suddenly, she looked more like a Hollywood party girl than herself.

"Hey," she said, smiling wide. "You busy?"

"Not really," I said softly. "Just grading."

"Why are we whispering?" She asked, mimicking my voice as she stepped inside my room.

"I like to keep things Zen while I work," I whispered back. But I'm not one hundred percent certain she caught my sarcasm, because she kept her voice dialed down to museum-slash-library levels of respectability.

We sat down together on my hotel suite's sofa. "So, were you just in the area? Or did you need something?"

"Well, neither, really." She flashed me her flirtiest grin, which is when I noticed she'd whitened her teeth. "I was just running around, finishing up my last minute shopping, and I thought I'd stop by to see you before you drive down to California. When do you leave again?"

"Hopefully Monday? I wanted to get my grades posted first so I could enjoy Christmas break without anything hanging over my head."

"Oh, haha! Right, right." Her laughter came out a little bit like a series of loud barks, which made me sit up a little straighter. The last thing I needed was Waffles the Sabre-Toothed Tiger to start howling again. I had exams to grade, sister. Nobody has time for puppy pity parties when they have sixty tests' worth of spelling and grammar errors to fix.

"Well, listen," she said, lowering her voice again as she began to rummage through her handbag. "I just wanted to stop by and give you your Christmas gift before you leave."

At which point she presented me with a perfectly wrapped, rectangular box.

Now listen, Sully, Brooks and I have never been the gift-exchanging type of friends. I don't think I've ever given *any* female friend a gift except for you, and that's because I was trying to win your undying love and affection. When Brooks handed me that box, I wasn't quite sure how to respond. So I did what I do best: I improvised.

"Oh!" I said, taking the gift from her hand. "Wow, thank you, Brooksie. Do you, uh… do you want me to open it now, or should I wait until I'm at the Logans' house on Christmas Eve?"

It was kind of dark in my suite, but that didn't keep me from noticing the girlish flush spreading into her cheeks. "You can open it now," she said softly. "I saw this today while I was shopping and it just screamed Pete Russell at me. I can't wait to see if you agree."

I slid the thin gold elastic band off the edges, then gently removed the wrapping paper and popped open the velvet-covered black box. For a second there, I thought Brooks had bought me some kind of ridiculously expensive watch. She's a low-key type of trust-fund baby, but she's a trust-fund baby all the same. And she does appreciate the finer things in life.

Like a three-hundred-dollar ball-point pen, which is what I found inside.

"It has blue ink, black ink, red ink, and a pencil," she said, taking the pen from the box to show me the clicking mechanism. "I know you prefer to grade things in green, but I figured this way, you could just carry one pen with you at a time instead of having five in your front pocket like you're president of the Nerd Herd."

"Wow, Brooks. This is just... wow."

Her face crumpled right before my eyes. "Oh, no. You hate it."

"No, I don't!" I protested, even though I absolutely did. "I'm just... you know, surprised or whatever. We've never bought each other gifts before."

"I know that," she frowned, the blush on her cheeks flaming bright crimson red. "But we were never really in the same place at the same time before, were we? I mean, you know, existentially speaking."

I watched her watching me for a few seconds and suddenly realized the subliminal reason behind the hair and the eyelashes and the nails. For whatever reason, Brooks had picked that day to cash in all her chips. Like, *would you look at me, you big dumb lug? I am totally into you, and I want you to see me as girlfriend material, not just the girl next door.*

Which is when it dawned on me that giving gifts is a two-way street. But apart from the nice-smelling bath products the hotel left in my bathroom every day, I had nothing to offer Brooks Darby.

Or maybe I did.

"Stay here," I smiled, grabbing the pen from Brooks' hand and all the wrapping from the table as I headed into my bedroom. "Don't move, okay? I'll be right back."

When I walked back in the room holding a perfectly adorable English cream golden retriever puppy, Brooks didn't notice the blood dripping from my finger or the scratches on my face from where Waffles had just mauled me on the way out of her crate.

She didn't notice the relief on my face as I passed that demon spawn into her arms.

The only thing she noticed, in fact, were the puppy's eyes. "Aw, look! She has your eyes! Wait, did you buy this little sweetie for me?"

"Of course I did!" *Liar, liar, liar, liar, liar, liar.* "Her name is Waffles. Do you like her?"

She was too busy staring into Waffles' eyes to hear my question. And maybe what they say about dogs is true – that they have a sixth sense about humans – because Waffles never shot me a look of betrayal as she nuzzled into Brooks' neck. She didn't wriggle around or bite her ear. She just hung her head over her new owner's shoulder while Brooks closed the distance between us and kissed me.

You read that right. Brooks Darby – the former destroyer of Baby Pete's chill – finally kissed me after twenty-four years.

All because of a *puppy,* Sully. That is the lamest first kiss story I've ever heard.

It's also the story of how I accidentally ended up with a girlfriend while I was still googling last-minute tickets to Ireland to track you down over my Christmas break.

A guy can go crazy examining how many random decisions thwarted his own happiness.

ADDISON

When I arrived at the Logans' house on Christmas Eve, James answered the door. This may sound logical to you, because *duh*, it was his parents' house. But James rarely spent Christmas at home anymore. And I had no clue until that very second how much I'd missed him.

I hugged my buddy before I even dropped my duffel bag on the ground. "What are you doing here?" I half-laughed, half-shouted. "I didn't think I would see you again for years. Not in person, at least."

"You wouldn't have." James clapped me hard on the back. "But the US Postal Service recently delivered five of the best Christmas presents ever to this particular address, so my parents invited me home to watch you open them in person."

You know those decisions you make sometimes and you wonder later, *what was I thinking?* When I'd applied for grad schools, I'd given them the Logans' address instead of the Restoration Initiative's because US mail is cheaper than international. Then I'd selected snail mail as my official form of communication. Not e-mail. Who would do such a thing?

Oh, Past Pete. You and your illogical decisions.

The thing is, in my rush to get home, I'd completely forgotten to alert the five graduate schools about my change of scenery. So all five letters had arrived the week before Christmas, and the Logans, being the good people they are, had never opened them. They just booked their son a *very* expensive last-minute flight home from China to watch me open them in person.

Acceptance to Yale.

Acceptance to University of Wisconsin at Madison.

Acceptance to Stanford.

Acceptance to Columbia.

Acceptance *and* a full-ride scholarship to Addison College, because I was a legacy three times over. (Gigi, Pops, and my mom went there.)

Without hesitation, I chose Addison. The moment I read the letter, I realized it was always going to be my choice. Why had I applied anywhere else? Even without the scholarship, that was where my heart expected to be. I wanted to share an experience with my people, you know? They weren't here anymore; this was the only way to connect with them now.

So I posted a letter on Christmas Day to the name and address provided, even though the USPS and the Addison offices were closed. And that evening, James and I sat at the Logans' computer and booked my flight to Boston for Addison's orientation one month later, held on their main campus in Vermont.

DEAR SULLY

When I got back to Portland after New Year's, things with Brooks were easy. I went to her apartment every day after soccer practice. We cooked dinner together and graded papers or took Waffles on walks in the snow. At school, we hung out whenever we could and tried not to be obvious in front of the kids that we'd taken our relationship beyond the professional.

The night before I left for orientation, I told Brooks I needed to fly to the East Coast to meet with one of James' big donors. Which wasn't technically a lie, because I *was* meeting one of his big donors: Pete Russell 2.0.

I know. Lying by omission still makes you a liar. But Brooks and I weren't officially official yet. We were just two old friends hanging out, sometimes with our lips attached.

Oh, yes. I really do know I'm the worst.

WHY ARE YOU STILL READING, SULLY?

Friday morning of orientation weekend, Kelly and Harper picked me up at Boston's Logan Airport. They'd both taken a vacation day from work to drive me up to Vermont, and I have to tell you, it was *really* good to see them. My memories of the Addison girls were pleasant but distant, eclipsed by the overwhelming presence of a certain Meredith Sullivan. But that weekend I realized they were two of my biggest fans. Yours, too.

You know who is *not* my fan? Anne Wilder. Harper and Kelly made some lame excuse about her work responsibilities, but I knew why Anne wasn't there. She may be quiet, but she's a mama hornet where you are concerned. And I had a sneaking suspicion she was still #TeamDan4Lyfe.

"So Pete," Kelly said, a mere twenty minutes into our drive north. "Does this visit mean you've officially decided on Addison?"

185

"Either Addison or Stanford," I lied, though I'm not sure why. "Hopefully this weekend will decide for me."

"Mmm-hmm. Taking your time, exploring your options. Good, good. Very wise." Kelly strummed her fingers against the passenger door. "Speaking of your wisdom or the lack thereof, remind me again why you and Meredith broke up?"

I squirmed in the backseat. "Do I have to answer that?"

Harper shot me a look in the rearview mirror. "That depends. Do you want to walk the rest of the way to Vermont?"

"Uh... no."

"Then start talking."

And since I knew Harper never made an idle threat, I answered their question. And then I answered all the questions they hadn't asked, like what it felt like when Ian died. Why I disappeared. How you walked out on me at the Treehouse and never looked back.

But you know what? In retelling our story to the Addison girls, my mistakes didn't feel like mistakes anymore. I remembered all the reasons I'd set you free.

"Okay." Harper nodded at me in the rearview mirror. "*Okay*. I get it now."

"Me too," Kelly nodded. "You know, you could have asked us for help. We could have flown out to Oregon to take care of you guys that summer. Neither one of you gave us a chance."

"I know. I *know*. We should have done a lot of things differently, me especially. And I'm sorry, okay?"

Kelly shot me a look over her shoulder. "I suppose you're forgiven. But don't sit here and act like you don't miss Meredith. You're in the presence of two highly sensitive empaths, you know."

DEAR SULLY

I looked out my window at the snow-covered farmhouses rolling past. "I *do* miss Meredith. I'll *always* miss her. She was my first love."

"Does she know that?"

I turned back to face them. "Look, she's better off without me, okay? Meredith is... well, she's a glacial lake – all calm and peaceful. And what am I? Nothing but a tornado, stirring up the silt. Think of all the bad things that have happened since she met me."

"But what about all the *good* things?" Kelly countered, eyes pleading. "The two of you take the edge off one other. You push each other without getting ugly. You believe in each other. But the very best thing? You make her *laugh*, Pete, and I love Meredith's laugh."

Oof. Kelly's words punched me right in the gut, because man, Sully, so do I. Especially the one that starts off really slowly, like you can't believe someone like me could humor someone like *you*. Or the silent one that happens when you're laughing so hard you can't catch your breath.

As Kelly waxed poetic about you, I noticed Harper watching me in the rearview mirror. Did you ever notice that when Harper watches you, it's like she can actually read what's going on in your mind? Like, the muscles around her eyes twitch in rhythm with your thoughts?

No? Well, they do, and her creepy gaze made me squirm again in my seat. She shot a brief, sidelong glance at Kelly, then she returned her eyes to the road. "Guess it's just as well," she said, almost too quietly for me to hear. "Especially considering..."

She gave a pointed look at Kelly's phone, which she was clutching to her heart. And maybe Harper's telepathic skills work for reading minds *and* sending silent messages because in the same instant, Kelly's eyes widened. "Oh," she yelped. "Yeah, I guess you're right."

"Right about what?"

Kelly shot me a helpless glance, then she tapped in the lock screen password on her phone. She clicked here, tapped there, and four seconds later, she handed the phone back between their seats.

"These are Meredith's latest Facebook posts. Scroll from here up and tell us what you see."

I scrolled slowly back up the page in chronological order. Your posts were brief, contained no photos, and your check-ins were repetitive. Same place every day.

But then my feeble mind picked up on the anomaly: it wasn't just the place that repeated itself. You'd tagged the same person every single time.

Revising at Gus O'Connor's Pub – **with Jack Kelly.**

Hating Past Meredith's words at Gus O'Connor's Pub – **with Jack Kelly.**

Taking a break from my word salad at O'Connor's Ceilidh Night – **with Jack Kelly**.

Ding, ding, ding! "Who is Jack Kelly?"

I may have added a four-letter word to that question, which is probably why the girls ignored me. And when I shoved the phone back onto the armrest between them, Harper changed the subject so fast I halfway believed I'd imagined the whole thing.

I don't have to tell you this: I have excellent compartmentalizing skills. For the rest of that weekend, I managed to focus on Addison College and my near future. It didn't hurt that several of my new classmates were Addison graduates who knew Harper, Anne, and Kelly. Every second of every minute that I was in Vermont, my horizon felt rife with possibility. I managed to ride that wave all the way back to Portland, and for the next several weeks, Brooks must have thought an alien had replaced me from the inside out.

I asked her to be my girlfriend. Officially or whatever.

I let her change my lock screen to a cringeworthy selfie of us kissing on the couch. I also let her change her name in my contacts from "Brooksie" to five kissy lip emojis.

I spent time with her parents, and not just because her dad held the keys to my kingdom until the day I turned twenty-five.

I hung out with her friends.

I watched *The Bachelor* without complaining.

When Amy Harrington decided she should be a full-time mom instead of returning to the classroom, I didn't even hesitate when the principal offered me her job for the rest of the year. Nor did I hesitate when Brooks invited me to join her in Cabo for her best friend's wedding in June, four whole months in advance.

And when I finally admitted the truth about Addison-in-Paris, Brooks was so crazy supportive that I wondered why I needed a Master's degree at all.

So what if my life didn't look the way I'd planned it once upon a time. Does anyone's life resemble their dreams? Of course not. Why do you think there are so many podcasts dedicated to that topic?

People rarely chase their bliss, yet the average person manages to find contentment all the same. And after half a decade of struggle, my life was better than most. I had no right to be greedy.

At least, that's what I kept telling myself, right up until the last week in May when the Highgate Alumni magazine found its way into my mailbox and I discovered this announcement in our class notes:

Meredith Sullivan, recent graduate and recipient of the Beckett Endowment scholarship, has sold her first novel, Night and Day, *to Reardon Publishing. According to her agent, Michael Brady,* Night and Day *will debut next October in North America, Australia, New Zealand, the United Kingdom, and Ireland, where Miss Sullivan resides.*

Two sentences. That's all it took to pulverize my allegedly happy life. Because while I knew you'd taken creative writing senior year, I'd only managed to focus on the "Meredith's ditching French" factor rather than the "Meredith's a right-brained wizard" truth.

That announcement was proof that you were not some mythical fairy from my past. You're a real person – a woman manifesting her dreams despite the Ian-shaped hole in her life. And somehow that single paragraph about your moxie made my average, normal life feel very average and normal indeed.

ELLIE WHITMAN

Google is the modern equivalent of Wonderland's rabbit hole. Type in *Meredith Sullivan* plus *novel*, for example, and boom! Your author website appears. Click the link, and hey! Guess whose official Instagram is a work of art? Yours, of course. Last I checked, you follow thirteen accounts: your publisher, and twelve other authors. One of whom is @doolinjack.

But here's something you may not have noticed: both @meredithsullivanbooks and @doolinjack share a follower named @ellie.whitman.123. Her profile picture is a Robert Doisneau photo of a couple swing dancing. She posts inspirational quotes, shots of her adorable Golden Retriever, Waffles, and sometimes on Mondays, she features Jonathan Crombie as Gilbert Blythe, because duh, he's her #ManCrushEVERYday.

Ellie Whitman has seventeen followers. Twelve are bots. The rest are creepers trolling for lady friends. But Ellie only follows you and Jack.

She hearts all of your writing posts. She does *not* heart any candids featuring #TheBoy.

Oh, come on, Sully – how can you be so oblivious?

I. Am. Ellie. Whitman.

On Memorial Day, after months of searching online, I tracked down a used copy of Jack's novel which I had overnighted from Ireland to my hotel because DUH.

One hundred and seventy-five dollars later, *Time To Go* was in my hands.

Jack is talented, Sully. I can see why he's won so many awards.

I can also see why the two of you clicked.

What? I can be the bigger person when I feel like it.

Two nights after I finished reading Jack's novel, I woke up drenched in sweat. At first, I thought I was having a heart attack, but no. It was just Passport Pete taking over the helm again.

You remember that guy, right? The one who runs for the hills whenever life gets weird?

Yeah. He's a peach.

Side note: Dr. Keating and I spent most of the summer getting to the bottom of this particular freak-out because it doesn't follow my usual pattern. For once in my life, I wasn't running away from my own pain. If anything, I was running *toward* you.

Keating believes that from the day I flew home last November, I was just... well, coasting. Checking off the days on my mental calendar until it was time for graduate school. Filling up the empty hours with Brooks.

DEAR SULLY

But somehow, seeing your name in that alumni magazine set the inner clock of my heart ticking once again. Because for better or for worse, you always make me aim higher, Sully.

So the day after teacher in-service ended, I packed my suitcase and booked myself a one-way flight for the following Monday.

Except when I told my girlfriend, I left out that pesky never-coming-back-again detail.

RUE GUENEGAUD

For the first two weeks after I moved back to Paris, I was either at my apartment, overseeing renovations, or I was at Marie-France's, doing odd jobs in your old room on the seventh floor.

When I walked through the doorway that Friday morning to find you standing under the gable of your *chambre de bonne*, every English and French word I'd previously possessed flew right out of my brain and skittered down the back staircase, because Meredith, *you were there.*

And for the record, I immediately spotted the claddagh ring on your right hand. I understood what it meant – that you and Jack were serious – but that didn't stop me from hugging you so hard that I cannot believe you didn't shove me away.

You could have shoved me away. I would have deserved it. But I wouldn't have cared, because MEREDITH. You. Were. There.

In Paris. With ME.

Dear Sully

All day Friday, I tried to get the words inside my head to form on my lips, but… nothing. Nope. Just nonsense and awkwardness and oh my word, why *didn't* you slap me, Sully? Somebody needed to slap me! I'm fairly certain Anne would have stepped up if only you'd asked.

Also for the record, I HATED watching you stare at my phone when Brooks' five kissy faces popped up on the *bâteau-mouche* that night. The light actually left your eyes, and not in an *OMG-I-hate-that-girl* kind of way. No, it was far worse than jealousy.

Your empty expression screamed: *who* are *you?*

I didn't know anymore, Sully. I only knew I was no longer the Pete you'd once loved.

When I got home Friday night, I went to my mom's jewelry box and pulled out the *Fee* charm I'd ordered for your twenty-second birthday. For a good half-hour, I sat on the sofa, running my thumb over Ian's quirky scrawl, imagining how disappointed he'd be in the man I'd become.

Good times, right? Thirty minutes well spent.

Then on Saturday morning, during the Louvre tour, I couldn't concentrate. The Addison girls said you were back at the hotel e-mailing your editor.

What? Who were *you?*

That's when I decided we needed a few hours alone together. Why? I wasn't exactly sure. But nevertheless, when the opportunity arose, I volunteered the two of us to solve Tour Guide Valérie's change-of-venue debacle.

In the taxi headed toward the rue Guénégaud, I noticed you staring at my bicep, and for a minute, I was flattered. "Did I spill coffee on my t-shirt or something?"

"What? No. I just noticed… did you misplace your favorite tattoo or something?"

"What are you talking about?" I tried to deadpan. "I never had any tattoos."

You lifted an eyebrow at me, then perfectly mimicked nineteen-year-old Pete, flexing your own arm and shoving your elbow in my face. "Bro, check out this ink. It says *mercy* in Mandarin. So awesome, right? Hey, don't mock me, Merry Merry Quite Contrary. It's bad luck to make fun of noble concepts, especially when they're written symbolically."

Merry, Merry, Quite Contrary. Oh, man, Sully. I wanted to laugh so badly. After all that time, you could still capture the essence of my former self.

"Okay, okay. You win, Sully. Maybe I did have a tattoo. And if I remember correctly, a certain redhead insisted my precious new ink probably translated as *super-duper American loser* instead of *mercy*."

"I said *gargantuan American loser*. And in my defense, you never told me your minor was Mandarin until a couple years later."

"Hold the phone, ladies and gents – I think the queen just tipped her crown."

"Hey, I'm no queen and there's no crown. But I do need all my luck nowadays, so I've given up mocking noble concepts."

"Right." I rubbed my fingers over my t-shirt sleeve, tugging it downward. "See, the thing is, I was nineteen when I got that *mercy* tattoo in Shanghai. My Mandarin wasn't very strong, so I had to trust the English translation at the tattoo parlor."

You covered your mouth in horror. "Don't tell me it actually say *gargantuan American loser*?"

"No, it did not. It said *panda*."

DEAR SULLY

You actually gasped, Sully. And then you covered your face with both hands, because I am completely ridiculous. And the two of us laughed the rest of the way to my house.

When we got inside my apartment, I watched you puttering around, checking out all the changes inside. You looked confused, like you couldn't decide if a designer had made choices on my behalf, or if the gray walls and contemporary furniture were manifestations from my own mind.

Both, actually. In my mind, the renovation symbolized freedom.

But I wasn't free, and neither were you.

I knew it was wrong to daydream as I watched you salute the photo of Lucky playing mahjong. Or when you trailed your finger along the dots on my China map. Or when your eyes lit up at my secret stash of Epiphany gnomes.

I knew it was wrong, because every time I tried to pretend you were mine, I'd catch a glimpse of that silver Claddagh ring on your right hand. And every time, my daydream went all hazy.

I was still in love with you, Sully. But you belonged to Jack.

So I threw a metaphorical three-pointer from center court. I gave you the silver charm with *Fee* written in Ian's handwriting that I'd commissioned for your twenty-second birthday.

Your eyes, Sully – the second I handed you that box, I could have sworn something shifted between us, because when you looked back up at me, your eyes made me believe you'd give me another shot, if only I'd ask.

But then Brooks called on the landline, and that look in your eyes disappeared. So I hurried into my bedroom to defuse the ticking time bomb on the other end of the line.

How long did you listen before you ran away? Fifteen seconds? Thirty? An entire minute?

However long you waited, I applaud you. I didn't do enough that day to convince you to stay.

Two days later, I started therapy. I had finally hit rock bottom.

DAN (IS STILL) THE MAN

Remember where this journal began? With my (literal) cliffhanger of a trip to Ireland in July?

Well, here we are again. Let's pick up where we left off: a week after you left my apartment.

Once upon a time, Grand Duke Pyotr Petrovich embarked upon a very impulsive trip to search for Fee, the Fairy Queen of Dún Aonghasa. However, upon arrival (and much to his chagrin) Pyotr discovered his beloved in the arms of an enchanting bard named Jack.

Sigh, Sully. Sigh. That was a dark day for poor Pyotr.

As you already know, I lost my mind in Dr. Keating's office the following day. And as you also know, Dr. Keating suggested I return home and clean up my mess. Which I did.

Except I didn't start with Brooks. I started with Dan.

That Sunday was July 8th, the sixth anniversary of the accident. I picked Dan up at his apartment sometime after nine that morning, and as we drove to Lincoln City, I didn't waste time on small talk. Instead, I told him the full story of the accident, including Sullivan's, you, and the thousand ways our lives have intersected over the years.

I explained why four Highgate delegates spent junior year in Paris instead of three. Why I freaked out after Ian died. Why I ran.

I talked about therapy and my ill-fated trip to Dún Aonghasa.

When we reached Highway 101 in Lincoln City, I turned south to Sullivan's. And there, in a booth at your parents' old restaurant, Dan resumed his role as the voice of reason in my life.

"So," he said, crossing his arms over his chest. "If I've read correctly between the lines today, you've finally realized you're an idiot. Yeah?"

"Oh yeah. One hundred percent."

"So now what?"

"What do you mean? Now nothing."

"Why not?"

"Did you not hear me, man? I flew to Ireland with my heart on my sleeve last weekend and found our favorite redhead tangled up with some hipster dude. If that image isn't disturbing enough, imagine two lanky supermodels with arms and legs akimbo doing their best impression of a lovey-dovey spider. Game over."

Dan took off his glasses and rubbed the bridge of his nose. "Look, I know you don't want to hear this, Russell, but the so-called lanky hipster is no Drew Sutton. His name is Jack, and he isn't some player trying to mess up your game. He was really good to Meredith, and they were happy together – so happy that I sort of assumed she'd end up with his last name."

Whoa. I concentrated hard on pulling in oxygen, because *what?* The artist-formerly-known-as-MY-best-friend was all of a sudden #TeamJack? How dare he, Sully? He didn't even try to mask his betrayal. He just sat there watching me for a long moment, one eyebrow raised as if to say *you reap what you sow, buttercup.*

But then a light bulb switched on. "Hold on a minute," I gasped. "You said you *assumed* they'd get married. That Jack *was* good to Meredith. That they *were* happy. All past tense."

"Hey, look who's actively listening for once in his life? Therapy looks good on you, bro." Dan's smirk was brutal, but his eyes were dancing behind those glasses. "For the record, Meredith called me a couple of days ago. She and Jack broke up, and from the wobble in her voice, I'd say they're officially over."

"Did she say why?"

"Even if she did, I wouldn't tell you."

"Why not?"

"Because it's none of your business, Pete. You're with Brooks."

"Are you in cahoots with Dr. Keating or something?"

Dan narrowed his eyes. "Listen, I can see that you're eager to fix all your problems and get your life back on track, but even if you and Brooks break up, you couldn't possibly fix things with Meredith overnight. You really hurt her, man. A bunch of times, actually."

"I know that."

"Do you? Because a week ago, you flew to Ireland without an invitation, and now you're mad at Jack, Dr. Keating, me... even Meredith for daring to love another man after *you* broke up with *her.*"

"Didn't you hear me, bro? We had a *moment* when I gave her that silver charm with her brother's handwriting. I could see it in Meredith's eyes! She *misses* me."

"So what if she does? Your job right now is to mind your own business. End things with Brooks, keep seeing your therapist, and focus on *your* life. If you're lucky, when the time is right, a giant heart-shaped clue will drop in your lap that Meredith's forgiven you."

"That sounds suspiciously like you think I should give up."

"Just trust me," he smiled from across the booth. "Have I ever let you down?"

BOOK REPORT

After I dropped Dan off at his apartment later that afternoon, I went to Darby Manor to speak to Vick. I explained all the reasons we needed to part ways, and like a pro, he gave me the business card of an American estate attorney in Paris. "I'm proud of you, son," Vick said, squeezing my shoulder. "Your parents would be proud too."

It was the single most adult conversation I've ever had in my life.

When Brooks opened the door to her apartment fifteen minutes later, Waffles nearly knocked me over. Aw. Sadly, all the puppy love in the world couldn't save me from facing the proverbial music.

"Welcome back, stranger." Brooks shut the door behind me and wrangled Waffles away from me, nudging her aside. "Good thing my dad texted to give me a heads-up that you're back in town. Otherwise I might've keeled over from the shock."

Past Pete would've bolted straight out the door at the tone in her voice. He would have hopped on the first rocket ship headed toward the Milky Way, never to visit this galaxy again.

But I was evolving, Sully. So I cooled my heels and gave Brooks a polite smile.

"Do you have a couple of minutes?" I asked, gesturing toward her living room. "I'd like to talk to you, if that's okay."

She eyed me suspiciously for a moment, then motioned me inside. At some point, Waffles wriggled free from Brooks' grasp, zooming around the living room, attempting to bury me in toys as her owner and I settled on opposite sides of the couch in silence.

"Listen," I finally managed. "I never should have left for Paris last month without saying goodbye. I know we kept chatting and texting and pretending everything was fine, but you're smart, Brooksie. I know you're smart. Which is why I should have admitted the truth instead of disappearing again."

Her face shuffled through a series of expressions: surprise, anger, annoyance. A million little things. But one thing's certain about Brooks Darby: she knows exactly how to distract me.

"What is your favorite French novel?" She suddenly asked, a propos of nothing.

"I'm sorry, what?"

"Come on, Pete. You're starting graduate school, which means you obviously know your way around a literary deep dive. But I realized the other day we've never talked about *why* French Lit is your thing. So I'll ask again: what is your favorite French novel and why?"

"Uh… well, I have a lot of favorites, I guess. But if I had to pick one, I'd pick this one called *L'Envers de L'Histoire Contemporaine* by Honoré de Balzac. I think the English title is *The Seamy Side of*

History, or maybe *The Wrong Side of Paris*? I don't know. They never quite get the English titles right. Have you heard of it?"

"I believe I can say with absolute certainty, no. Definitely not."

"Huh. Well, I guess that doesn't surprise me. It's not one of Balzac's most famous works."

"Considering I've never heard of this Balzac person either, that's sort of a moot point." She scratched Waffles behind the ears. "*The Steamy Side of History,* huh? You're into sordid romance novels?"

"What? No. Just ignore the English title." My ears burned. "Look, it's not a romance. It's about this grown-up orphan who squanders his family fortune trying to meet society's expectations on his life. A fancy job, the right wife… you know the drill."

"I think I'm vaguely familiar with the concept, yes."

"Well, the next thing you know, the rich orphan's a cautionary tale: penniless, jobless, loveless, and in need of a cheap place to live."

"Hmm. Where have I heard that before?" She pretended to tap her lip. "Oh, yeah. Sounds like this Balzac guy ripped off Dickens."

I gaped. "No, no, no, you are missing the point. See, when this orphan dude moves into his new digs somewhere near Notre Dame, he finds himself tangled up with a covert charitable society, and... hold on, I don't want to spoil the ending if you're gonna read it."

"Oh, I promise you won't spoil a thing." Her lips quirked upward. "But you still haven't answered why it's your favorite."

"I don't know, really. Half the time, you feel like you're walking down the street in nineteenth-century Paris, and the other half, you're chasing Balzac down a tangent in the middle of his own story. But I guess I love this story in particular because you just can't help rooting for that Godefroid kid. Despite his goofy name, he's got moxie."

She smiled wistfully. "You're never coming back to Portland again, are you?"

Leave it to Brooks to put such a fine point on things. A long moment stretched between us where I couldn't answer – at first because I didn't know *how* to answer, and then because I did.

"I mean, I wouldn't say never," I finally admitted. "I definitely won't be coming back anytime soon, but *never* is a word I hate to use these days. You just don't know where life will take you. You could be minding your own business one minute and standing in front of a long-lost friend the next."

The muscles in Brooks' forehead relaxed. "Fair enough, Russell. Fair enough."

I reached across the empty space between us and squeezed her right hand. "If you ever find yourself standing in front of me again someday, no matter where we are, promise you'll look me in the eye, okay? Because you matter to me, Brooks Darby. You always will."

She didn't reply – not really. She just sort of smiled halfway and gave me a brief nod. The not-so-tiny puppy hopped up between us on the sofa and the three of us sat there together for a few more moments, with me scratching Waffles' belly and Brooks scratching her ears. Twenty minutes later, I gave Duchess Waffles Von Wartburg one final pat on the head, then I walked out the door.

This might sound weird to you, but on the plane home to Paris, I typed up a transcript of the above conversation specifically with you in mind. Maybe you don't care how things ended with Brooks; I wouldn't blame you for that. But the fact that you *might* care was enough of a reason to get the details right.

Because the thing is, Sully, I wrote these letters in part to answer a question you've never asked me. Yes, Brooks and I have known each other our entire lives, and yes, we once had a connection. But I'm hoping, now that I've filled in the blanks, that you'll see the difference between Brooks and you. Flying sparks are nice, but they've never been enough.

Not for me, at least.

For example, you never would have asked why I love *L'Envers de L'Histoire Contemporaine*. You were there with me in *Promenade Parisienne* the semester I first read it.

You walked beside me the Friday we explored the rue Chanoinesse, where Balzac set the novel, right around the corner from Notre Dame. And you were the one who convinced Monsieur Salinger to join us for lunch after class so we could learn more about Balzac's *Comédie Humaine*, just for funsies.

I can't think of anyone in the world who understands me better than you do. And now that I've read your novel, I know you feel the same way about me.

I've got room in this notebook for one more letter. Hopefully, I saved the best letter for last.

Night and Day

For the next six weeks after I returned home, I visited Dr. Keating every single day. Who knew I had so much to talk about? Not me, my friend. But talk I did. And Dr. Keating listened.

Paris emptied out in August. The whole world seemed to be on vacation except for Dr. Keating and me. When I wasn't in his office, I explored different neighborhoods of this city I'd always loved. Don't ask me to name a favorite. I have too many now.

School started in September. It was weird to be in class *in Paris* without you and Dan and the Addison girls. Luckily, the Centre Bellechasse is right by the Musée d'Orsay, which has given me a good excuse to brush up on the Impressionists and Post-Impressionists every day after class.

Caillebotte is still my favorite. Van Gogh, too. And sometimes Toulouse-Lautrec.

The leaves began to change all over town before I noticed. The autumn air was crisp and smelled like… well, pollution, but the very best pollution you ever smelled in your life.

On Sunday, October 8th, I was tying my tennis shoes to head out for a midmorning run in the Luxembourg Gardens when a FedEx delivery guy rang the buzzer downstairs.

Who gets FedEx packages on Sundays?

Well, me apparently. And inside, I found a book-shaped package from Dan Thomas, wrapped like a present in what looked like the remains of a paper grocery bag, with this Post-It note attached:

> REMEMBER THAT GIANT
> HEART-SHAPED CLUE I PREDICTED?
> CONSIDER IT DROPPED, OLD MAN. ☺
> THE AUTHOR OF THIS BOOK WILL BE
> AT THE CENTRE LAFAYETTE ON
> TUESDAY, OCTOBER 16TH, 11 AM.
> MAKE IT COUNT, OKAY?
> I BELIEVE IN YOU.
> -D.T.

I stripped the brown paper away. Inside, I found a guy and a girl twirling off the front cover of a book, the Pont des Arts in the distance behind them as twinkle lights snaked up the bare limbs of two gigantic trees framing the couple on either side.

Night and Day. By Meredith Sullivan.

I don't know how long I stood there staring at your book, Sully. An hour? It took me a while to breathe. But at some point, my newly-tied tennis shoes carried me to our bridge, where I sat for a few hours reading Luke and Allie's tale. By midafternoon, I'd relocated to our chairs in the Tuileries. And by dusk, I'd read the last line of your acknowledgements:

And finally, to P.B.R. – thank you for giving me Paris.
This story's for you.

I don't know a lot about publishing, but what I do know is that you must have written that last line before your publisher created the advance copies they send out to bloggers or whatever. Which meant you wrote me that message before you and Jack called it quits. Why did you do that, Sully? Why would you risk everything like that?

Maybe because *Night and Day* is a love letter to me.

And now you've read all my love letters back to you.

The Centre Lafayette anniversary shindig is tomorrow afternoon. Real talk: I'm scared out of my mind right now. When I walked away from you after Ian died, I never dreamed our paths would continue to cross. But Gigi was right – there are no coincidences. Maybe it's time we figure out how to walk through this life together instead of time zones apart. I can't wait to see you tomorrow.

LOVE,
PETE

Sunday, October 22nd, 3:03 am

Dear Pete,

Or should I call you Ellie Whitman?

I know I'm not supposed to laugh at you when you're being all angst-y and emo, but this second set of letters is hilariously adorable. And you, my charming friend, are adorably clueless.

Let's start with the obvious: I am so sorry for what you saw this summer at Dún Aonghasa. That was goodbye, plain and simple. Please don't let it mess with your head.

On a related note: I suppose I should care that you and Brooks have such a colorful past. And yeah, maybe I should feel betrayed that you downplayed your history with her all these years, but in this case, I understand. In another life, Drew was Brooks and I was you.

Same song, different verse. Only my verse sounded a little more Taylor Swift (the country years), a little less Justin Bieber (the lost years).

What? Don't try to claim you're not a Belieber. I've seen your iTunes, mister.

By the way, you know what glaring flaw comes through loud and clear in both your letters and my novel? You and I are *terrible* communicators. Let's work on that, okay?

No secrets. No lies by omission. Because when you look objectively at the reasons we've spent all this time apart, it's painfully obvious we *both* share the blame.

Promise me we'll never do that again. I *miss* you whenever you're not around.

Speaking of promises, I swore not to cheat this time (no texting!), so I'm posting this letter before I fly to New York tomorrow... er, today. I like this old-school letter-writing tradition. You think there's a chance we could do it again sometime?

love,

Sully

THREE YEARS LATER

MONDAY, MAY 7TH

DEAR SULLY,

HAPPY THIRD ANNIVERSARY TO US! i LOOKED IT UP AND THE TRADITIONAL GIFT FOR A THIRD ANNIVERSARY IS LEATHER, WHICH MEANS IT'S TIME FOR ANOTHER JOURNAL. THIRD TIME'S THE CHARM, RIGHT?

DON'T BLAME ME, SISTER. YOU'RE THE ONE OBSESSED WITH ALL THINGS THREE.

AND THREE SQUARED IS NINE, SO i PICKED NINE MORE SULLY/PETE STORIES. i'M AWARE THAT YOU KNOW THEM ALL. BUT THEY WERE FUN TO RETELL ALL THE SAME.

LOVE,
PETE

AUTUMN LEAVES

You stayed in Paris for four and a half days after the Centre Lafayette anniversary shindig. Which meant that I only had one hundred and eight hours to convince you that the handsome young devil holding your hand was actually Pete Russell 2.0 – the upgraded, limited edition.

Wednesday, we went to the *Musée Marmottan*. You'd never been there before, which is just wrong considering how much you love Monet. But what you didn't know was that the Marmottan has an early sketch of Caillebotte's *Paris Street, Rainy Day*. That little surprise earned me enough points that you stuck around 'til Thursday.

That day, you came with me to class. The doodle notes you took on the left-hand (back) side of the page were the best ones in my spiral all trimester. And Thursday night, we walked along the river.

On Friday, we took the train down to Chartres and made out like teenagers the entire hour and a half down and back. That night, even though we were tired from the best day ever, we went swing dancing at *Caveau de la Huchette*. No one puked afterward.

Basically, it was the most perfect week of my entire life.

So when it came time for you to fly back to Ireland on Saturday evening, I'm not gonna lie, Sully: I was bummed. No wait – make that devastated. Shattered. *Verklempt.*

"Listen up, frowny face," you scolded as we stood near passport control – the point of no return – poking the corners of my lips upward with your index fingers. "Nowadays, they have these newfangled inventions called airplanes, and guess what? By some miracle, they fly east *and* west. So we can see each other as often as we want. Twice a week if necessary."

"I know that," I muttered, pulling you close. "I just miss you, Sully, and you're standing right here. Why'd you have to go and make my life better this week? When you're not around, Paris smells like car exhaust but when you're here, everything smells like pumpkin spice lattes."

"That probably has less to do with me than it does your Starbucks addiction, but okay." You draped your arms around my neck. "Now listen, I don't like to be bossy, but on Tuesday, you gave me a journal full of letters and then promptly ripped your gift right out of my hands. You promised to give it back before my flight home, so come on. Hand it over, Hemingway."

You stepped backward, one hand on your hip, the other outstretched, waiting. So, I unzipped my messenger bag and pulled out a blue journal decorated with dozens of old-fashioned skeleton keys. When I placed it on your palm, you immediately opened it, just as you had earlier that week on the Pont des Arts. Only this time, you read the Post-It note on the inside cover.

DEAR SULLY

"*Dear Sully,*" you read out loud. "Night and Day *told me your side of our story. I hope the letters in this journal tell you mine.* Aw." Your eyes scanned the rest of the Post-It. "Remind me again why you mailed the other journal to Ireland?"

"Oh, you know," I shrugged. "I figured the other passengers on your flight might not want both halves of my toxic soul in such close proximity to one another on a plane. Flammable materials don't mix well with all of that canned up oxygen, you know."

You smiled so sadly at me in that moment, Sully. "Don't say that."

"What? That oxygen is flammable? Hey, I don't make the rules, sister. That's science."

"Your soul is the opposite of toxic, Pete Russell." You stepped forward, wrapping your arms around my waist. "Your soul is a beautiful, old warrior who has survived the very worst days and still fights onward. And one of these days, you're going to believe that, all by yourself."

You hadn't even read my letter about Dr. Keating yet. How is it possible you guys both saw me the same way? Mind. Blown.

So I hugged you, Sully. I held on so tightly I have no idea how you could breathe. Every single second in Paris that week, the new thing between us – well, the newly *renewed* thing – had felt unbreakable. Solid. Like nothing had ever split us apart. But also all week, I'd been dreading that moment at the airport. And not just because you were leaving me.

No. I dreaded the moment those journals left my possession. Because once you read them, my Pete-shaped mask would be stripped away forever.

But you totally get that hey-I'm-naked-in-the-middle-of-Times-Square feeling, don't you, Sully? When you wrote *Night and Day*, you placed *your* soul on display too. Only I hadn't made that connection yet the Saturday you were leaving me to head home.

I didn't understand my own fears that day. But you did.

"Thank you for trusting your words with me," you whispered, lips brushing against my neck. "I promise to keep both halves of your soul safe. Your heart, too."

Nope, that definitely was *not* a tear you saw in my eye when you pulled away. Can I help it that you'd spent all week flicking fairy dust in my eyes, you crazy Irishwoman? Some of it probably landed in your hair and flew up my nose while you were whispering nice things to me. Good grief, Fiona. Real men only cry at bowl games.

You're smiling right now, aren't you?

Well, fine. I suppose it's possible that your future husband did go all misty-eyed in the airport that day, but he didn't stay that way for long. Because you, young lady, are a shameless flirt. Sure, the average person believes you're an uptight book nerd, but me? I know the truth.

"So, hey," you said, slipping my journal inside your carry-on. "Does Addison College observe Thanksgiving, or do they take their French cultural immersion one step too far and ignore all American holidays?"

"They don't ignore it. We only have class on Tuesday that week."

"Lucky you. And lucky me, because I have Wednesday through Friday off too."

"Really? Huh. I never would've guessed you three Irish Sullivans would still celebrate American holidays."

Dear Sully

"Oh, *we* Sullivans don't. But my employer these days is Reardon Publishing, and they specifically told me to take Thanksgiving off. As in, *that's an order, young lady. Go somewhere nice and clear out that cobwebby right brain of yours so we can finally read some new stories.*"

"Somewhere nice, huh?" My pulse began to race. "Like where – Tahiti?"

"Oh, sure. That's a swell idea. Let's invite melanoma to join us while we're at it." You flashed the backside of your hands at me, freckles glittering everywhere. "No, instead of Tahiti, I was thinking somewhere in this time zone."

"This time zone? Well, that narrows it down. Andorra? Lichtenstein? Luxembourg?"

"More like Italy," you replied. "Venice specifically, but I'm not opposed to Florence or Siena either. Possibly Cinque Terre, but not Rome. Okay? We're too old to chase down pickpockets in the subway, no matter how romantic the Spanish Steps might be at sunset."

My mouth quirked into a grin. "Meredith Sullivan, are you asking me out on a five-day date to the most romantic city in the world?"

"A date? Pfft. This is a research trip. I was commanded *by my employer* to find some inspiration. It just so happens that I need an assistant to follow me around and fetch me espressos while I work, and since you already live on this continent, I figured what the heck? You can come along too. If you're not busy, that is."

"No, no," I smiled, tugging you toward me by your waist. "I'm all yours that weekend. I'll even bring Kelly's itinerary if you like. We never got to use it back in the day."

"Nah. Itineraries are for losers," you smirked, lips inches from mine.

You kissed me, Sully – scandalously, I might add, right in front of the *gendarmes*. And for the rest of the day, I could still taste your pumpkin spice Chapstick on my lips.

It wasn't until I got on the train home that I discovered the tiny drawing you'd slipped inside my jacket pocket while you were distracting me at passport control. On a piece of hotel stationary, you'd sketched your girl Edith de Nantes, the buxom waitress with the winning smile, and her boyfriend Hugh Guennot, cuddled up together on a gondola in the middle of the Canale Grande, both with heart eyes for days.

You knew I'd never say *no* to Venice.

But just for the record, they do say Lichtenstein is terribly romantic in carly winter.

PAPER WISHES

Venice is our town, Sully – maybe even more than Paris. Remember how the sun sparkled off the lagoon and lit up your gray-blue eyes? Well, I guess you couldn't remember *that*. But I bet you do remember letting me kiss you in front of the other passengers on the *vaporetto* from the airport into town. We kissed for so long that we missed our stop. So we rode it another ninety minutes until our stop came around again.

I figured the whole weekend would swoosh past us in a romantic haze, but that's not true, is it? Turns out that when you have no set agenda, you end up making the best memories ever. Like when you insisted we eat gelato that first night, even though it was five degrees Celsius and our lips turned blue. Or on Thanksgiving Day, when we noticed cameras trailing some guy through the Piazza San Marco, and it turned out to be Chris Pratt filming a commercial for some luxury Swiss watch.

I told you there was no way it was the *real* Chris Pratt. Why would Mr. All-American Family Man skip out on the second most important national holiday? But you ignored me. Then you strutted right up to him during a filming break and convinced him to take a photo with "his real-life doppelgänger." Never in my life would I have predicted that moment. But Venice is our town, Sully, and in Venice we lived out loud.

I can still smell the brine of the water mixed with the caramel apple of your hair Friday evening as the gondolier propelled us slowly along the tiny canals of the Castello district. You leaned back against me, tugging my arm tight around your waist. Maybe it was the wintry fog creeping in around us, or maybe it was just your heart beating in time with mine, but that night, I finally believed we could last forever.

On Saturday, we ended up at the Peggy Guggenheim Collection. Neither of us had ever been there, and to my surprise, it's one of the coolest museums in the world. I dug the Giacometti sculptures, you went nuts over Magritte's *Empire of Light*. And then you spotted that paper-laden olive tree at the far end of the courtyard.

"Oh, look! Yoko Ono donated this tree," you said, inspecting the placard. "How cool is this? You write a wish on one of these pieces of paper, then you tie it on a branch for safekeeping."

I watched the silvery leaves fluttering in the breeze for a moment, then smiled. "This seems like the exact level of *formaggio* to warrant your contempt, Little Miss Cynical."

"What do you mean, *formaggio*? Making wishes isn't cheesy!" You punched me softly in the stomach. "I think we should do this, Pete. Separately, of course. I don't want any of your silly wish germs hopping onto my paper."

"Only you could insult my wishes and get away with it." I grabbed us a couple of stubby golf course pencils from the stack, two sheets of paper, and two ribbons. "I'll go over there, and you can stay here, but take a picture of yours, okay? We'll text them to each other tomorrow night."

"But that's cheating! What if I want mine to come true?"

I glanced around. "Am I missing the sign prohibiting wish discussion?"

"Everybody knows that when you make a wish, you're not supposed to tell anyone."

I slid a stubby pencil behind your ear. "You believed in the tooth fairy until you were twelve, didn't you?"

You gasped. "The tooth fairy's not real?"

"Take a picture," I said, spinning my finger in front of your paper. "Take a picture, or it never happened. That's an order, Sullivan."

And with that, I skulked away to my corner of the courtyard.

Guess which one of us texted her wish first on Sunday night? Spoiler alert: it was you.

Now listen, you've accused me several of times of scribbling up a fake wish after I saw yours. I know, I know, it would be easier to believe that my wish would be something basic like "I wish they'd invent calorie-free kettle corn" or something equally nonsensical.

I understand why you think I updated my wish to be as schmoopy as yours. But you can check the time stamp on my photo, Sully. The image I sent you was the image I took in the courtyard that day.

It's not my fault that great minds think alike.

Here's yours:

> I wish Pete would come to the
> Juniper House for Christmas.
> (For real though – you busy?)

And here's mine:

> i WISH i COULD SPEND
> CHRISTMAS iN iRELAND WITH SULLY
> (FOR REAL THOUGH – YOU BUSY?)

All i Want for Christmas

A week before Christmas, the day before my last final, a crazy winter storm hit the North Atlantic. To be honest, I never knew storms like that made it this far east. I thought they hung out in the Caribbean and maybe *occasionally* hit the northeast coast of the United States. But apparently, this is why the Juniper House does most of its business from May to September, because every flight headed west from Paris was shut down for so many days that I almost missed Christmas full stop.

But on Christmas Eve morning, I arrived at Charles de Gaulle by five a.m. so I could hop the first flight to Shannon. Ten hours later, I walked out of customs and into your arms. I swear, Sully, I've never hugged *anyone* the way I hugged you that day. I'd missed you so much in that month we were apart that my classmates started calling me Eeyore.

Please never tell another soul. Thank you in advance.

The storm that had kept me from you had also dumped two feet of snow on the western coast of Ireland, so instead of the carpet of green I'd been expecting, the road to Doolin had transformed into a magical fairyland of snow and stardust and twinkling lights.

Jamie and Molly had blocked off the last two weeks in December so there were no guests in the inn. I remembered the Juniper House from those two weeks we'd spent in Doolin with your brother and Kate, of course, but when we pulled up to the canary yellow house built into the side of the hill, I had the distinct feeling that I was *home*.

Before you'd even pulled up the emergency brake, your dad was opening my car door, then pulling me into a hug so warm that my eyes threatened to leak. Your mom had dinner ready, and even though it was only five o'clock, I was starving (thank you, time change). The two elder Sullivans piled half a kilo of roast on my plate while they asked me a million questions about Paris. I was well on my way to a food coma when they started bragging about you and your book.

"Meredith's agent Isabelle is an actual angel," Molly cooed. "Why, just last month, she negotiated *three* new foreign rights' deals."

Isabelle? I thought. *Hmm. The Highgate magazine said her agent's name was Michael.*

Blah blah blah, Poland. Blah blah blah, Sweden. Blah blah blah, Estonia.

Now, looking back, I can think of twenty times that day I should have noticed something was off. But I never did, Sully. Not even when we were late to the Christmas service because you stayed in the bathroom twenty minutes longer than usual.

DEAR SULLY

Ladies and gentlemen, meet Pete Russell. Dreamy-eyed, oblivious, and stuffed to the gills with Molly Sullivan's Christmas roast.

Clueless, I tell you. When that tiny kid nailed the high note on the chorus of *O Holy Night* at your tiny village church, I took your hand, because in that moment, I believed we'd finally put the past behind us. And when you squeezed my hand back, I bit my lip to keep myself from tearing up again, because oh my word, we were *finally* back together.

So, no. I did *not* find it odd when you nudged me out the back door before the music ended. Nor did I notice you fidgeting while your parents dawdled in the courtyard, introducing me to every townsperson who stopped by to say hello.

A few moments later, a buxom blonde walked up and grabbed you in her arms like you were her long-lost sister. And when you hugged her back, I felt… well, a little bit sick, to be honest. As I watched you with this woman, I suddenly realized that there were people in Ireland who loved you. A family of your own choosing.

From the looks of it, a friend you loved as much as (or maybe more than) the Addison girls.

"Well, aren't you gorgeous," the curvy blonde said into your shoulder. "I've missed you so much that I hate you with my whole heart." She smiled primly at me over your shoulder, then pushed away from you, stretching out her hand in my direction. "Hello. I'm Emma. And you are?"

"Pete." I reached for Emma's hand. "Pete Russell. Nice to meet you, Emma."

"Hello, Pete," Emma said, squeezing my hand as she shot you a not-so-subtle look. "Well, my goodness, it's nice to finally meet you as well."

There was something in the way that Emma said *finally* that made me realize she didn't need any further explanation of who I was. But you simply met her gaze and smiled.

"How's life, Ems?"

"Grand," she said warmly. "I was really hoping I'd see you tonight. I've missed you loads. Or maybe I've just missed the way you always left my tea kettle turned the wrong way, you weird lefty." Emma turned to face me. "Sorry. Meredith and I were flatmates in Galway earlier this year."

Now look, I'll admit that any normal person would've known right away who Emma was, but I was still riding high on cow meat and pheromones. *Sully and I are back together on a snowy, Irish Christmas Eve! Woo hoo! But who is this blond girl and why is she ruining Sully's chill?*

"Did you?" I sing-songed like a complete chucklehead. "I've never been to Galway, but I hear it's nice. Lots of festivals. Buskers on every corner. Claddagh rings. Yep. That's all I know."

I don't know if you know this, Sully, but you and Emma both looked at me like I'd morphed into a three-headed dragon. Suddenly, I felt like an intruder on a very private club.

"So," you said, turning to Emma. "Is… everyone else home for Christmas, too?"

Her lip twitched. "Um… not this year, no. Maeve and Adam took the twins down to Cork to visit his family. And my brother lives in Donegal now. With his *wife*."

"His…" You choked on the word. "Your brother got married?"

Emma nodded. "They eloped earlier this month. He bought back the rights for *The Long Walk* and *Time to Go* from County Down Press. Hannah quit her job in London, and they've moved up north to start over again, all shiny fresh and new. He's hoping to write cozy mysteries now."

No lie, Sully – I thought you might vomit right there in the church courtyard. Emma stepped beside you, wrapping her arm around your waist as she fixed me with a bright smile and distracted me just long enough to let you catch your breath. "So, Pete, are you staying in Ireland long?"

"Until Epiphany." I looked at you, then back at Emma. "I, uh… I go to school in Paris."

"Do you really?" Emma's expression brightened as she squeezed your waist. "Hear that, love? Maybe you should join him. I hear Paris has inspired a best-seller or two. What do you say?"

You turned in to Emma, wrapping your arms around her as you curved your head into her hair. "I love you," you said, choking back a sob. "You know that, right?"

Emma's eyes brimmed with tears as she hugged you back. "And I love you. I always will, no matter what."

The two of you clung to each other for so long that my throat clenched up. When Emma finally pulled away, her eyes twinkled through the tears.

"This bloke had better be worth my broken heart." She tilted her head in my direction, patting your cheek. "Not that I blame you. Tell me, do they put growth hormones in your food in America? I've never seen someone as wide across the shoulders as this fellow. At least, not in real life. And those teeth, my word! Somebody comes from a long line of healthy genes."

And just like that, the two of you were laughing. I hadn't heard you laugh like that since your brother died, which is how I finally realized who Emma was: Jack's sister. And that quip about her broken heart? When you and Jack cut ties, you lost his sister too.

Until that moment, standing there in the snow, I'd never quite realized how far out my bad choices rippled. Here's hoping I never forget the pit in my stomach that night.

Your parents headed upstairs a few minutes after we returned to the Juniper House that night, so I decided to set up *It's A Wonderful Life* on the living room TV. "I'll fix us some tea," you said, a grimace-like smile plastered on your lips.

I stood numbly in front of the TV for a full ten minutes, my brain scrambling for what to say next. When the tea kettle whined its lazy whistle, I walked into the kitchen to find you leaning against the kitchen sink, your back to the doorway. I laid a hand on your shoulder. "You okay?"

Every muscle in your back seized, Sully, and a tiny noise escaped you – a controlled sob. "I'm sorry," you whispered. "I don't know what's wrong with me right now."

My first instinct was to run out the door, up the hill to the highway, and hitch a quick ride to the Shannon airport, because hello! Why were you freaking out about Jack?

But you see, Emotionally-Educated Pete was much wiser than College-Educated Pete, and he knew it was perfectly healthy and normal to grieve your dreams. Even after you'd moved on.

So I turned you around to face me and took your face in my hands. "Listen to me for a second. I love you. Not because you're hot, which you are, and not because you're talented either, even though you are my superior in every way. I love you because when I'm with you, my soul feels easy. Even in the hard times. Did you know that?"

"No." You lifted your eyes to mine and smiled. "Do you know I love you too?"

"I do. So, look, now that we're both clear on that issue, why don't you tell me what's going on? I promise nothing you could say to me right now could change the way I feel."

"You don't know that."

"Uh, yes. I do. But if you don't want to tell me, why don't you pick someone else, and I'll pretend to be that person. Go on."

"Like who?" You frowned. "Oprah?"

"Oprah, Obi-Wan Kenobi, Chris Pratt... whomever you like."

You looked up at me with a crooked smile. "What about Pete Russell?"

"Really? *That* guy?"

"He smells nice. And I like his hair or whatever." You watched me for a long moment, then sighed. "Okay, okay. So, my blonde friend tonight? That's Jack's sister."

"Emma?"

Without another word, you took my hand and led me back to the living room bookcase, pulling a leather-bound book from the shelves. You handed it to me, and when I opened to the front page, I found a silhouette of a young woman bouncing along a row of buildings as the snow fell around her. The sky was midnight blue, and leafless trees glittered with Christmas lights.

"*The Long Walk*," I read out loud. "Hold up, Sully... is this redhead on the cover *you*?"

You nodded grimly. "Jack wrote this novel at the same time I was polishing up *Night and Day*. We, um… we sat in O'Connor's Pub every day for a month, for hours and hours on end."

"It only took him a month to write a full novel?"

You took the book from my hands. "Jack gave me this copy that day you saw us together on Inishmore. It was… you know, like a parting gift. I guess now it's the only one in the world."

I watched you staring at the cover, and after a moment, I finally understood why you'd been acting so weird all day.

The streets on the cover were decorated for Christmas.

You met Jack on Christmas Eve.

Man, Sully. A lot can happen in a year, can't it?

I scratched my neck and met your gaze. "Um… so, why is this the only copy?"

"That's what Emma meant earlier: *The Long Walk* will never be published, because Jack bought back all the rights to his books. With all the foreign deals Michael had already negotiated, Jack must've spent at least fifty thousand euros to make both of his books disappear."

"Wait, what? Why would he tank his own career like that?"

You lifted your eyes to mine. "For Hannah. He did it for his… wife."

I blinked at you for a few moments, because suddenly, I understood what you meant. Jack loved this Hannah person so much he didn't want *your* story out in the world. And as much as that obviously stung your heart, I wanted to hug the man. Because the truth is, Sully, I think he did it for us as well.

"I would do that for you, Pete," you said, slipping your arms around my waist. "If you asked me to tear up every single contract

I've signed this year and pay them all back, I would do it. I mean, I might need a tiny loan, because I've been living on my advance, but I'd do it, I swear. All you have to do is ask."

I lowered my forehead to yours. "No way," I smiled. "I've already booked my tickets for every stop on the Meredith Sullivan Victory Tour next October and I've ordered a different color #TeamAllie shirt for each stop. That's a *lot* of cotton we'd be wasting."

"I'm serious, Pete."

"I'm serious, too. I want you to publish *Night and Day*. Luke plus Allie forever."

I stepped back and stuck my fist out for you to bump knuckles. And you smiled – so big and bright that I half-believed I'd dreamed the rest. Then you bumped my knuckles with yours. "Yeah, yeah, whatever you say. Luke plus Allie forever, divided by zero, times infinity."

"You can't divide by zero. That's basic math."

"I know that. It's a metaphor. Like, no one can divide them? Get it?"

"What's a metaphor?"

You sighed, Sully, and I scooped you into what I hope was the greatest Christmas kiss you've ever known. Because the truth was, I understood how razor-close we were to the edge that night. And I made myself a promise as my lips touched yours that I would never lose you again.

See also: that diamond ring on your finger, Mrs. Russell.

AULD LANG SYNE

The rest of that week was perfect like Venice. Your parents drove us through the Burren and over to the Rock of Cashel a couple of days after that. The weather stayed so cold that the snow never melted, and oh man, sister. My insides were reduced to molten goo from all the love.

Fun fact, Sully: do you know that you have the best phone manners of any person I've ever met? If someone told me you'd arrived here fully formed in a time machine from the fifties, I would believe them. Because while some people I know check their phone every two seconds even when it's *not* buzzing, you rarely check it even when it is.

So imagine my concern on New Year's Eve afternoon when you not only looked at your phone during tea time, you actually swiped open a notification. We were in the parlor, and your dad was knee-deep in an anecdote about the Irish parliament. For the next thirty seconds, I tried to split my attention evenly between the two of you. But then your face drained of color.

"Everything okay?" I muttered.

"Hmm?" You glanced at me quickly without meeting my eye, then returned your gaze to your phone. "Oh, um… yeah. It's nothing, just some minor formatting crisis at Reardon. You wouldn't believe how many times this has happened already."

Listen, I may not be a published author like that last guy you dated, but everyone on the planet knows the publishing world shuts down in December. And yeah, maybe that's a little like saying school teachers only work until three o'clock, but still – it was New Year's Eve.

And a Saturday.

Your mom turned her attention to our side of the room. "Are you feeling well, love?"

"I'm fine," you smiled, though it looked a little like a sneer. "No worries."

Molly set her teacup down on the table beside her. "White cheeses," she tutted, shooting me a sympathetic look. "I blame that cheddar company up the road from us in Oregon. She refused to eat anything but cheddar growing up, and now… well, you might want to move over to this side of the room, dear."

"Mother!" You groaned, and you have *no* idea how hard I had to fight to keep my chill that day, Sully, because NO. WAY. Your mom had just warned me you might fart.

Why yes, Pete Russell, I thought. *Welcome to the family.*

Hold on, hold on, STOP. Just one minute. You know I am sitting here laughing so hard that I'm crying, right? If you don't believe me, check out that tear stain a couple of lines up. My stomach hurts. Oh wait – maybe it's the *fromage blanc* I had for breakfast.

I just fell out of my chair.

Now wait, before you make the obvious joke – that the French verb *peter* means "to pass zee gas" – I'm already ahead of you. Do you think Liz Russell forgot that nonsense when she named me Peter? No way – my whole identity is a double entendre. My first diaper in life was a blowout. I can prove it to you! My dad documented it *photographically.*

"I have to take care of something upstairs in my apartment," you said, sliding your phone back in your pocket. "Pete, can you, um… you know, entertain yourself until dinner?"

"Sure he can," Jamie chirped as he got to his feet. "Would you like to pop over to Ennistymon with me, Pete? The shops will be closed tomorrow and we don't want to run out of toilet paper if Meredith is…"

"DAD!" You bellowed and ran out of the room, letting the back door bang behind you.

Your mom and dad laughed so hard that I had to join them, Sully. It would have been *rude* not to. I love you. Not as much as I love white cheese, but you're a close second.

FINE. FINE. I'll get back to the story.

You stayed up in the garage apartment until we had dinner that night with your parents, and afterward, you asked me to go on a drive with you. Dude, I was freaking nervous. Could you tell? I felt certain you were going to break up with me, although I couldn't imagine why.

Apart from the fart jokes, obviously.

Though it was barely eight o'clock, night had settled over Doolin town. We passed Fisherstreet, winding our way up a rocky back road up to Doonagore Castle. Suddenly you turned left, then five-point turned the car back around. The entire Doolin coastline spread out below us from whatever driveway we'd just blocked. Even from that distance, we could see the sea sparkling in the moonlight.

You handed me your phone. "Open it. The code's 1-0-0-8."

"One thousand eight? Is that some important date in Irish history?"

You smiled timidly. "October 8th. That's the day we danced in the Tuileries junior year."

I wanted to kiss you so badly in that moment, but I held it together and tapped in your code. There on the screen was an e-mail from kbeauchamp@centrelafayette.fr.

"Read it," you said into the silence between us. "Read it, and tell me what you think."

Without arguing, I did what you said – or at least, I tried. I had to read it three times to make sure I was understanding correctly, because my blood was thundering so loudly in my head that I had a hard time deciphering the letters on the screen. They said:

Mademoiselle Sullivan,

I'm so pleased that you've considered my offer of part-time employment beginning 9 January. You will shadow Danielle for the rest of the academic year, and in June, if things go as planned, you will become my assistant. I'm afraid I can't pay you very much from January through May, but Marie-France de Clavéry has offered to house you rent-free through the end of the school year as a thank you to Danielle and me for our decades-long friendship.

I wish you and Pete the very happiest New Year together. Please don't hesitate to contact me should you have further questions as you make your final decision. I look forward to your reply.

Meilleurs voeux pour une très belle année,

Kathy Beauchamp

A strange sort of muffled sob escaped me, and just like that, gigantic tears began to tumble down my face. "Is this for real? Did Kathy just offer you a job in Paris?"

"Yes." Your expectant smile faltered. "Hey! Why are you crying?"

"I'm not crying." I shoved the tears off my cheeks. "The car heater just irritates my eyes."

You laughed, Sully. That low, rumbling laugh you make when you think I'm super cute. You reached across the space between us and cupped your left hand under my jaw, brushing a stray tear that I missed. "You want me to fill in the blanks here?"

"Uh, yeah," I half-sniffed, half-laughed. "That would be nice."

"Okay, when I came to Paris this fall for the anniversary shindig, Madame Beauchamp asked me to arrive three hours early. She took me to breakfast and explained that Danielle wants to retire at the end of this year. At first, I just thought she was shooting the breeze with me."

"Really? Does that seem like something Kathy Beauchamp would do?"

"Well, no, but you know I'm slow on the uptake sometimes," you smiled sheepishly, playing with a curl behind my ear. "She did finally spell it out for me and asked about my book schedule, like how many hours a week I usually devote to revisions, how often I travel to the States for scheduled events – things of that nature. So I pulled out my planner –"

"Of course you did."

You pinched my cheek playfully. "Mock all you want, but Kathy Beauchamp appreciated my organizational skills. After she glanced through my spring commitments, she said my schedule seems reasonable and that there's no need to rush my decision. We've talked several times since October, and this morning, I e-mailed to let her know I was interested in the job, but that I needed to speak to you first. When I went up to my apartment earlier, I crafted a preliminary response."

"It took you two hours to write a response? Really?"

"Listen up, Judgy McJudgerson. Unlike you, I never use my French anymore, and this was important." Your eyes searched mine for a few seconds, like you didn't know if you should ask the question on the tip of your tongue: *What do you think, Pete?* But I already knew my answer.

I leaned across the car to kiss you, breaking the silence between us. "I am one hundred percent on board with this plan," I said against your lips. "Let's go back to your place and start packing your things right now."

"Be serious for a second here – what about your thesis? Won't I be in your way while you're trying to work?"

"Are you kidding me? I need you now more than ever. Between the two of us, maybe we can finally make sense of my thesis topic."

"You've already chosen?"

"Well, not exactly. My advisor chose for me: Gaston Bachelard's *La Psychanalyse de Feu* and its influence on Jean-Paul Sartre's *Being and Nothingness*.'"

"The Psychoanalysis of Fire? What does that even mean?"

I started to explain but your eyes actually glazed over, which made me laugh inside. Because PREACH. What *does* it even mean? Even now, three years later, I still don't get that title.

My mom used to say, "You may have deep feelings for someone, Peter, but it's your choices *together* that make those feelings count." I decided to include this story in our anniversary journal because that night, you gave me a voice in your decision. Maybe you didn't know it at the time, but that meant more to me than Venice and the Juniper House Christmas *combined*. Because without saying a word, you'd asked me to be on your team.

RELATED: We still don't have a couple hashtag. Why, Sully? Why? #MerePete #Russivan #ButSeriouslyHelpMe

ROMEO AND JULIET

You have an unusual disdain for Valentine's Day, Miss Sullivan, and while I generally respect your opinions, there once was a time when my foolish heart vowed to change your mind. Because as everyone knows, I enjoy the corny side of life. So I needed you to get on board with Cupid's holiday. Except I hit a roadblock along the way: I had no idea where to take you out.

"Dude," Dan said when I called him in desperation. "You're in Paris! This is the no-brainer of the century. Look up the Palais Garnier website and see which ballet they're running. Meredith's a dancer. She loves beautiful stories. How have you not come up with this on your own?"

Why *hadn't* I thought of that on my own? No clue. But I marched myself over to the box office that very second and bought us the best tickets they had for *Roméo et Juliette.*

Quick side note here: can you explain to me why everyone thinks *Romeo and Juliet* is romantic? They die. Not only that, their deaths were completely avoidable. Why does Western Civilization value this story so much? I have no freaking clue.

Anyway, I was so psyched about our date. I shaved twice that afternoon and wore my light blue sweater, because you said it was your favorite. And when I got to Marie-France's building, I nearly fainted when I saw you waiting in the lobby, because you looked like you stepped right out of a time machine from mid-century America.

Your hair was pulled off your face in a bun, and you were wearing a black dress that could have been Grace Kelly's. Most of the time you don't wear high heels but this night, you were nearly my height and so completely gorgeous that I wanted time to stop, right then and there. Forever.

While we waited for our Uber, I leaned in to kiss you, and you stepped backward a little. "Sorry," you muttered, frowning as you laid a hand on my chest. "I've been coughing my head off all day and I don't think it's contagious, but since I'm never right on those things…"

"What? You're sick?" I lifted the back of my hand to your forehead. "Hey, you're warm. And maybe a little bit clammy."

You swatted my hand away. "Stop that. You'd be clammy too if you had to navigate this dress. It has three different zippers." Then the Uber pulled up, and off we drove into the night.

My end-of-the-night plan that night was genius, if I do say so myself. The Palais Garnier is only a thirty-minute walk from your apartment, and guess what's smack dab in the middle of said route? The Pont des Arts. So on the way home, I figured I'd casually steer you over the bridge and once we were there, I'd present you with the teeny, tiny padlock charm I'd bought for your bracelet to symbolize *our* padlock. You know, the one buried in silt at the bottom of the Seine.

So sweet. So thoughtful. Soooo over the top.

Except the ballet was a bust. By intermission, we were both ready to leave. So I took your hand as we left the main entrance and asked, "Hey, how are those heels treating you?"

You glanced down at your feet, then back up at me. "Wh-what?"

Your eyes were watery – not in the way they get when you're feeling weepy, but... glazed, really. That's the best way I can describe what I saw. Not to mention your teeth were chattering so loudly that even *my* head hurt.

I slipped my jacket around your shoulders. "Aw, man, you *are* sick."

"No, I'm n-n-not," you stammered. "Where to n-n-now?"

I pressed my cold hands on either side of your face. Your cheeks flamed so hot against them that my skin immediately warmed against yours. "Nope, that's it. We're ordering an Uber to take us back to Marie-France's right now."

"Pete, no –"

"Yes. No fussing, okay? Let me take you home." I took one step down and turned to reach for your hand... just as you puked all over me, my blue sweater, and yourself.

Oh, man, Sully. You broke my heart when you started crying. But I managed to flag down an usher from inside to clean up the steps. And while we waited for our driver to arrive, we used the inside of my jacket to wipe ourselves down, which must be when that adorable padlock charm fell out of the pocket.

R.I.P., Valentine's Day.

"Rue Guénégaud," you mumbled when our driver arrived, and thirty minutes later, you were asleep in my bed, cuddled into my pillow. Which is not nearly as romantic as it might sound out of context, is it?

As I pulled in an armchair from the living room to keep watch over you, I nearly woke you up church giggling like a teenage boy. Why? Oh, come on, bro. Imagine me traveling back in time machine to take such a picture back to Freshman Year Pete™.

"Greetings, younger self! I bear news from the future. Number one: buy all the bitcoins you can, and number two: DUDE. This is Meredith Sullivan, your Valentine's date when you're twenty-five years old."

Maybe this is why they don't allow time travel. You'd give your younger self cardiac arrest.

MORE THAN YESTERDAY

The first Thursday of every month was my thesis advisory board meeting. Why did an entire board of professors need to discuss my work with me? Why not just one or two? I don't have a clue, but you know I secretly loved it. And even though they required us to dress up, the meeting itself had quite a family feel. Plus, my advisors were next-level brilliant.

So of course I always came to find you immediately afterward.

The April meeting happened to fall on the type of Paris spring day that would inspire Gene Kelly to tap dance along the Seine, singing at the top of his lungs. I may have done a little bit of that myself on my way from the Centre Bellechasse to the Centre Lafayette that afternoon.

When I crossed the threshold into the entry hallway, I spotted you immediately through the glass wall. You were hiding at the far end of the courtyard, reading under the shade of the giant oak trees, ponytail high, your trusty turquoise blue pen in your left hand.

It was noon, and as always, the building was abuzz with kid energy. Guys and girls from probably every state in the Union scampered past me, speaking in the requisite French. I strolled down the familiar hallway past the *Grande Salle* to the coffee machine and ordered two *cafés noirs* – one for you, and one for me. And as I cut through the secret faculty passage to the back part of the courtyard, I could finally make out what book you held in your hands.

It was *Night and Day* – the latest proof copy, judging by the pristine spine.

"Hey," I smiled as I settled down beside you, but you kept your eyes on the page. "*Night and Day,* huh? I heard that Luke guy is major swoon *avec* sigh."

"Shhhhh. Things just got interesting."

"Oh yeah? Did Allie just give Luke her sock to free him from his master's creepy kitchen?"

"Listen, *Luke,*" you said, placing the book by your left side as you took one of the coffees. "Sass me all you want, but I've got twenty-four hours to refresh my memory on my own book before I speak to some bookish podcaster who gets half a million downloads a month."

"Half a million? Whoa. Do you know what questions she might ask?"

"Besides why I abuse ellipses and em-dashes? Yeah, no clue. So this should be fun." You took a sip of your coffee. "You look nice. How'd your meeting go?"

"Oh, you know. Too many ellipses and em-dashes, just like you."

"Mmm-hmm." You sipped again, assessing me. And then your lips spread into a knowing smirk. "I can't believe it. Your advisors didn't find a single error, did they?"

I lifted the plastic cup to my mouth to hide my smile, because *no*, Sully. They did not find any errors. In fact, the advisory board let me turn in my thesis a month early, which meant that I was done with my Master's degree. But you knew that already, didn't you? You'd read and reread my work so many times that you probably could have written your own hundred-page paper.

"Doesn't matter," I lied, drinking the rest of my coffee before I crumpled it up and pitched it into the nearby trash can. "So what were Luke and Allie up to when I interrupted you?"

"Hmm?" You sipped your coffee distractedly as your eyes tracked the two students ambling past us. "Oh, right. Well, I hadn't gotten very far yet, but it was the first time Allie sees her *chambre de bonne*."

"Ooooooh. I like that chapter. Luke's got game."

"You always say that."

"What? It's true!" I took your (mostly) empty cup from your hand and chucked it next to mine in the bin. "You're the storyteller, Sully. If you didn't want Luke to resemble a super hero in that scene, you should have dialed it back a little."

"Okay, smarty pants. You tell me your version of Allie's first moments in her new bedroom, and if you can do a better job than I did, I'll rewrite that section."

In October, or November, or even December, I might have panicked when you threw down such a gauntlet. Back in the early days of our reunion, I was terrified that you might pull a Pete Russell and run away from me if I breathed the wrong way. But by April, we were a team – solid, steadfast, and headed in the same direction. Which meant I knew you *actually* wanted my side of the story.

"Alrighty, if you insist," I grinned, sliding my arm behind you on the bench. "But fair warning: in the real-life version of that scene, Luke was the opposite of cool. He was sweating so hard that he can't believe you left the malodorous pit stains out of your description."

"Don't talk about yourself in third person, Pete. You sound like a politician."

"Whatever, Sully. Now, listen, play nicely for a minute and close your eyes. I need you distraction-free while you imagine yourself back in your old bedroom."

"*Old* bedroom? It's also my current bedroom."

"Details, details." I lifted my free hand to your face and pretended to close your eyes. "Now then, think back with me to that day. Tell me what you remember."

You sat there obediently for a few seconds, then smiled, eyes still closed as I removed my hand. "Well, the first thing I remember is that you made a lot of racket stumbling into my room."

"Hey, now! That wasn't me. It was the two-hundred year old floorboards! They were completely rotted, you know. Marie-France made me replace them last summer."

"Only you would blame ancient floors on your lack of stealth." Your eyebrows drew together in a scowl, but you kept your eyes shut. "Okay, I remember that you shoved your hands into your pockets when you approached me, which I actually thought was pretty cute."

"Yeah? How come?"

"I don't know. You just seemed… intimidated, maybe? Surely not, though."

"Oh, I was definitely intimidated. You were standing there all brilliant and beautiful in the middle of the room, looking around like you owned the place."

"I did not."

"Uh, yes, Sully. You did. You looked like the queen of your own castle, and I might have bowed at your feet if I hadn't been terrified that you might kick me in the skull."

"Yes, well, if I'd kicked you in the skull, it would have hurt. You'd just shaved off an entire helmet of curls and you had no buffer left."

"I know. Gigi made me go full Sampson just so I could impress you, Delilah."

"I know. You told me about it in your letters." You opened your left eye, the right one still squinting. "Hey, how come you didn't write me a letter about this day up in my brand new room?"

"Good question. I didn't leave it out on purpose. Maybe it didn't occur to me last summer."

"Maybe." You closed your left eye. "Keep telling me now, please. I want to hear this story."

"Yes, ma'am. Where were we?"

"I was standing in my room, looking like a boss."

"Yes, you were." I kissed you gently on the temple as I leaned in closer. "When I saw you there in the middle of your room, I wanted to wrap my arms around you and squeeze you tight because you'd made it, sis. After all that hard work, you'd finally made it to Paris."

You opened your eyes as your lips curled into a smile. "Thanks to you."

"No, thanks to yourself." In one fell swoop, I got to my knees and slipped the ring box out of my front jacket pocket. "From the second I met you that day in Lincoln City, Meredith Sullivan, I have admired you. You are whip smart. You're not impressed by money or fame or beauty or anything else the world values. All you care about is fighting for your dreams. And I want to spend the rest of my life making sure all of your dreams come true."

You do realize you didn't actually let me ask you to marry me, right? You also never answered.

Rude.

Instead, you grabbed my face in between your palms and started that laughing-crying thing you always do when you're so happy that the feels have nowhere else to go. Then you pulled me to standing and kissed me right there in front of every single kid you'd spent a semester bossing around.

I can't believe you've never accused me of high-def chicanery in the three years since I spontaneously proposed in the middle of the school day. What was I thinking, popping the question out of the blue like that on a Thursday? And it wasn't just any old Thursday, either.

Only a crazy person would propose on April Fool's Day.

DISTRICT SIX

You're not one to obsess over material things, Sully. It's one of your best qualities. But one thing I'm particularly proud of is how you flipped out over your engagement ring. (In the best way possible.)

As you know, I found a jeweler in Paris who made custom rings from heirlooms that had been damaged or flawed in some way. I brought him four items: my parents' wedding bands, my grandparents' bands, my mom's engagement ring, and Gigi's.

A month (and one molten gold casting) later, he'd created the ring you never saw coming: Gigi's diamond, my mom's diamond, and a third one just for you because *duh*. You're all about the threes.

I'd been carrying it around with me for days looking for the right moment to drop to my knee. I knew the words I wanted to say, but I absolutely did not know when to say them.

Not until that moment under the shady trees of the Centre Lafayette on April Fool's Day.

The Sunday evening after I proposed, you were hanging out in my apartment, just like every other Sunday that semester. Your dark clothes spun their way through the rinse cycle in my washing machine while I pulled ricotta-filled pasta shells from the oven and you filled out paperwork at my kitchen table.

"That smells so good," you sang in a falsetto, scribbling something onto the page. "What's with the sudden interest in cooking, Russell? You think you can trick me into marrying you?"

"Hey, no homework at the table, young lady. Those are Russell house rules."

"Oh, this isn't homework," you smiled to yourself. But you still wrangled your papers into their folder, setting them aside. When you joined me at the kitchen counter to pick up your plate, you kissed me. "*Grazie*, you beautiful genius. My fiancé is better than your fiancée."

Um, NO. He was not. But I made a mental note that carbs and cheese are the way to your heart.

While we ate, you chatted away about the decision-making trick your office intern Julia – a Highgate student – had taught you earlier in the week. "I don't know how it works, but it totally does. You distract someone with silly questions so their subconscious brain can tackle the real issue. Kathy wants to introduce Julia to the U.S. Congress. We're both convinced she can help them get stuff done."

"Come on, Sully. You can't distract someone *that* easily."

"Oh, but you can, *Monsieur* Russell. Julia's tricked me every single day this week into making decisions I wasn't ready to make." You hopped up from your chair and bounded across the living room to your purse. "She recreated her method on some index cards so I could practice on you and Marie-France. You want to try?"

"Uh, sure?" I answered dubiously. "But I don't know what decisions I have to make."

"Oh, you have decisions, my friend." You held those cards to your chest like an evil mastermind. "Now listen, you're supposed to keep your mind occupied with a mindless task while you answer the questions. So, I don't know. Maybe you could do the dishes? That's pretty mindless."

"I thought the one who *didn't* cook dinner had to do the dishes?"

"Normally, yes. But this is for science." You handed me your plate, and smiled. "Come on, chop, chop! This will only take a minute, I promise."

I obliged and headed to the kitchen sink, turning my back to you. As I kept the water pressure low, you cleared your throat.

"Okay, Russell. No thinking! Just answer. Here's your first question: blue or red?"

"Blue."

"France or Finland?"

"Hello! France."

"Tacos or burritos?"

"Duh. Tacos for the win, forever and always."

The first lightning round went on for about a minute, and after ten or eleven questions, I was no longer actively thinking about anything. Then you shifted gears a bit.

"Live off-grid or live in a mansion?"

"Off-grid," I answered, then laughed. "Hey! I didn't know that about myself."

"I did. Break your left arm or your right?"

"Right."

"Shipwrecked on an island for the rest of your life or locked in a magical castle?"

"Island, one hundred percent. Magical castles are creepy. Plus I look better with a tan."

Completely fascinating, Sully. How did Julia the Intern come up with these questions? Did she find them on Pinterest? Was Julia an only child who had no friends, and therefore had time to come up with value-based questions that had no bearing in real life?

No bearing, that is, until you asked, "Traditional wedding or elope to city hall?"

"City hall," I blurted. And then the apartment went as silent as the eye of a storm.

At least it did for a couple of seconds. And then I felt your arms wrap around my waist from behind. "City hall was my answer, too."

Here's the deal, Sully: I did not believe you. Everything about you screams traditional, from your good girl, rule-following vibe to the way you love your parents and school and everything in between. So when you claimed you wanted to elope, I smelled a rat.

I turned around and pulled you toward me. "Are you just saying that because I'm a guy and you think I'm not down to plan the wedding of your dreams? Or are you telling the truth?"

"Option B," you answered. And when I looked in your eyes, I knew it was true.

You grabbed my hand and tugged me toward the sofa, grabbing your little folder along the way. "I know we just got engaged," you said as we sat down. "But I am a planner, Pete."

"You say that like I'm not one hundred percent aware."

Your cheek quirked up in a half-smile. "Yes, well, as a planner, I am also an information gatherer. Which means when I haven't been hanging out with you, I've started to compile some research."

"I would expect nothing less." I grabbed the folder from your hands. "Is that what you were doing earlier? You were taking notes on your research?"

"Not exactly," you smiled. "See, I knew that if your subconscious brain could vote, he would admit that he wanted to take the simpler route. The only question we need to answer now is *when*. And for the record, I'm up for it whenever you are. Well, after you fill out your part of the paperwork and we wait the mandatory forty-five days. Rules are rules, after all."

"But Sully, what about your mom and dad? You're their only child now. Won't your mom want to go dress shopping with you? And doesn't Jamie want to walk you down the aisle?"

Something flickered across your expression, and just like that, I understood why your traditional heart couldn't bear the thought of planning some big ceremony. Because *no*, actually. You already knew that your mom and dad did *not* look forward to an enormous ceremony on the hillside behind the Juniper House. There would always be an Ian-shaped hole in your family, which had changed all your family plans forevermore. And as I read your expression in that moment, I realized the three of you must have talked through all the possibilities a long time before I put a ring on it.

See, this is one of the pitfalls of navigating the world by yourself, without older and wiser parents to guide you into adulthood. I had never considered how it would feel to stand in front of two hundred guests without a single member of my family sitting nearby. How was it possible after all those months working through my stuff that I hadn't imagined such an important moment without them?

You must have read my thoughts, because you took the folder back, then you wrapped your fingers around mine. "You and me forever," you smiled. "We can wait forty-five days or forty-five years. I don't care how long it takes. Just tell me when, and I'll be there."

According to Google Maps, the sixth *arrondissement* town hall is only ninety meters from Marie-France's front door. Which made it pretty convenient to walk down there with you thirty-five days later.

Yes, that is correct, Mrs. Peter Beckett Russell – thanks to your immaculate paperwork, we shaved ten days off the mandatory forty-five day waiting period. Between your dual citizenship and my family's longstanding tax record on the rue Guénégaud, the District Six paper pushers could find no reason to postpone a *mariage civile* between the cutest American lovebirds that Paris had ever seen.

A couple of hours later, right at sunset, we got married again on the Pont des Arts – just you, me, and that young priest Marie-France knows from Saint-Sulpice church.

You wore an emerald green sundress and an ivory cardigan to both ceremonies. I wore a black suit. And my tie matched your dress.

We stood together on the exact spot where we'd thrown our lock in the river junior year, and then we threw the keys in two years later. The same spot where my parents stood and let fourteen-year-old Pete take their picture back in the day. Where Pops and Gigi got engaged.

You made that baby priest cry with your vows, Sully. And maybe you made me cry a little bit as well, but I'll never admit that to anyone who wasn't there. Because the moment you promised to be my wife, you also became my family.

You and me. Forever.

EMMA WOODHOUSE

Fun fact: did you know @ellie.whitman.123 still follows you on Instagram? I mean, you do have a few thousand followers now so you may not realize Ellie still hearts your posts. Especially the ones featuring that guy you call #GilbertBlythe.

Major swoon *avec* sigh.

So when you announced that your official book launch would be at Albertine, a French-American bookstore on the Upper East Side, my girl Ellie took note. She made a gigantic countdown poster the size of her refrigerator door, and every morning, she would X off another date until October 17th – book launch day. (Pssst. That was me. Your husband. On our refrigerator. In our kitchen.)

Your mom and dad came, of course. And since our Brooklyn apartment was so small, we decided to celebrate by booking two rooms at the Surrey Hotel – one for them, one for us. It was only a four-minute walk from the bookstore, and hey, how often do you launch your debut novel?

Only once, Sully. Only once.

For weeks leading up to the launch, I kept hearing people say how calm you seemed. "Oh! Meredith! I can't believe you already have all your bookmarks printed! You're so organized!" Blah blah blah. Do they know you at *all*, Sully? Have they not seen your planner? Good grief. It was like watching the whole world looking up at the sky and exclaiming, "Oh, my! How blue!" Of course you were prepared. You're the planner queen. But calm? Mmmmm, no.

But as I would soon find out, your nerves had little to do with your book and more to do with the launch party itself.

I wish I could capture the light that flooded your parents' faces when you stepped up on the tiny makeshift stage that evening. Or the way your loopy grin shifted into a smirk when you noticed Dan's and my #TeamLuke and #TeamJosh t-shirts under our professorial-looking blazers.

Too bad Dan was wearing the #TeamLuke shirt and I was wearing #TeamJosh, though. Did you know there's like five Tumblr pages dedicated to *Dan* as Real-Life Luke? WHAT? Do these people not recognize me? I'm your own personal #GilbertBlythe, featured regularly on Instagram as your #OTP. Your #ManCrushEveryday. We share a last name! Come on, Fans of Meredith!

I. AM. LUKE.

Anyway, ninety seconds into the Q&A portion of your event, I heard the tinkling of the bell above the store's front door. *Rude*, I thought. *This is my girl's VERY FIRST book launch, and you want to show up fifteen minutes late?* But then I noticed your face morphing into the heart-eyed emoji, and oh, Sully. Without even looking behind me, I knew what you'd done.

Yes, hello again, Emma Woodhouse. Up to your old tricks, I see?

My first thought when I saw Anne was *whoa.* Her pretty dark curls were extra pretty, and her outfit was… well, let's just say I couldn't wait to watch Dan squirm.

Except he didn't squirm. Not immediately, at least. He just sat there beside me, cataloguing the gilded astronomical symbols on the midnight blue ceiling, oblivious to the reunion headed his way.

I learned a long time ago never to stand in your way where Dan and Anne were concerned. So as you moved from the interview to the signing table, I decided to kick your plan into high gear. My mistake? Assuming Anne was in on your scheme.

Oh, Emma. You are either the worst friend on the planet or the best. I still can't decide.

Without a single glance your way, I gestured for Dan to follow me to the back of the line.

"Don't you want to sit with Meredith?" he asked as his forehead creased into a question mark. "You're the hero of her novel!"

"*Luke* is the hero," I corrected. "Besides, we have a job to do."

"We do?"

"Yeah. Meredith doesn't want the line to drag, so she asked us to hover at the back and intimidate all the people in front of us with some well-placed huffs and menacing glares."

He laughed. "Sounds about right. Hey, maybe we could –"

We'd reached the back of the line by then, which is when Dan finally noticed his own personal Lauren Bacall standing alone.

I always forget that Anne's at least six inches shorter than you are until she's standing right in front of my face. But that night, she seemed even smaller as she squeaked, "Pete! Hey!"

"Anne!" I said, half-laughing as I hugged her. "Did you drive up from Boston?"

"I took the train," she smiled as she pulled away. Then she looked behind me. "Hi, Dan."

He didn't respond for at least a few seconds... maybe longer. When I finally turned around, Dan was still ten feet behind me, his features schooled into an expression so soft that I wanted to laugh. He claimed later that he was temporarily plotting both our demises, but I saw it with my own two eyes, Sully. Dan Thomas was still loopy for his Paris girlfriend.

Which is when I got my grand idea.

Now look, I know you want the whole world to believe your favorite movie is *Star Wars*, and while I generally like to indulge your personal blind spots, I refuse to indulge this one. Because despite how cool it sounds to pretend you're everyone's manic pixie dream girl, your *actual* favorite movie of all time is *You've Got Mail*.

It's cool, sister. Your secret's safe with me... says the sappy dude whose favorite movie is *The Princess Bride*.

Anyway, your obsession with *You've Got Mail* reached a fever pitch after we moved to New York, and because you were the Kathleen Kelly to my Joe Fox and the Buttercup to my Westley, I had booked us a post-signing reservation for eight at Café Lalo on West 83rd Street.

You. Me. Your parents. Agent Isabelle. Editor Angie. Dan Thomas. Plus one empty seat for the Holy Spirit.

Actually, I don't know why I booked the extra seat. Maybe eight's easier to say than seven. Or maybe I just know you intuitively enough to plan ahead.

So I put on my most charming smile and launched my plan. "Are you heading back to Boston tonight, Anne?"

"Um, no." She shot a quick look at Dan, who was still frozen in place. "I'm staying at the Excelsior because Meredith told me about your dinner reservations at –"

"Café Lalo! Great!" I grabbed Anne's elbow, steering her gently toward Dan. "Listen, could you guys do me a favor? I know my wife. She can be a little too indulgent with people's time, and I don't want to lose our reservations if things run over here. Do you think you could head to the restaurant and save our seats?"

Over Anne's head, Dan lifted an eyebrow at me. "What about getting our books signed?"

"That's the beauty of knowing an author personally, Danny," I smirked. "She can sign your book at dinner. Or next week when you come over to do your laundry, if you like. Whenever, man. It's cool."

He raised his eyebrow even higher. "Why is your voice squeaking, Russell?"

Anne, who was standing with her back to Dan, simply smiled at me. "We'll make sure nobody steals your table, Pete," she assured me. "Just make sure Meredith knows we're there waiting."

"Oh, I will," I winked, hugging her once again. "Did I mention how gorgeous you look?"

"Cut the charm, Russell. She already bought Meredith's book." Dan narrowed his eyes at me as he tugged her out of my grasp. "Come on, Anne. Let's get out of here."

I watched them leave, then headed back to your table, pulling up a chair from nearby. "Well done, Emma Woodhouse," I muttered into your ear. "Operation D'Anne Part Deux is in motion."

"I know," you smiled to yourself as you scribbled your signature into a book. "Thanks for sending them out into the night. I knew you'd do the right thing."

"Wait, what?" I blinked. "You knew I would send them over to the restaurant without us?"

"Of course I did. You're ten times the romantic that I am, and Dan's your best friend."

"Yeah, but... hey, did you just play me?"

You smiled up at the person before you and thanked them for coming, then signed their book. Then you nodded to Isabelle to pause the line before you turned back to face me. "Of course I didn't *play* you, Pete. I just banked on your usual behavior and made plans accordingly."

"What's that supposed to mean?"

"It means that this morning, I called Café Lalo to change our reservations from eight people to two. Because as soon as the initial shock wears off, both Dan and Anne will remember that they're both single and living in the same time zone. And all will be right again with the world."

And you know what? You were right, Sully. By brunch the next morning, Dan and Anne were back on track. By January, she'd moved to Brooklyn, and that April, they threw a small wedding in Anne's parents' backyard, six months after their reunion.

Speedy and expeditious. Just like you and me.

Look at us, Mrs. Russell. We're *trendsetters*.

DEAR SULLY

CHANGLE LU

We spent our first married Christmas back in Paris at the Guénégaud apartment with Molly and Jamie. When we invited them, I made them swear they wouldn't bring gifts. But of course your mother ignored me, and these days, I kind of think her rebellion was providential. Because one of her gifts – a book called *Street of Eternal Happiness* – changed our future for the best.

You read all three hundred and fifteen pages on the flight back to New York from Paris. For weeks afterward, you'd tell me everything the author had taught you about life in the former French Concession. Thanks to this Rob Schmitz fella, Changle Lu – the Street of Eternal Happiness – became Shanghai's equivalent of the rue Cardinale Lemoine in Paris, where Hemingway and Hadley first lived as a young couple. At least in your mind.

"Promise me," you insisted. "If we ever move to Shanghai, we'll live on Changle Lu."

I made that promise, Sully. And I kept it. (You're on our balcony overlooking it right now.)

Changle Lu, a.k.a. Changle Road, is a tree-lined boulevard with colorful old buildings on either side and million bicycles dotting the cobblestoned sidewalk. Along certain sections, it wouldn't take much to imagine that we still live in Paris, so strong is the former French influence on the architecture.

Our apartment is… well, if the Brooklyn apartment was miniscule, our Shanghai apartment is only just slightly less tiny. When the apartment agent brought us here that first week in town, I expected you to be disappointed. I should have known better.

Instead of all the inconveniences, you only saw the charm. The furniture is shabby-chic, tone-on-tone white, and every slipcover is washable. The hardwood flooring is original. And it's in that herringbone design you love. The exposed ceiling beams seem straight out of some medieval tavern in Rouen, France.

And the light pouring inside through the trees? "We'll take it," you said, without hesitation.

Most mornings, I wake up to find you sitting on the balcony with your laptop, writing (and rewriting) a high-stakes thriller that has nothing to do with *Night and Day*. The new story features six linguistically-gifted individuals who function as the intellectual equivalent of the Navy Seals, if the Seals worked for Interpol. Three men, three women, each raised in a separate safe house across the globe by fifty "parents" representing the world's fifty most popular languages, plus one coded language that only the agents know.

There's mayhem. There's romance. There are irregular verb jokes and chapters full of nerdy fun.

DEAR SULLY

But, as you so often remind me, we're not here to write thrillers or learn Mandarin, are we? We came to Shanghai to help James and Sarah Logan, whose twin girls arrived just days before we did. I figured we'd only be here a few months – organizing laundry, canvassing the train station to find new residents – but to your surprise (and my relief), you love Shanghai as much as I do.

Two years later, we're still here, eternally happy on *Changle Lu*.

That isn't to say that you've stopped finding me ridiculous. For example, remember when you asked me for a Mandarin/English *dictionary* for your twenty-fifth birthday? Simple and practical, right? Right. But come on, Sully. How could I disappoint Amazon's data scientists when they offered me same-day delivery on a creepy, pointy-eared Elf on the Shelf at checkout?

Hello, Ducky Shincracker. Welcome to the fam.

To your credit, you humored me temporarily. When Ducky pooped chocolate kisses across our kitchen counter, you laughed. And when Ducky made snow angels in a cup's worth of spilled flour, you found it adorable.

But then he hung upside down from the shower head with a miniature (fake) video camera, and uh… whoops. After that, poor Ducky was banned from our flat until further notice.

Luckily for me, the guys at the Restoration Initiative appreciate Ducky's shenanigans. He moved in to the shelter after you kicked him out, and he stuck around until Christmas. But everyone missed him, so I brought him back for Chinese New Year. Then the Qingming Festival, Labor Day, the Dragon Boat Festival… until eventually, Ducky just became a part of daily life, much to your chagrin.

Some days, we find Ducky climbing his "rock wall" of magnets up the refrigerator or riding a bamboo surf board down the staircase banister. Other days, he spells out his name in M&M's.

This morning, Ducky is climbing up the branch of an aloe plant on the front desk, wearing a paper cowboy hat, chaps, and spurs that I tricked you into coloring for me last night.

Hey, if Ducky makes people happy, who are you to judge?

I'm gonna miss Ducky when we move to New Haven in six weeks. Remind me again why I decided to get my PhD?

Yeah, yeah, I know. It's been my dream my whole life, and when our old friend Dr. Sweeney took over Yale's doctoral program, he moved mountains to get my commitment transferred from Columbia. Not gonna lie – that was flattering. Whatever. I still think I'm crazy.

Anyway, we've reached the end of this journal. And as I've been writing this last letter, I've decided to give it to you a few days early. Why? Because A) I have no patience (shocker) and B) I'd like to revisit our dinner date plans for Thursday night. Are you *sure* you still want to eat greasy burgers and fries for our anniversary? I know you think five-star restaurants are a waste of money, but hear me out.

You've had a stomach bug off and on for days. And as much as I loved revisiting the Valentine's puke story a few pages back, I don't actually want to reenact it now that we're old geezers. So, you tell me: greasy burgers or a well-done filet mignon? It all comes from the same cow. Except one choice is more likely to end up on my clothes at the end of the night. Your call, Sully.

LOVE,

PETE

Thursday, May 10th, 11:43 am

Dear Pete,

Happy third anniversary, my love! Well, technically, today is our sixth anniversary. You kissed me on May 10th of our junior year in college, and because we eloped on that same date three years later, I don't count any of the (twenty-seven) months in the middle when we weren't together.

I am sitting across the room from you right now, watching you check people in for laundry day here at the Restoration Initiative. It's hard for me to remember now what my life was like before you. I must have been supremely bored. Because even now, when my daily tasks include sweeping floors and folding laundry, you make me laugh so hard that I cry.

A million memories float through my brain as I watch you making every person who walks through the front door feel like a celebrity. Do you know that you do that? I don't think you do. It's just who you are. And I'm so lucky to spend my days in your orbit.

Sometimes I wonder what Freshman Year Meredith™ would think if she knew that somehow, despite all the odds, Adult Meredith™ has shacked up in China with the ultimate frat boy. Ha! Could she wrap her mind around that possibility? No way. Yet here we are, living the dream, one hundred percent crazy in love.

And thank you for having zero chill when it comes to giving gifts. I'm super happy for once that you gave me that leather anniversary journal full of memories three days in advance. Nice one, Russell! But you should really leave the three references to me from now on. When are you gonna learn, bro? Pete Russell has never schooled Meredith Sullivan at her own games.

See, tonight, while we're eating burgers (*not* steak), your buddy James is taking Ducky Shincracker on a field trip. For once, I'm allowing that weird doll back in our flat, where you'll find him on your side of the bed, holding this letter and sitting atop of an innocent cushion of soft white cotton.

Is it a t-shirt, you're asking yourself? *A pillowcase*? Naw, look again, mister! If you unloop it, you'll see… oh, wait, guess who's catching on, ladies and gents! Have you figured it out yet?

Why yes, that *is* a onesie emblazoned with a giant barcode and the words: *Made in China*.

Hey, maybe you could take *this* back in your time machine when you visit Freshman Year Pete™ instead of the stalker-esque picture of me sleeping. Talk about blowing that kid's mind!

DEAR SULLY

"Greetings, younger self! I bear news from the future. Number one: buy all the bitcoins you can, and number two: DUDE. You're Meredith Sullivan's baby daddy."

Stomach bug INDEED. How about *this* for our couple hashtag? #BabyMakesTHREE

love,

Sully

ACKNOWLEDGEMENTS

It feels impossible now, but the first time I read *The Bridge* and *The Long Walk* back-to-back, I realized (to my extreme horror) that Pete Russell was only my **third** favorite male character.

First place: Jack Kelly. Second place: Dan Thomas.

I KNOW. I'm as shocked as you are by Past Jill™.

What?! No. Just… NO.

So I came up with a solution: I typed out Pete's backstory in his own words. Every night for three weeks that summer, I let Pete's version of things flow onto the page with zero censorship. It was maybe the easiest writing experience of my life (probably because I thought NO ONE would ever read it). And what I discovered on those pages changed who Pete became in later revisions of *The Bridge* and *The Long Walk*. In other words, the Pete you know and love today.

In 2017, I decided to revisit the secret Pete project. Only this time, I started off longhand in a notebook, just like Pete would have done while he was writing Meredith. And now, two years later, I'm sad to let *Dear Sully* go. Fictional or not, Peter Beckett Russell is a fiercely loyal friend. And I, for one, am thankful he picked me to tell his stories. I will miss listening to his voice inside my head. (Weirdo.)

Now that you know the story behind *this* story, here's the list of people who helped me place it in your hands. If you love Pete as much as I do, please tell them thanks.

Thank you first and always to my heavenly Father, who has shown me grace and mercy from the moment I was conceived. I should thank You also for the hard lessons along the way… although if I'm being honest, I'm not a fan of difficult things. *Sola gratia.*

To my parents: I think it's been more fun watching *you* two fangirl over these books than it has been to write them. *Thank you* will never be enough. I love you both.

Shout out to Sarah Oister for another gorgeous cover, and to Sharon Duncan for her consistently brilliant editing and her general life expertise. Both of you make my stories appear *way* better than they are. (BTW, Sharon gave *Dear Sully* its title, so tell her thanks, will you?) Also, mad props to Tarran Turner for the Tower 19 Press logo and to Eddie Renz for website support (and *The Bridge* cover!).

To any of my friends or family who have faithfully cheered me on from the sidelines: I see you. I hear you. And I'll never forget the way you've huddled around me on this particular word marathon. Also, big hugs to everyone who helped me keep this "secret project" under wraps until the very last second. (Although let's be honest: I did a terrible job keeping it secret myself.)

And finally, to you, the reader: Pete and Meredith made me believe in love again after a very, *very* long time when I did not. But you? *You* made me believe that dreams can come true. You're holding one of mine in your hands. Thank you from the bottom of my heart for your part in this journey.

ABOUT THE AUTHOR

Jill Cox studied French language and literature so she could move to Paris, and then taught high school French so she could convince others to join in on the fun. She has never been to China, but that didn't stop her from modeling the fictional Restoration Initiative after a real-life non-profit in Shanghai managed by her real-life cousin, James. Now that she's completed *The Bridge* series, Jill has run away to Neverland – or maybe just her neighborhood coffee shop – where she's drafting all the novels that stacked up in her brain while she was playing matchmaker for Meredith and Pete. You can find her on all social media platforms as @jillcoxbooks.

Made in the USA
Middletown, DE
28 September 2022

11377034R00168